HELENA DIXON

MURDER
at the
DOLPHIN
HOTEL

Bookouture

Published by Bookouture in 2019

An imprint of Storyfire Ltd.
Carmelite House
50 Victoria Embankment
London EC4Y 0DZ

www.bookouture.com

ISBN: 978-1-83888-063-7
eBook ISBN: 978-1-83888-062-0

Murder at the Dolphin Hotel is dedicated to my family, my husband, David, my daughters, Robyn, Corinne and Alannah, my parents, my brother and sister-in-law, and my mother-in-law. All of them have supported me and continue to support me in all kinds of ways and without them, *Murder at the Dolphin Hotel* would not have been created.

Torbay Herald

10ᵗʰ June 1916, Dartmouth, England

A reward is offered for information regarding the disappearance of local Dartmouth mother of one, Mrs Elowed Underhay. Mrs Underhay, aged twenty-seven, was last seen two weeks previously when she was thought to have departed from Kingswear station to visit friends near London. She has not been heard from since and her family and friends are keen to assure themselves of her safety. She was not thought to be in low spirits or to have any financial difficulties at the time of her disappearance. Mrs Underhay is described as five feet two, blonde, with blue eyes and was dressed in a rose-pink travelling costume with grey hat and gloves. Any information to be given to Mrs Treadwell, The Dolphin Hotel, The Embankment, Dartmouth.

CHAPTER ONE

Dartmouth, 1933

Kitty Underhay was on reception duty at her grandmother's hotel. Outside the revolving doors lay a fresh, sunlit afternoon. Inside the lobby there was the scent of beeswax and lavender with dust motes floating in the air.

'They fetched a body out the river this morning,' Cora murmured to Kitty as she whisked her duster across the top of the reception desk. The older woman glanced around the lobby to check there were no guests within earshot before continuing with her tale. 'Foreigner, Dutch they said. And it looks a bad business. Constable told me he'd had his head bashed in.'

'Cora, really.' Kitty glared at her employee. 'You are the limit.'

Cora loved a titbit of gossip, and in a small, sleepy riverside town like Dartmouth, foul play on this scale was unusual to say the least. She bustled around the desk, her round, middle-aged face avid with glee at being the bearer of news.

'Police is searching the banks down by the lower ferry. Mr Farjeon found him in the water when he went to open up his booth. Says he thought it were a dead dog, so he fetched a long stick and there was a face looking back up at him, all glassy-eyed and weed-covered.' The maid's stout frame shuddered at the thought.

Kitty sighed. Once Cora got started it was difficult to stop her, but she had to admit that her curiosity was piqued, even if she could have done without the details. As in any town that had a high number of holidaymakers and boats calling in to port, one expected some issues, especially with the naval college on the hill at the edge of town. Even so, a murder, especially of a stranger, was indeed news.

'You can't trust foreigners.' Cora pursed her lips and rubbed at an imaginary spot in front of the visitors' ledger. 'I heard as well, that—' Whatever else she was about to add was left unsaid as Kitty's grandmother, small and elegant in a tweed suit, silk blouse and pearls, swept up to the reception area.

'I think the desk is clean enough now, Cora, thank you, and Kitty dear, please pay attention to your work. You need to pay more notice when you're on duty at the front desk. People expect high standards at the Dolphin.'

Cora tucked her duster into the pocket of her starched white apron and hurried away, clearly piqued at not being able to finish her tale. Kitty couldn't decide whether to laugh or sigh as she tore her gaze away from the bustling river scene on the embankment outside the hotel. She wondered how many of the day visitors had been at the far end of the embankment watching the police activity by the lower ferry. 'Sorry, Grams.'

Her grandmother raised a perfectly groomed eyebrow. 'I wish you wouldn't keep drifting off into a trance. I'm worried that you won't be up to managing the Dolphin on your own whilst I'm away in Scotland. This tittle-tattle of Cora's doesn't help. One should feel safe in one's home.' The older woman ran her hand lovingly across the dark green leather visitors' ledger on the polished oak reception desk.

'Grams, I've worked with you at the hotel since I was old enough to hold a duster. There is absolutely nothing for you to worry about. I'm sure the police will catch the culprit very quickly.' Kitty did her best not to let her frustration show in her voice. She'd lived at the hotel since she was a small child. She had worked in virtually every role that her grandmother had felt suitable, from housekeeping to the kitchen, yet she still treated her like a child, and an incapable one at that. The Dolphin might be *the* premier hotel in the small Devon river resort, but she was quite confident about her ability to run things in her grandmother's absence. As for the news of a murder right on their doorstep, well, it was unsettling but nothing to do with the Dolphin.

'I know, darling, but running a hotel is a lot of work and responsibility for one person. You never know what kind of problem may arise, especially at the start of the summer season. Anything could go wrong, from the chef walking out to a linen crisis. We're very busy with bookings too. I do wish Livvy hadn't had her accident at such an inconvenient time; it's so difficult to get help when she insists on living in such an uncivilised place.' The older woman frowned and adjusted the neat set of pearls encircling her throat.

'Great Aunt Livvy needs you to go to her. I'll be fine. The Dolphin will be fine. You'll be back from Scotland before you know it.' She pinned her brightest and most professional smile to her face. It wasn't Livvy's fault that she'd slipped and fallen on the stairs and broken both her ankle and her shoulder.

'Hmm. I would have asked you to go to Livvy but since you've organised this new-fangled jazz thing with that American woman, you really need to be here to keep an eye on it all.'

'We're very lucky to have secured Miss Delaware to open the summer season. She was quite a hit at The Cat's Miaow club in London. That kind of music is all the rage now. That's partly why we're so busy.'

'I just hope she doesn't attract the wrong kind of clientele. News of a murder in the vicinity will not be helpful for business. This masked ball you're planning at the end of her engagement will also be quite a lot of work.'

Her grandmother still didn't sound convinced, especially about the American touring band and jazz singer that Kitty had booked for the first two weeks of the summer tourist season. It had been Kitty's idea to enhance their summer entertainment programme with some new acts, rather than using the same local performers who toured all the hotels in the bay in turn. She gritted her teeth, determined to prove all of her grandmother's misgivings unfounded.

Fortunately, one of Grams' friends entered the hotel through the dark oak and glass-plate revolving door and she was left in peace to get on with her work. However, when two more of her grandmother's oldest friends also entered the hotel a few minutes later and they headed for her private rooms, Kitty suspected something was afoot.

Her fears were confirmed with the arrival of Mrs Craven, a small, sturdy woman with iron-grey curls, an avant-garde little felt hat and a fox fur stole about her shoulders. There was a determined expression on her face.

'Kitty my dear, how is your poor grandmother?' Her clarion voice carried across the lobby.

'She's very well, thank you.' Of all her grandmother's friends, Mrs Craven was the one she liked least. A former mayoress of the town, she was on the board of all the civic societies, every charitable committee and was the ladies golf captain. Somehow, she always contrived to make Kitty feel like something she'd scraped from the bottom of her shoe.

'I don't know. Trust Livvy to get into a scrape. She always was accident-prone even as a girl. Thoughtless and reckless,' Mrs Craven pronounced. She tugged off her gloves and dropped them into her handbag. 'I presume your grandmother is in her salon?'

'Yes, I think she's just rung for tea.' Kitty struggled to get her head around her great aunt as an accident-prone girl. Livvy had turned seventy-four on her last birthday.

'I do hope you're supporting your poor grandmother with all this worry. This accident is typical of Livvy, never a thought for other people. Just like your mother.' Mrs Craven swept away before Kitty could reply, which was lucky under the circumstances as several very rude words hovered on the tip of her tongue.

'Here you go, Miss Kitty. You look like you need a cup of tea.' Cora reappeared and slid a tea tray onto the small bureau in the alcove behind the desk. 'There's a biscuit too if you want one.'

'Thank you, Cora.' Kitty smiled at her, willing to overlook her earlier gossiping. Cora had worked at the hotel since Kitty was a child. A plump woman who filled out her neat black uniform and white apron, her greying hair was fixed in a neat bun under her white cap, and she was incorrigibly nosey. Kitty's grandmother overlooked her impudence because she was a good worker and she knew Cora's home circumstances were not happy.

'I saw that old trout, Ma Craven, come in. I wonder how much we'll see of her once your Grams goes off to Scotland?' Cora mused as she fiddled about with the tea things.

'I'd rather not think about it. Grams has a full meeting of "the gels" today so I expect they'll be "popping" in and out to keep an eye on things, and on me too, no doubt. Especially after today.' Kitty grimaced. She knew her grandmother and her friends all too well.

'Excuse me,' a polite male voice interrupted their conversation. 'I was told to come here and ask for Mrs Treadwell.'

Cora melted away back into the lobby with the appearance of the man at the front desk.

He was clean-shaven, tall and rangy, in his mid to late thirties; his suit appeared worn at the elbows and he carried a small, battered leather bag. He didn't fit the profile for the Dolphin's usual clientele, or the description of anyone her grandmother would be likely to have an appointment with.

Kitty hesitated, unsure if she should interrupt her grandmother's morning gathering with her friends.

'Um… Miss? This is the Dolphin Hotel?' His blue eyes seemed to sparkle with amusement at her confusion.

'Yes, sir, of course. You said my grandmother was expecting you?'

The stranger's grin widened, revealing a small dimple in his right cheek. 'Yes, Mrs Treadwell is expecting me.'

Kitty's professional training kicked in. 'I'll just call through.' She picked up the telephone receiver and dialled the extension number for her grandmother's suite with a shaky finger. 'What name shall I give her?'

'Matthew, Mr Matthew Bryant.'

Her grandmother answered on the second ring. 'Grams, there's a Mr Matthew Bryant in reception. He says he has an appointment with you.' She noticed the stranger's lips twitch when she emphasised the Mr in front of his name.

'Wonderful, I've been expecting him. Ask Cora to show him through to my rooms.'

Kitty carefully set the receiver back in its cradle, a million unanswered questions buzzing in her head. Her grandmother was clearly up to something, and her sixth sense told her it was something that Kitty wouldn't like. There had been a lot of odd things happening lately. None of them very significant, but perplexing nonetheless, and her grandmother had not been keen to discuss them.

'I'll just call someone to take you through.' She was about to press the small brass call bell for the portering staff when Cora reappeared. Kitty wondered how much she had heard. She couldn't have been far away from the desk, no doubt doing her best to eavesdrop. Nothing pleased Cora more than being the first to know something.

'Cora, could you show Mr Bryant to Grams' rooms, please.'

The man hefted the leather bag. 'Nice to meet you…' he leaned in to read the discreet gold badge pinned to her lapel, 'Miss Kitty Underhay.'

Heat sizzled in her cheeks at the amusement in his eyes at her obvious discomfort at his impudence.

'If you'd like to follow me, sir.' Cora headed off across the lobby towards the stairs with the stranger following in her wake.

Thankfully the lobby was empty now of guests, so Kitty took advantage of the opportunity to take a sip of the tea Cora had left for her in the alcove. Although the drink was almost cold, it helped to fortify her nerves. She wondered who Matthew Bryant was and what his business with her grandmother could be.

She swallowed her last mouthful, shuddering slightly at the cold dregs. A faint tremor in her fingers which had started when he'd arrived, now caused the china to chatter when she replaced her cup onto the saucer. She wasn't certain why the stranger's arrival had affected her, but something about him unsettled her usual calm.

She peeped out of her hiding place at the glimpse of spring sunshine outside the lobby. On days like today, the centuries-old building seemed to close in on her, suffocating her and pinning her to the ancient walls like a helpless moth. The hotel was almost as old as Dartmouth itself, dating back to the fifteen hundreds and handed down in Kitty's family from generation to generation since it had first begun as a small tavern to the present day, when it was a large hotel, catering for the growing tourist trade. The half-timbered building faced the river not far from the upper ferry station, and a brisk walk from Warfleet Bay and the ancient Dartmouth Castle.

Outside, the sun shone on the water, the castle stood guard at the river mouth and people were enjoying the fine day. She was inside, trapped by her inheritance, doing the same mundane jobs, day after day.

'I'd better get rid of that tea tray, miss, before your grandmother spots it, or we'll both be in trouble.' Cora whisked into the alcove and collected the tray of dirty crockery.

'Thank you, Cora. Did you take that man to see Grams?'

Impudent as ever, Cora replied, 'Yes, miss, and I tried to find out why he was here as I was sure I'd seen him before, but he was as close-mouthed as an oyster.' She shook her head, a perplexed expression on her face. 'Sorry, miss, got no information for you.'

*

Matt shifted uncomfortably on the rose-patterned chintz armchair, the continued scrutiny of a half-dozen pairs of eyes boring into his skin.

'More tea, Captain Bryant?' Mrs Treadwell picked up the silver teapot and gestured towards his half-empty cup.

'No, thank you, and please, I prefer to be plain "Mister". The war is long over and my army service is ended.' He set the cup down carefully on its saucer on a small, highly polished mahogany side table.

Mrs Treadwell placed the teapot back on the tray and folded her hands onto her lap. 'Very well. Now, I realise my proposition is a little unusual, but as I leave for Scotland tomorrow, time is of the essence and Kitty's well-being is my prime concern. Even more so now there has been a murder only this morning so close to the hotel.'

Matt raked his hand through his hair and wished he'd thought to don a better suit and tie. Better clothes would at least have given him some kind of armour against Mrs Treadwell and her cronies. He'd faced a good many dangers in his past, but this group of old ladies was as scary as any he could remember. Especially the one with the fur stole and the gimlet gaze, seated like a queen on a throne in the best armchair. The other two ladies had the sofa and Mrs Treadwell had a straight-backed chair presiding over the tea tray.

'What does your granddaughter think of your idea?'

The older woman's lips thinned. 'I would prefer that Kitty remain unaware of the real reason for you being at the hotel. I am anxious not to trouble her.'

'But if she knew there was a threat of some kind to her, or to the hotel, she would be more alert.'

The other women exchanged glances.

'No.'

Matt sighed and tried again. 'Have you taken your concerns to the police?'

His question caused a series of half-stifled nervous titters to break out around the room.

'Unfortunately, our police force is not as one would wish it to be. The station in town is very small and covers a large area. I have raised my concerns with a senior officer but unless something actually happens, it would seem that the services they can offer are somewhat limited. Besides which, I do have the reputation of the Dolphin to consider,' Mrs Treadwell frowned.

'Are you sure you can't give me any more information?' He knew the woman was holding something back from him. The details she'd provided before his arrival at the hotel had been fairly vague. Mrs Treadwell was an old acquaintance of his parents. It had only been his own father's insistence that he accept the job that had brought him to the small Devon river resort. Since he had resigned his government employment a few months ago, he had been kicking about at a loose end and he suspected his father thought this might fill his time.

The elderly woman sighed and rose from her seat to cross the room. She opened the lid of a small mahogany writing box standing on her bureau and withdrew a slim bundle of papers.

'Here, this is all I have. My main concern is that Kitty is kept safe and the hotel protected. I'm not sure who this person is or what they hope to obtain.' She proffered the papers to Matt.

His gaze locked with hers. 'You *suspect* you know who it is, though?'

She broke eye contact first, confirming his suspicions that she knew far more than she had told him so far.

'Yes.' She turned away and crossed over to the tall bay window to gaze out at the river.

Matt glanced at the papers in his hand; typed notes on cheap white paper, all with unsigned variations of the same message. No envelopes, no signature or clue to who could have written them.

I'm coming back to claim what's rightfully mine.

'Who do you think it is?' he asked.

The older woman's spine stiffened and there was a tremor in her hand as she moved to straighten the edge of the dark green velvet drape framing the window. 'The person I thought it might be is dead.'

A chill ran through Matt's veins at the faint audible gasp that went around the circle of women.

'And who was that?' His thoughts automatically strayed to the petite ash-blonde girl with the shingled hair at the reception desk downstairs. This was connected to her, it had to be.

'My daughter, Elowed, Kitty's mother.'

CHAPTER TWO

A chilly late spring breeze blowing from the river cut through the flimsy silk material of Kitty's blouse when she stepped outside the hotel. Clouds scudded past in the bright blue sky and sunlight sparkled on the water as she hurried along the street. She paused at the corner and hesitated for a moment, wondering if she should return to get a heavier jacket. The melodic chimes of the town hall clock told her there wasn't time if she wanted to get all her errands completed during her lunch break and before the post office closed.

Ignoring the cold, she turned into the side street leading away from the river. The post office would probably be busy, and she had several pieces of mail which needed to go out today. The narrow street lined with tall eighteenth-century buildings was crowded with visitors making their way to the main shopping area. The upper ferry from Kingswear across the river had just unloaded, bringing locals and visitors, with a steady stream of vehicles; a mix of motors and carts all bumper to bumper, heading towards the centre of town.

Kitty walked towards the post office. The closer she got to the town centre, the harder it became to get through the people surrounding her on the narrow, cobbled pavements. Jostled by the press of the crowd, the parcels in her arms slipped and she made a wild grab to save them from landing in the gutter.

In the same instant, someone shoved hard into her side, knocking her off balance and out into the road. Her packages fell around her feet as she tried to save herself from falling. She hit the ground and there was a blare of car horns. She looked up and locked her gaze with that of the horrified male driver behind the wheel of the coal merchant's dark green truck, mere inches from her face. She was frozen in place, unable to move, when a strong arm took hold of her and yanked her to safety on the pavement.

Kitty's heart thumped against the wall of her chest as she gazed into her rescuer's dark blue eyes. 'It's not advisable to play with the traffic.' Matthew Bryant looked down at her. He still had hold of her arm.

'I… I don't know what happened.'

Matt released her and darted out into the road to retrieve her parcels before the coal truck moved on. 'You're in luck, nothing got squashed.'

'Including me.' Kitty attempted a laugh but to her horror it came out as more of a sob.

He offered her the packages he'd retrieved from the road and studied her face. 'You look pretty shaken up. Come on, let me buy you a cup of tea.'

Before she could protest, he'd led her inside one of the many tearooms along the street. A small table for two was vacant right at the back next to the doors leading to the kitchen.

'Thank you. I don't know what happened out there.' Kitty took a seat at the polished table and stared disbelievingly at the hole in the knee of her stockings. She must have grazed her leg when she'd stumbled. Blood oozed stickily through the fine, flesh-coloured silk, making her nauseous at the realisation of her narrow escape.

'Here, take a sip of water; you look as if you're about to pass out.'

She hadn't noticed him collecting a glass of water from one of the uniformed waitresses. The water splashed against the glass as she raised it to her lips. 'My hands are shaking.'

The corners of his mouth lifted in a faint mockery of a smile. 'I'm not surprised. You had a pretty close call there. How did you end up in the road?'

Kitty shook her head and tried to gather her thoughts. 'I don't know. I was on my way to post my parcels and as you saw, it's really terribly busy out with visitors. The one o'clock upper ferry must have unloaded. Someone bumped into me and I almost dropped everything.' She paused and took another sip of water. 'It's strange, it felt like someone shoved me hard from the side and I overbalanced and fell out into the road.'

'It's a good thing I was passing.' He sounded concerned.

She nodded slowly. 'Yes, or it would have been a pretty nasty accident.' She started to feel better now she was safely seated inside the comfortable tearoom. It was certainly a happy coincidence that Mr Bryant had been there to rescue her. She shivered when she thought of what could have happened if he hadn't saved her.

Matt flagged down the waitress once more and ordered a pot of tea and some sandwiches, ignoring Kitty's protests and offer to pay.

'You're sure it was an accident?' he asked as the waitress returned with their lunch.

Kitty frowned. 'Why wouldn't it be?' It was a strange question to ask. No one would deliberately try to push her under a truck – except she had definitely felt someone shove hard into her side.

He shrugged. 'Ignore me. Security is my business, so I suppose I simply have a suspicious mind.'

'Is that why you were meeting my grandmother, Mr Bryant? To discuss security?' She was relieved to see her hand had stopped shaking as she poured tea from the pot into the dainty floral-patterned china cups that the waitress had set out in front of them.

She thought she detected a flash of something in his expression before he answered her. Annoyance? Irritation? She wasn't sure.

'Please, call me Matt, and amongst other things, yes. Your grandmother has hired me to look after security at the hotel. As she is leaving for Scotland soon to go to your aunt, she was worried about leaving you to look after the Dolphin alone.'

Her indignation must have shown on her face as he held up a hand to stem the protests and outrage that threatened to spill from her lips.

'It isn't that she doesn't think you capable of managing the hotel, but she's heard from other hoteliers of several incidents lately that have worried her, and with the summer visitors' season just getting underway, she wanted a visible deterrent to protect the hotel. I think the recent murder has added to her concerns.'

'The deterrent being you, presumably.'

He nodded and grinned at her. A small dimple flashed briefly in his cheek, making him appear quite boyish for a moment.

Kitty took a bite of her sandwich. 'Grams hasn't mentioned any incidents to me.' She may not have mentioned anything but there had been a strange undercurrent lately, even before the body in the river had been discovered.

He shrugged again and picked up his cup. The delicate china nestled, incongruously fragile, in his large hand. 'She probably didn't want to worry you.'

Kitty wasn't convinced. It was probably the tale her grandmother had given him, but that didn't mean it was the truth.

*

Matt finished his tea. He wasn't sure Kitty had believed his explanation of why her grandmother had hired him. It had been pure chance that he'd been only a couple of paces behind her when she'd stumbled out into the road. There had been a crowd of people on the pavement at the time. He'd been close enough to save her but too far away to determine if she had been deliberately pushed, and if so, who had done it.

At least the colour had returned to her face now. She'd been ghostly pale when they'd first entered the tearoom.

'I should get back to work, there's a lot to do today. I still have to get these parcels into the post.' Kitty touched a napkin to the corners of her mouth.

'I'll take the packages to the post for you if you like, I was heading that way.' He wanted to see if there was anything in the parcels that Kitty's attacker might have wanted to obtain.

At first, he thought she was about to refuse but then she slid the stack of brown envelopes and packages across the table. 'Thank you. I'll reimburse you for the postage from petty cash later. I really need to get back and clean up before Grams spots the state of my stockings.' She grimaced as she looked at the ugly graze on her knee.

'Will you be all right walking back by yourself?'

She gave him a look that he suspected she'd learned from her formidable grandmother. 'I think I can manage.'

'I'll see you tomorrow then.' He watched her limp away as he paid the bill for their lunch. When his father had asked him to help Kitty's grandmother, he'd thought the job would be simply babysitting a rather air-headed young woman whilst her grandmother was away. Something that would fill his time while he considered his next steps. Kitty, however, appeared far from irresponsible. He hadn't thought there might be some substance to the older woman's fears for both her granddaughter and her business.

Mrs Treadwell had shaken him slightly with the story of Kitty's mother, Elowed, and her mysterious disappearance in 1916, but he couldn't see how that could be connected to the strange letters. Unless someone wanted to use that tale to their advantage somehow.

He quickly sifted through the small bundle of parcels that Kitty had left on the table. From their size and shape they all appeared to be brochures, nothing that anyone would want to prevent from reaching the mail. That left only the possibilities of the incident being an accident after all, or that someone had wanted to harm Kitty. He quickly discounted the accident theory. Kitty had definitely felt someone push her. That meant he had to take Mrs Treadwell and her theories much more seriously. Even if that theory involved a woman who was probably dead.

Matt gathered up the packages and took them to the post office. Afterwards, he wandered back through the narrow streets towards the river and the embankment. He hadn't been sure about taking this job. Since leaving the army and his government post he'd been without a clear focus. After everything he'd been through during the war and afterwards, his father's suggestion of a short-term position in a beautiful, peaceful location had sounded like a good idea.

It would give him time to decide what he wanted to do next. Time to finally grieve and to move on with his life, away from places and people that kept reminding him of everything he'd lost. Whilst he'd been busy with work, distracting himself with other people's problems, the passing of the years still hadn't filled the empty space inside his chest. Matt stood on the embankment, lit a cigarette and stared out across the river. The trees on the far bank were bright with the promise of new foliage, and bluebells and primroses peeped out from the unruly clumps of grass beneath them. In the reeds, a small group of fluffy yellow-brown ducklings were barely visible as they paddled around their mother. Matt sucked in a breath and tried not to think how unfair it was that Edith and baby Betty weren't there to see it.

*

Kitty made it back to the hotel and hurried up to her room to bathe her leg and change her damaged stockings. Her room was at the top of the hotel, right in the eaves on the third floor. The ceiling was lumpy and uneven, with wooden beams running lengthways. Her furniture was a mishmash of older dark Victorian pieces left from when the hotel had been modernised. The dark pink satin eiderdown on her double bed added a cheerful feminine note to the room, matching the rose that stood on her dresser in a crystal vase. Grams had been disappointed when she'd refused the spare room attached to her own suite, but Kitty preferred the privacy and peace that living in the attics gave her. There were only storerooms and a couple of empty bedrooms used occasionally by staff on that level. Plus, she had a view right along the river of the open farmland and tree-covered hills down to where it opened into the estuary below the castle.

She unlocked her door and dropped her handbag on her bed before rushing into her bathroom to clean her leg. It wasn't until she came back out and opened her drawer to find fresh stockings that she had the feeling that something was wrong.

The hairs at the nape of her neck prickled as she glanced around the room. Someone had been there, she knew it, and not simply the chambermaids. On the surface, everything looked exactly as she had left it. She frowned and looked back down into the open drawer. Her stockings were still neatly stacked but the packet on top was a pair that she always kept at the bottom of the pile. She'd been keeping them for a special evening occasion as they were too fine and expensive for every day.

Unnerved, she opened some of her other drawers. The contents appeared neat and undisturbed, but they definitely weren't in the order she'd left them in. Her favourite satin pyjamas were at the back of the drawer and the ones she'd singed with the iron were at the front. She checked her jewellery box. Not that she possessed anything valuable, but the few items she did own had huge personal meaning for her.

The silver locket her mother had given her was still there along with her great aunt Livvy's sapphire ring. Her mother's picture was still there in its silver frame. Someone had searched through her room, though. But who? And why? Her grandmother wouldn't snoop. She would interrogate Kitty to death if she wanted to know anything, but she would never search through her things.

Her little Bavarian clock cuckooed the hour. Her mind whirring, Kitty changed her stockings and removed her hat before leaving her room, double-checking that she'd locked the door behind her. She would have to find out if anyone had borrowed her spare key from Mickey, the maintenance man. The idea that some unknown person had rifled through her personal possessions was scary.

Perhaps her recent misadventure had affected her more than she thought but she had always felt safe and secure in her home before. Now with a death on her doorstep, a brush with the coal lorry and someone tampering with her possessions, she was suddenly afraid. Perhaps her grandmother had been right to hire Mr Bryant; extra security might be in order after all. Something terrifying was going on at the Dolphin.

CHAPTER THREE

The discovery that someone had been in her room going through her possessions left Kitty feeling twitchy and uneasy. Her skin crawled at the idea that someone had casually managed to gain entry and touch all her personal belongings. Seeing her things so carefully replaced had left her feeling grubby and dirty. Why would someone have searched through her things? Theft, she could understand, but nothing was missing.

Spare keys to all the rooms – including hers and the one for her grandmother's suite – were all hung on a pegboard in Mickey's office, along with spare keys to the various storerooms. Kitty stopped off on her way to her office. Mickey was in his small room, sitting at his desk with a newspaper and his sandwiches in front of him. He was a small, wiry local man, getting on in years; he had lost both his sons in the war. During her childhood he had been very kind to her, allowing her to trail after him as he carried out his various maintenance jobs. A fug of cigarette smoke filled the air from the ashtray on the desk.

He looked up and immediately rose to his feet as she tapped on the open door. 'Did you want me for something, Miss Kitty?'

'No, I just wondered if anyone had been in my room in the last couple of hours?' She could see her key hanging from its hook on the pegboard on the far wall.

Mickey scratched his head. 'Don't think so, miss, the maids were in yesterday to give it a turn out and early this morning to make the bed and leave the towels. I haven't been out of here much this morning except to help Cora with a delivery for a couple of minutes. Why? Is something wrong?'

Kitty forced herself to smile. 'No, everything's fine. I've heard there was a spate of burglaries at some of the local hotels and guest houses. Grams has hired a new security man, Mr Bryant. But even so, please make sure your office is locked whenever you leave it, to be on the safe side.'

The elderly man raised his eyebrows. 'Very good, miss, I'll be on my guard.'

'Thanks, Mickey.'

She left him to finish his lunch. It was difficult to know what to do next. Should she raise her concerns with her grandmother? Or should she talk to Mr Bryant – Matt – about it, since he was now apparently in charge of security at the hotel?

Kitty mulled it over as she seated herself at her desk in the small wood-panelled back office behind reception. Perhaps the solution would make itself plain while she worked out the staff rotas for the next six weeks. But despite her best efforts, by the time she closed the files, placed her pen back on the stand and finished her shift, her head ached and the problem continued to niggle,

Kitty's grandmother expected her to come to dinner in her suite at seven. There were still quite a few things to sort out before she left for Scotland. Kitty planned to ask about Matthew Bryant, and how he had been hired. Normally she knew in advance if any staff were needed and had some input into the interviews. There was something going on that didn't feel right and she intended to find out more.

Her headache had subsided to a dull throbbing in her left temple by the time she had changed into a plain black evening gown and joined her grandmother in her rooms.

'You look pale, darling. Are you feeling well?' Her grandmother greeted her with a kiss on her cheek and a glass of dry sherry.

'Just a headache. I'm sure it'll go soon.' Kitty frowned at the sherry. It was all part of the pre-dinner ritual. Her grandmother always insisted a small glass improved the appetite and aided digestion. Kitty wasn't so sure, but sipped obediently to please her. She would have preferred a cocktail.

A tap at the door signalled the arrival of the trolley containing their dinner. The mouth-watering smell of grilled salmon escaped from below the ornate silver cloches as Kitty took her place by her grandmother. The oak table, which had been owned by Grams' father, had been laid in the wide bay window, affording an evening vista of the river. Coloured electric lights hung on strings glowed orange and yellow, marking the edge of the waterway; an improvement on the old gas lamps. Some of the boats were lit for the first evening cruises of the summer visitors' season and a few couples walked hand-in-hand along the footpath.

Her grandmother took her seat and the waiter served them both with minestrone soup before leaving them to eat their first course.

'I bumped into Mr Bryant at lunchtime.' Kitty smoothed her white linen napkin across her knees and picked up her spoon. 'He told me you'd hired him to look after security here and that some of the other guest houses had been having problems.'

'And?' the older woman queried.

'I was surprised you hadn't said anything about taking on staff so early in the season, or that you hadn't mentioned that you were worried.' Kitty took a spoonful of her soup and waited for her grandmother's reply.

'Matthew is the son of an old friend of mine, General Bryant. He has considerable expertise in security; he worked for the government after the war and has recently resigned from his post. It appeared to be the perfect solution, considering there was so little time before I leave.'

'It would have been nice if you'd mentioned him though, or your concerns with security.' Kitty knew she sounded childishly resentful, but it was a fair comment. She was supposed to be running the hotel jointly with her grandmother, after all.

'It didn't seem that important, darling. It's really reports of petty thefts, some vandalism. Of course, with the murder of that poor man found in the river this morning, it seems I made a wise decision. By the way, I gave Matt the vacant staff room on your floor.' The older woman rested her spoon in her empty dish and dabbed at the corners of her mouth with her napkin, leaving red smudges of lipstick on the linen.

Kitty's headache kicked up a notch. 'Grams, I thought we'd agreed that those rooms were to be used for storage.'

'Well, darling, he has to live somewhere, and this is only a temporary position. I expect he'll find somewhere else in time. His parents would like him to settle down permanently.' Her grandmother collected the soup dishes and carried them over to the trolley. She then lifted the silver cloches from the plates containing their main courses and returned to the table. Kitty silently counted to three as she stared at the plate of salmon and salad that her grandmother had placed in front of her.

When she'd turned twenty-one, she'd insisted on taking a room on the top floor where she could have privacy. Now she would have Matthew Bryant just a few doors away from her at the other end of the corridor. That thought was more than a little disturbing. There had been something about the self-mocking gleam in his eyes when he'd looked at her at lunchtime which had ruffled her senses.

Her grandmother changed the subject to her forthcoming trip to Scotland and they spent the rest of the meal finalising the arrangements. Once the remains of dinner had been cleared away and a tray of coffee deposited on the low table in front of the fire, they moved to the sofas.

'What have you done to your leg?' Her grandmother leaned forward to peer at the dressing on Kitty's knee.

'A silly accident at lunchtime. Someone barged into me as I was on my way to the post office and I had a close encounter with a truck. Luckily your Mr Bryant happened to be there to catch me. Typical clumsy me, completely ruined my stockings.' Kitty attempted a laugh so her grandmother wouldn't be alarmed.

Her grandmother didn't smile. 'Please be more careful, Kitty. I've enough to worry about with Livvy.'

'I'm fine, Grams, honestly, it was one of those silly accidents that happen sometimes.' She wished she hadn't told her the whole story. She should have made something up to stop her grandmother from worrying. Then again, if she had bumped into Matthew, he could well have mentioned the incident, so whatever she'd decided to do would have been wrong.

'Hmm, it sounds as if it was a good thing that Matt was there.'

Heat mounted in Kitty's cheeks as she recalled the strength in his grip as he'd pulled her to safety and the frisson of electricity that had hummed between them in that brief physical contact. 'Yes, I suppose it was.'

Silence fell as both women sipped their coffee.

Her grandmother sighed. 'Kitty, I am worried about going to Scotland and leaving you here. I know you think I'm a bossy, fussy old woman, but you and Livvy are all I have and as one gets older, I suppose it's natural to think of the worst things that can happen in life. This American jazz singer, well, it's not like having one of our local entertainers, it's a lot of work for you.'

Kitty swallowed. She'd never seen her grandmother's expression quite like this before; a mix of fear and worry highlighted by the fine wrinkles around her eyes and mouth.

'I promise I'll take care, Grams. And Miss Delaware will give us a wonderful start to the summer season. Room reservations are up already and tickets for the ball are selling briskly. You said yourself that the hotel was busy.' She reached out to give her grandmother's hand a reassuring squeeze. The older woman's fingers felt frail and cold in her grasp and a sliver of fear iced through Kitty's heart.

'Since your mother went missing all those years ago, it's made me even more aware of how things can change in the blink of an eye. She's been in my thoughts a lot again lately.'

'I know, Grams.' She wondered what had made her grandmother suddenly think of Elowed. Her grandmother might exasperate her, but she still loved her dearly and was grateful for everything she'd done to raise her after her mother's disappearance.

She'd also thought about her mother a lot recently. Over the years her grandmother had spent a small fortune trying to trace her, without any luck. As Kitty had grown older and each landmark birthday had passed with no news or contact, both she and her grandmother had been forced to conclude that she had to be dead. Indeed, one of the private investigators her grandmother had hired had come to that same conclusion, even giving them details of what he thought may have happened. It was all conjecture however, as he had not provided a shred of proof.

Her mother had vanished when Kitty was six. She'd arrived at the Dolphin from London with Kitty, stayed for a few months and had then disappeared from the face of the earth. Kitty often wondered what her life had been like before then. She vaguely recalled a brownstone building with stairs and a park. She had no idea where her father might be, she couldn't recall him at all. The name on the birth certificate had led her nowhere and her grandmother had never appeared to have any information other than she believed he had gone to America.

Kitty finished her drink. 'I'm going upstairs to finish reading the book I started yesterday. It's a Dorothy L. Sayers, and I had to leave it at a good bit.' She placed her cup down on the tray.

'I don't know how you can enjoy those dreadful crime novels, so gory. I think I'll get an early night too, though. It'll be a long day tomorrow with all the travelling.' Her grandmother's voice was vague, as if her thoughts were elsewhere.

Kitty bent and kissed her cheek, savouring the familiar scent of the roses in her grandmother's favourite perfume. 'By the way, did you pop into my room earlier for something?'

The older woman frowned. 'No, why?'

'Nothing. I thought you might have been looking for something you needed to pack.' She gave a small shrug to show it wasn't important. 'Night, Grams, see you tomorrow.'

*

Matt made his way to Mrs Treadwell's suite as soon as he received her message.

'Tell me what happened to Kitty at lunchtime,' she commanded as soon as he entered her room.

He took a seat on the sofa opposite her and told her about the incident with the truck. He guessed from the empty cups on the tray in front of him that Kitty had just left. The older woman paled as he told her his theory that Kitty might have been pushed deliberately.

'I don't like it. I don't like it at all. I have to leave tomorrow, but it worries me that Kitty might not be safe.'

'At this moment the best you can do is trust that I will be looking out for her. You truly have no idea who could have been behind this or the letters?'

She shook her head in response to his question, but her gaze didn't meet his. 'No idea at all. I've lain awake at night racking my brains trying to think what this could be about. Kitty is the only thing of value that has ever been left with me, when Elowed disappeared without a trace. Painful though it was, I have accepted that my daughter is most likely dead, and even if she were alive, there is no reason she would send these notes instead of coming herself.'

Matt leaned back in his seat. He could see she was genuinely worried, but he still felt she was keeping something from him. 'Thanks for all the information you gave me about the letters. I've started to sift through it all, looking for pointers.'

Mrs Treadwell nodded, the creases on her brow showing she was still troubled, and making her look older than she had previously seemed. 'There's one more thing. Kitty asked me if I'd been looking for something in her room. She made something of a joke about it, but it has me worried. Why would she think I had been in her room?'

'You think someone else might have got into her room?' This was concerning. It meant whoever was behind the strange happenings might have access to the hotel, and really was targeting Kitty.

'It struck me as an odd thing for Kitty to say. Mickey, our maintenance man, has spare keys in his office.'

Matt turned the information over in his mind. 'It's a good thing I'm on the same floor as Kitty. At least if there is a problem, I'm close at hand. She's quite isolated up there from the rest of the hotel.'

The old lady smiled for the first time during their interview. 'Thank you, Matt. Though I'm rather afraid that Kitty doesn't feel quite the same way about having you as a neighbour.'

CHAPTER FOUR

Kitty was surprised at how alone she felt when her grandmother's hired Bentley finally drove away. She blinked back the tears which unexpectedly prickled beneath her eyelids.

'What is the matter with me? I'm not usually this maudlin,' she muttered to herself. She tugged the edges of her neat navy-blue cardigan closer together to protect her from the spring breeze blowing across from the river and turned to re-enter the hotel.

A lock of her hair blew across her eyes, the blonde tendril further blurring her vision. She put up her hand to return her hair to order and promptly cannoned into an older man just leaving the hotel.

'Oh, I'm so sorry,' Kitty apologised.

She'd only seen this particular guest a few times before, although he'd been staying with them for a few weeks. A thick-set middle-aged man with glasses and a surly expression, he'd stood out from their usual guests. He dined alone and never appeared to receive any post or messages. She had assumed he must be a commercial traveller in the area on business of some kind.

The man nodded and grunted a brief acknowledgement before hurrying off down the street towards the centre of town. Kitty walked into the hotel lobby, rather discomforted by the man's brusque reaction. Usually guests at the hotel were cheerful and chatty. This man had seen her several times before when he'd come to the desk for his room key. It was clearly going to be one of those days where everything seemed out of kilter.

When she reached her small office tucked away at the back of reception, she discovered Matthew Bryant seated and waiting for her in the chair opposite her desk, obviously refreshed from a night's sleep and wearing a well-tailored dark grey suit.

'I see you've made yourself at home.' Irritation at his presence in her office warred with the involuntary jump her heart gave when his gaze locked with hers.

He ignored her barbed comment. 'Good morning to you too. Your grandmother mentioned something to me last night that I wanted to talk to you about.'

Kitty took her place behind the desk. 'I'm not sure I understand. Is it to do with your contract of employment?' She supposed she would have to try and do some kind of induction for him, although he seemed to have made himself pretty familiar with everything already.

His brow furrowed. 'No, my contract is fine. Your grandmother and I agreed terms when I accepted the position. It is to do with my job here, though. Mrs Treadwell told me she thought you were worried that someone may have had access to your room yesterday.'

'What made her say that?' She held her breath for a moment as she waited for his answer. She'd thought she'd managed to avoid alarming her grandmother.

'I gather it was a feeling she got about something you said to her.'

'Okay.' Kitty leaned back in her chair. 'Yes, someone was in my room yesterday and I don't mean the chambermaids. I think it was while I was with you at lunchtime. Whoever it was searched through my things. Nothing was taken as far as I can tell, but it was odd and… creepy.' She had tried not to think too deeply about it, convincing herself that she must have been mistaken.

Matt's gaze grew more intense, forcing her to look at him. 'You've no idea what they might have been looking for?'

She shook her head. 'No clue. Unless of course they were after money or expensive jewellery. My jewellery was untouched, but most of it is costume, and I don't keep any money in my room. But they were tidy about it. Everything was neatly replaced in my drawers and cupboard, but things weren't quite in the right place. That's how I knew my things had been tampered with and I hadn't imagined it.' There, she'd admitted the truth out loud, and it scared her.

He rested his elbows on the arms of the chair and steepled his hands together beneath his chin. 'If you don't believe it was a member of staff, how do you think they got in?'

Kitty shrugged. 'I don't know. My first thought was that maybe they'd found the spare keys in Mickey's office.' Her pulse speeded as he dropped his hands and leaned forward in his seat, his dark blue gaze calling heat into her cheeks.

'I've asked Mickey to order a proper key cabinet. The question is, why did someone take the key to your room? And then having carefully searched your room, place the key back on its hook in Mickey's office?'

The implications of his questions hit her like a bucket of ice water. 'You think they deliberately chose my room? It wasn't a random thing?' She'd been so stupid, of course it couldn't have been random if whoever it was had gone to that much trouble. This was even worse than she'd imagined.

'You've had nothing go missing from other guests? No comments or questions to suggest their possessions have been disturbed?'

'No, but, it could just have been someone taking a random key and trying their luck. My room is quite isolated.' Her voice faltered. That wasn't quite true any more. Matt's room was only separated from hers by a couple of storage closets. The key had also been replaced, and why would a thief only try one key or leave her few bits of jewellery and her mother's picture frame? If they wanted money, then even those things would have provided a few shillings.

The gleam in his eyes told her he didn't believe the theory of a random thief any more than she did. She suspected that he also knew her feelings about sharing her floor with him, which perhaps was somewhat ungrateful as he'd saved her life.

*

Matt knew it was risky alerting Kitty to the potential threat to her safety, especially when her grandmother had asked for his discretion. In his view however, when someone had attempted to push Kitty under a truck, that had changed the rules. She had to be made aware that there was a potential threat, without alarming her unnecessarily or giving away too much.

It had been his idea to secure accommodation on the same floor as Kitty. Her self-imposed isolation at the top of the hotel bothered him. Something else bothering him was the niggling feeling that Kitty's grandmother hadn't been entirely frank with him about her suspicions of who might be behind the threats. She had mentioned Elowed, Kitty's mother, but had remained cagey on the subject of Kitty's father.

'What about any of the current hotel residents?' he asked.

Kitty blinked. 'I'm not sure what you mean.'

Matt studied her face. 'Is there anyone who you think may be responsible? Anyone who makes you feel uneasy at all for any reason?'

Confusion clouded her grey-blue eyes. 'At this time of year, a lot of our guests are regulars who travel with a touring motor coach company or via the train. They come every spring and autumn before the main rush and the prices rise. Our main visitor season starts soon though, when Miss Delaware launches our summer entertainment. We have a few private guests, and again, some of them are regulars. They have business locally and stay with us several times throughout the year.'

'So, there isn't anyone that you can think of who might be worth keeping an eye on?'

Kitty caught her lower lip between her teeth. She hesitated for a moment before speaking. 'There is this one man. I just bumped into him actually, outside the front entrance. He hasn't done or said anything that makes me think there's anything wrong but…'

'But?' Matt asked when she hesitated again.

'He makes me feel uncomfortable and I don't know why. He has an unusual accent, although he registered with an English name and address. I suppose he could be ex-colonial.'

Matt could tell from the delicate pink flush shading her cheeks and the scrunching of her shoulders that the conversation made Kitty feel awkward.

'I know it's not nice to think that one of your guests might be responsible, but I have to look at the possibilities. That's why your grandmother employed me. Tell me which guest you mean.'

Kitty sighed and pulled out the visitors' register. In a few seconds she beckoned Matt to come around to her side of the desk and view the page.

'This is the man. Mr Brian Smith from Essex, room twenty-one on the second floor.'

He stood behind her to peer at the details. 'Can you make me a copy of the register entry?' He was close enough to smell the fresh soapy scent on her skin and to notice the tiny mole below her earlobe. Matt forced his attention back to the screen and tried not to think about his proximity to Kitty or why she ruffled his senses so much. He hadn't thought about a woman this way for a long time, not since Edith.

He straightened and took a tiny step back, only to bang his heel against the office wall. 'Smith is not the most original choice for a surname,' he commented.

'Maybe not, but it could be his real name.' Kitty removed the top from her fountain pen and copied the details onto a fresh sheet of paper.

Matt barely waited for her to finish blotting it before taking it from the desk. He knew she was right; Smith might well be the man's real name. It was one of the most common surnames in England. He moved away from the back of her desk to stand near the door. It was too disturbing to his peace of mind to spend much time alone with Kitty in a small space. Perhaps that was the problem; he disliked small spaces, something else that was a legacy of the war.

'What do you plan on doing with that?' Kitty asked, looking at the copy of the register entry that he held.

'I'm going to do a little probing and see what I can find out.'

Kitty looked alarmed. Matt spoke quickly before she could change her mind and retrieve the information she'd given him.

'Don't worry, I'll be discreet,' He didn't tell her that not all his investigative methods were strictly legal. Some of his sources of information were definitely of the shadier kind and somehow he didn't think Kitty would approve. 'He'll never know, and if he turns out to be on the level then it'll put your mind at ease. If it makes you feel any better, remember that someone caused you to ruin a pair of stockings yesterday by pushing you in front of a coal truck.'

'I can't help thinking this is all a bit of a fuss over nothing. We have no real proof that anyone tried to shove me in front of that truck and there might be some explanation for the things being moved in my room.' Her eyes held an anguished plea for him to agree with her.

'We've already talked about this, Kitty. Your grandmother hired me to look after the security of the hotel. You've reported something unusual and I have to try to get to the bottom of it.' He wished he could be completely honest with her about the messages her grandmother had received but he had given his word that he would say nothing. He was already starting to regret that promise.

*

Kitty blew out a breath and slumped back in her chair as soon as Matt left the room. He was as bad as her grandmother for treating her like a child and not giving her the full picture, and she knew from her gut that he wasn't telling her everything. Although what on earth could be going on in a sleepy old-fashioned hotel like the Dolphin was beyond her comprehension.

She stayed where she was for a moment, spinning herself gently from side to side in her wood and leather office chair. Matt wasn't the only person who could do some investigating. Maybe she ought to do some snooping herself, and her first port of call would be to try and find out a bit more about Mr Matthew Bryant and why Grams had hired him.

Kitty decided to leave the rest of the staff rotas until later. It wasn't as if she had any plans for the evening, so she could always finish them then. Instead, she opened her desk drawer and hunted around for the spare key to her grandmother's suite. It was time she went and did some research of her own.

A sliver of guilt stilled her hand as she turned the key in the lock to her grandmother's suite. Perhaps she should leave well alone and go back to sorting out the paperwork in her office. She shook the thought away, squared her shoulders and entered the suite. The salon seemed empty without her grandmother's small but formidable presence. Although her grandmother had done away with many of the frills and furbelows, the room still had a distinctive Edwardian look, with chintzy chairs and heavy drapes framing the windows. The ticking of the handsome silver gilt carriage clock on the mantlepiece appeared to reproach her presence.

She locked the door behind her and crossed the room to the small rosewood writing bureau where her grandmother kept all her private and business papers. Kitty slid the palm of her hand along the side of the bureau, feeling for a small notch in the wood. She pressed firmly and a tiny hidden drawer slid silently open to reveal the spare key.

Kitty took the key and closed the drawer before unlocking the front of the bureau. Inside the cabinet was a neat arrangement of drawers and pigeonholes where her grandmother stored her documents. Moving swiftly Kitty began to sift through the paperwork, looking for Matt's contract, or any correspondence he had had with Grams. She hated herself for snooping but couldn't bring herself to stop. All her life secrets had been kept from her. Secrets about her mother, her father, about her life before she came to the Dolphin, and now, it seemed, secrets about what was going on at the hotel and why Matt was really there.

Nothing. There was nothing there. Frustrated, Kitty closed and secured the bureau before returning the key to its hiding place. She stood, ready to leave and return to her office, when she heard someone at the door.

Before she had time to think things through, Kitty stepped silently across the salon and hid in her grandmother's bathroom, leaving the door slightly ajar to peer through the gap. Even as she moved, she berated herself for being stupid. She had every right to be in her grandmother's room. Regardless, her instinct told her that whoever else wanted to enter the suite had no right to be there and Kitty intended to find out who it was and what they wanted.

CHAPTER FIVE

She froze in place, wedged in a narrow space between the sink and the doorframe, as the intruder unlocked the door and entered the room. To her frustration, she discovered that her view through the gap between the door and frame was more limited than she'd hoped. She tried to control her breathing, her heart thumping in her chest as she heard the familiar sounds of drawers being opened and closed.

It was hard to know what the burglar might be looking for. Kitty was certain that this wasn't some random break-in. Thank goodness she had relocked the bureau. From the sounds of papers being shuffled, items being moved, and the earlier systematic search of her own room, someone was looking for something they believed either she or her grandmother had. What that something could be, she had no idea.

Cautiously, Kitty shifted her position, glad she had opted for her understated pale grey dress and navy cardigan that morning instead of her favourite cherry-red print. She tried to catch a glimpse of whoever was in the room, hoping she was inconspicuous in her hiding place. She toyed with the idea of bursting out and confronting whoever was out there. Only the terrifying memory of her life flashing before her when she'd almost been flattened by the lorry prevented her. Whoever the mystery burglar was, they could be dangerous; they had obviously gone to a lot of trouble to get hold of keys and to sneak around the rooms.

The sound of footfall on the Turkish carpet caught her attention and she held her breath as the intruder drew nearer to her hiding place behind the door. She released the air from her lungs slowly as he headed instead towards her grandmother's bedroom. The palms of her hands were sweaty with fear and she rubbed them on the front of her skirt to dry them. What if he tried to get into the bathroom next?

The intruder was a man, she was sure. The sounds of his breathing and a muffled curse when his search of the lounge had proved fruitless had told her that. She glanced around the bathroom. There was nowhere to hide and a quick look along the marble countertop next to the sink didn't reveal anything useful that she could use as a weapon either.

The sound of her grandmother's telephone ringing made her jump and her heart rate leapt in momentary panic. She clutched at her blouse and held her breath, only to exhale slowly when the ringing stopped. Her knees trembled when she realised the telephone had rung once and stopped, then rung again immediately afterwards.

The intruder had responded to the code and answered the call. Kitty strained to try and hear the conversation going on in the next room. Whoever had called him on the internal line had to be a staff member as all external calls went through reception.

'Nothing. The place is empty. I've checked it all except the bureau, it was locked.' His voice sounded closer and Kitty shrank back against the cold, white tiles of the bathroom wall.

'Yes, I looked there, I told you. No, nothing in the bedroom.'

She hardly dared breathe. The man was right outside the bathroom door. Outside, in the corridor, she heard the distant rumble of the elevator. The intruder cursed.

'I have to go. The maids are coming.'

A few seconds later Kitty heard the door of her grandmother's suite click. She waited for a minute in case the man should return. Once she was certain the coast was clear she stumbled into the lounge and sank down on the sofa. Her hands and legs trembled, and her thoughts were jumbled with fear and relief.

She picked up the receiver and dialled the extension to reception.

To her dismay her voice wobbled slightly when the receptionist answered. 'Please ask Mr Bryant to come up to my grandmother's suite. It's urgent.' She hoped it wasn't the receptionist who had rung earlier.

She barely had time to replace the handset when Matt let himself into the suite.

'Kitty? What's happened? I was in the lobby when you rang down.' He was out of breath as he hurried straight to her side; his expression anxious.

She managed to give him a brief report on what she'd seen and heard.

'Did you manage to see anything at all that could identify who the man might be?'

Kitty shook her head. She felt calmer now Matt was with her. For some reason, since her encounter with the lorry, she seemed to trust him instinctually. 'I couldn't see anything through the crack in the door. He sounded like an older man, though.'

'Anything else you could tell from his voice?' Matt asked.

She frowned in concentration. 'I got the impression that he might be local. He had a very faint accent.'

Matt rubbed his chin. 'He was clearly acting under orders from someone, whoever he might be. What on earth are they looking for and why here?'

His question echoed her own thoughts. 'It makes no sense.'

'Would you recognise his voice again if you heard it?'

Kitty sucked in a breath. 'I don't know. I think so, but I can't be sure. He only spoke a few words.'

'Is he a guest here?'

She had been trying to think if his voice had been familiar ever since Matt had joined her. 'I don't know. I don't think so. But who could have called him on the telephone? It has to be a staff member to know he was in here, and the internal telephone number. There are only a few places within the hotel with a telephone extension. There is one in reception, my office, in the kitchen, my bedroom, Grams' suite and the honeymoon suite.' She knew most of the guests and she was almost positive she would have known if she'd heard the intruder's voice before. It was more disturbing that someone she employed could be involved.

'Okay. I'll need to get a staff list from you, and we'll see if we can work out who it might be. It wasn't reception as I was there, and the phone wasn't used. The most likely extensions would be the kitchen or the honeymoon suite.' Matt sounded frustrated as he raked his hand through his hair, making the ends spike up like a disgruntled hedgehog.

'The kitchen is busy this time of day so someone would notice the telephone being used. The honeymoon suite is empty as Miss Delaware will be using it for her residency.'

'Then a member of staff who knows that suite is vacant is the most likely option. One of the maids, perhaps?'

'Did Grams say anything to you about this before she left?' Kitty wondered where the urge to smooth down Matt's hair had come from. She rested her hands in her lap and waited for his response. She was sure her grandmother must have had some inkling that something odd was going on. Why else would she have hired Matt? The story about thefts in the town had never really sounded very convincing.

He slumped back against the sofa, his eyes narrowing slightly as he studied her face. Kitty could almost hear the cogs turning in his mind as if he were weighing up how much he should tell her.

'Your grandmother gave me some strange notes she'd received.' His gaze was wary.

'I don't understand. What kind of notes? What did they say?' Kitty frowned. The conversation had taken a surreal turn and she began to feel as if she were starring in some cheap thriller.

For answer he dug into his pocket and pulled out a piece of paper. 'This is one of the letters. They all said much the same thing.'

She scanned the note, struggling to take in what was happening. '"*Give back what is not yours to keep.*" This is bizarre, how can anyone respond to this? Do the police know about these notes?'

'Yes. There doesn't seem to be enough for them to do anything; cheap paper, common type, no distinguishing features, unsigned and your grandmother destroyed the envelopes. She says they were typed with a local postmark. The police arranged extra patrols after your grandmother pulled a few strings with the chief constable, but that was all they could offer.'

*

He noticed that Kitty didn't seem surprised that her grandmother had used her influence to get extra patrols.

'I don't understand. What on earth could Grams or I possibly have that would interest a criminal gang? I assume this must be the work of more than one person given what I heard when I was in Grams' bathroom.' She stared at the paper in her hand as if she hoped it would tell her the answer.

'I'm not sure. I wondered if perhaps your grandmother's friends might have some ideas?'

Kitty lifted her head to look at him. Her clear grey-blue eyes met his gaze.

'I don't know. I suppose they might have. The gels, as Grams calls them, have been her friends for years. If anyone knows anything, I suppose they might.'

Matt was satisfied from the frankness of Kitty's countenance that whatever lay behind the mystery, she wasn't privy to it.

'Is there any one of them she is especially close to? One she may have confided in more than the others?' he asked.

Kitty sighed. 'Mrs Craven is probably the one who would know more than the others.'

He picked up the hesitancy in her voice. 'But you don't like her? I believe I have met her; she was the one wearing the dead animal?'

She laughed and shook her head, a stray tendril of her soft blonde hair falling onto her cheek. 'Yes, to the fox stole, and no, I don't like her particularly. She's an awful old snob and she always treats me as if I'm some kind of burden to Grams. She didn't like my mother either.' A rosy pink blush swept across her pale face.

Again, there was the mention of Kitty's missing mother. He remembered the awkward silence that had fallen before at his interview with her grandmother and her friends when Kitty's mother had been mentioned.

Maybe she was the key to this mystery. 'Your grandmother mentioned your mother in connection with the letters.'

'My mother? I suppose it could be someone being malicious or trying some kind of con trick. There is still a reward for information.'

'What about your father?'

A wry smile curved the corners of her mouth. 'My father had gone before my mother came back to the Dolphin with me. I haven't seen or heard from him since.'

He had no reason to disbelieve her. 'Do you have a telephone number for Mrs Craven?'

She recited the number and he added it to the list in his notebook. 'I think I'll call her and see if I can go and see her to ask a few questions.'

'When Grams rings next I'll see if there's anything else she can tell me.' Kitty hesitated. 'I don't want to worry her, though. She has enough on her plate with Livvy, and although she may seem like a tough old bird, she isn't.' Her eyes held an unspoken plea.

'I know. Just find out what you can without alarming her. I wasn't supposed to tell you any of this.' He couldn't help flashing Kitty a small smile, hoping to reassure her.

She smiled back at him. 'I'll be tactful.'

He left Kitty to finish her afternoon's work. His mind was busy filing and sorting all the odd scraps of information. He doubted if Kitty would get much from her grandmother when she called. Although he was certain the old lady hadn't told him everything she knew, he wasn't sure if she had the whole picture. If she did know who was behind the threats and why, then she wouldn't have employed him. His brief hadn't merely been to protect Kitty but to uncover the mystery.

Mrs Craven answered his call on the first ring, taking him by surprise. 'Mrs Craven? We met at the Dolphin Hotel the other day. Mrs Treadwell employed me—'

She interrupted him before he could get any further. 'There is no need for you to beat about the bushes, Captain Bryant, I remember perfectly well who you are. What can I do for you?'

Matt blinked and continued. 'I wondered if I might call on you and ask you a few questions. There have been some very strange things happening here at the hotel and I'm concerned for Kitty's safety.'

He thought he heard Mrs Craven snort. 'You may call today at four o'clock, although I doubt if I shall have anything to say which might be useful to you. Please ring the bell as it is my maid's afternoon off.'

'If you do think of something, anything at all concerning Kitty or her mother, it would help.' Matt could see why Kitty didn't care for the woman.

'I very much doubt if I can add much of use and I'm sure most of the town could tell you about Kitty's mother,' the elderly woman remarked in a dry tone. 'But I shall do my best.'

'Nice piece of work,' Matt muttered as Mrs Craven hung up, the decisive click of the receiver going down seeming to echo on the line.

He glanced at the time on his wristwatch. He had less than two hours before he was due at Mrs Craven's home. Not much time.

Kitty looked up from her desk when he entered her office a little later in the afternoon.

'How did you get on when you called Mrs Craven?' she asked.

'I'm on my way to go and see her now. Do you have her address?'

Kitty scribbled it down on a piece of paper and passed it to him. 'Do you think she knows anything that could help?'

Matt shrugged. 'I'm not sure, but it's worth a try.'

'I suppose so.' Uncertainty showed in Kitty's eyes as she attempted a smile.

'I did a little bit of digging around earlier this afternoon. When I get back, can we meet? There are a few things I found that I'm not sure about.' There were a lot of things he wasn't certain about. Every lead he followed up seemed to throw up more questions than it answered.

Kitty nodded. 'Of course. I'll be in the hotel, just give me a call.'

The shadows under her eyes had grown darker during the afternoon and Matt wished he could take her away from the Dolphin and place her somewhere safe until the mystery had been solved. The impulse surprised him.

'I'll see you later.' He headed out of the hotel to take the short walk through the town and up the hill to where Mrs Craven lived in one of the new houses that commanded a view of the river valley.

He wished he could shake off the feeling of unease that seemed to grow with every step he took closer to Mrs Craven's home – the same sense of unease he used to feel in the war zone right before something bad would happen and the same sense he'd had the night his wife and child had died.

CHAPTER SIX

The street was empty and seemingly devoid of life. The breeze which usually cooled the air down by the waterside was absent here, up on the hill. Mrs Craven's house was at the end of a street filled with large, middle-class houses, imposing in their isolated air of self-importance. The windows surveyed him blankly through diamond leaded panes as he reached the foot of the drive. Matching stone tubs sat either side of the dark oak front door, scarlet tulips standing to attention, guarding the entrance.

Matt sucked in a breath and straightened his shoulders before raising the polished brass door knocker. There was something about Mrs Craven that reminded him of being called to the headmistress's office when he'd been at primary school.

The staccato rat-a-tat-tat of the door knocker broke the eerie silence in the deserted street. Matt checked his wristwatch; he was two minutes early. The door remained resolutely closed. The prickly sense of unease that had dogged him all the way to the house intensified. Mrs Craven was not the kind of woman who would break an appointment.

He stepped back from the iron-studded front door. There were no signs of life from inside. A gate set in a wooden fence stood at the side of the house, which he guessed gave entry to the back garden. A quick glance up and down the street revealed no trace of anyone watching him. Moving swiftly, he headed for the gate.

He expected to find it locked, but to his surprise the wrought-iron handle turned easily in his grasp. The prickling sense of danger at the nape of his neck intensified as he pushed the gate open a little way.

'Mrs Craven?'

There was no reply.

Tentatively, he pushed the gate open wider, granting him a view of the neatly kept rear garden. A blackbird chirped from a nearby flowering cherry tree, breaking the silence. At first glance, everything appeared in order: the lawn was a lush, pristine emerald green, mown and clipped to bowling-green standards; wallflowers stood in rows along the flower border.

The only alien object in the peaceful scene was the crumpled mound of blue at the far end of the garden path. Matt sprinted forwards. Mrs Craven lay in a small, still heap on the riven stone flags. Her eyes were closed and her lips pursed as if annoyed to find herself in such a position. A sticky puddle of blood oozed from her temple, staining the grey stone and emerald turf dark red. A trowel lay discarded in the flower bed next to her gloved hand, along with a collection of mare's tail weeds.

Matt dropped to his knees and felt the elderly woman's neck for a pulse. To his relief, there was a faint fluttering beneath his fingers. He scanned the garden quickly for any clue as to what had taken place. There was no sign of a weapon, no footprints or anything out of place. Her rings were still on her fingers and a gold watch on her wrist. Robbery wasn't the motive.

The ambulance arrived at the same time as the police. Matt gave what details he could to both services as the ambulance staff prepared to take Mrs Craven to the local cottage hospital. Whilst answering the policeman's questions, his mind whirred. Had the old woman simply had some kind of fit, or fainted, causing her to bang her head on the path when she'd fallen? The timing was suspicious, and Mrs Craven was not the kind of person who would faint easily. When or if she regained consciousness, he might get some information but for now another lead had been halted, and another layer added to the mystery surrounding the Dolphin Hotel.

He accompanied the police and ambulance crew back round to the front of the house. A small knot of bystanders had formed at the end of the driveway and were gazing with avid curiosity at the ambulance. Matt stayed behind and tagged along nonchalantly behind the police officer as Mrs Craven was driven away. He would have liked to have questioned the onlookers to discover if any of them had seen or heard anything out of the ordinary that afternoon. Instead, he had to be content with trying to overhear anything useful from the questions the policeman was asking.

He loitered for as long as possible, slipping in a few questions of his own in between answering the concerned enquiries of Mrs Craven's neighbours and their staff. It appeared that no one had seen or heard anything, including the lady whose telephone he'd used to alert the authorities.

Kitty was at the front reception desk when he returned to the hotel. She looked up as he entered the lobby, an eager expression in her eyes.

'What did you find out?' she murmured as soon as he was in earshot.

Matt glanced around the lobby. A family with two young children were having afternoon tea in the corner seats and an elderly couple were browsing the tourist brochures in the rack by the elevator.

'We need to talk, but not here.' He kept his voice low as he leaned against the polished dark oak counter. The sooner she knew what had happened, the better.

Her forehead creased into a frown as she slid a small key across the countertop towards him. 'Meet me in Grams' salon, two minutes.'

*

When Kitty arrived upstairs at her Grams' quarters, she found Matt standing at the window, staring out at the view of the river. 'One of the girls has taken over from me downstairs a while. Now, tell me how you got on this afternoon.'

He turned to face her. 'Mrs Craven wasn't able to tell me anything.'

Kitty stared at him. 'You could have told me that in the lobby.' She folded her arms and tilted her chin upwards to glare at him.

'She couldn't tell me anything because when I got there, she was lying unconscious in the garden.'

Her knees turned to cotton wool and she sank down onto the plush sofa. 'I don't understand.'

Matt crossed the room to take the seat next to her. Kitty could barely take in the information as he told her about what he'd found on his visit to Mrs Craven's home.

'Will she be all right? I mean, I don't like the woman, but I don't want anything bad to happen to her.' Her mind raced and the cup of tea she'd drunk earlier threatened to reappear. It would be too much of a coincidence for something to happen to Mrs Craven just as she was about to speak to Matt. If it wasn't an accident however, then someone had taken care that it shouldn't appear suspicious. She tried to suppress a shiver when she recalled her own near-miss with the truck.

'I don't know, she's an elderly lady, even if she does appear to be as tough as old boots.' Matt raked his hand through his hair.

'It could just have been an accident though, couldn't it?' She knew she was grasping at straws. Her gut instinct told her loudly and clearly that someone had wanted to stop Mrs Craven from talking. But who and why? And how had they known that Matt was going to see her today? The elderly woman had lived in the area all her life – what could she have possibly had to say now that she couldn't have said at any time in the past?

'Maybe if and when she comes around we'll find out what happened. Truthfully though, I don't think either of us believes she accidentally fell and banged her head.' His gaze locked with hers and a chill ran down her spine.

'You think the incident with the truck was deliberate too, don't you?' There, she'd said it.

The look in his eyes supplied her answer.

'Did you find anything else out this afternoon?' Her voice sounded scratchy and she coughed to try and restore it back to normal.

'I did some poking around the hotel and called in some favours from some friends to try and find out a bit more about your mysterious Mr Smith.'

'He's not my Mr Smith, and I hate feeling that I'm suspicious about a guest who is probably a perfectly innocent holidaymaker.'

Matt sighed. 'The problem seems to be that he isn't anyone's Mr Smith. Mr Smith does not exist.'

Kitty frowned, not understanding quite what Matt meant. 'Of course he exists, we have an address for him and everything in the register.'

Matt shook his head. 'I made some calls this afternoon. The address is real, but Mr Smith doesn't live there. No one does. The house has been derelict and boarded up for the last ten years.'

She felt her jaw drop and closed her mouth with a snap. 'That's impossible.'

Matt shrugged. 'We don't know of course if it's connected to the anonymous notes or to Mrs Craven's fall.'

'It has to be. Why else would someone come here with a fake address?' She slumped back on the sofa. She felt more uncomfortable than ever now, knowing one of her guests had set out to deliberately deceive the hotel.

'It may be that he has other reasons for wanting to conceal his identity that aren't connected to what's been going on, but whatever his reasons, it's definitely suspicious.'

'I don't think I'm going to sleep tonight with him staying here and knowing he isn't who he says he is.' She worried at her lower lip with her teeth as she thought about it.

'At least he doesn't know we're on to him and we can keep a watch on his activities. Is he out at the moment?'

'Yes, he handed in his room key to the desk just before you got back.'

'Great, come on then.' Matt reached out his hand and tugged her to her feet. 'Let's go and search his room.'

She snatched her hand free. 'We can't do that. It wouldn't be ethical.'

Matt grinned at her, the dimple in his cheek deepening. 'And you think it's all right for this man to register under a false name and address and to possibly be a suspect for conking a defenceless old lady over the head? Suppose he does a runner without paying the bill? Or steals all your towels?'

Kitty glared at him. She knew he was right but the idea of searching a guest's room didn't sit well with her. 'Fine, you win. What do we do if he comes back while we're in there, though?'

'You're the boss, you'll think of something.'

She could hear Matt humming to himself as he followed her along the winding corridor at the rear of the hotel leading to Mr Smith's room.

'Will you stop that! You sound like a badly tuned bumble bee.' She pulled the bunch of master keys from her jacket pocket and unlocked the door.

'Our friend is right at the end of the corridor here,' Matt observed, looking around.

'I think he asked for this room. Something about being a poor sleeper and needing a quiet room. This room has a private bathroom too.' Kitty had forgotten that request until Matt had commented. This part of the floor was very quiet, and the rooms were cheaper as the only view from the window was of the small rear garden which backed onto the foot of the sandstone escarpment which started at that end of the hotel.

'Hmm,' Matt pushed past her and into the room.

Kitty rubbed at her arms, trying to eliminate the goosebumps that had started up the instant she'd opened the door. Everything looked neat and tidy, the double bed turned down, no clutter on the polished rosewood nightstand. She glanced out of the sash window at the empty garden and the small wooden gate set into the cliff. It closed off the entrance to an old passageway that was rumoured to have been used to avoid the customs men back in the seventeenth century.

Matt was busy, systematically searching carefully through the contents of her guest's drawers, giving her a running commentary as he searched. 'Underwear, navy socks, some er, pictures, ugh, nothing in this one.' He moved to the bedside cabinet, checking the folder containing the hotels complimentary stationary. 'Oh, what's this?'

To Kitty it looked like a blank piece of paper. Matt folded it carefully and tucked it in his pocket. 'Just going to check the bathroom.'

'Hurry up, you're making me nervous,' Kitty hissed and checked the corridor once more.

'Keep your hair on. You own the place, remember, you have a right to be here.'

CHAPTER SEVEN

Kitty glanced back along the corridor towards the elevator. The metal master keys were sweaty in her palm. Inside the room she could hear Matt clanging around in the bathroom. 'Matt, get a move on.'

'Just checking on something.'

More scraping and bumping sounds followed. Kitty's heart was beating so hard she thought she might be about to have a panic attack.

'Ha!' Matt's triumphant exclamation diverted her attention.

'What?'

'Hang on, I'm coming out.' Matt appeared at her side; a boyishly triumphant grin plastered across his face. 'Let's go.' He set off along the corridor. Kitty stifled a frustrated shriek as she locked the room door and hurried after him.

She caught him up at the elevator. 'Well, what did you find?'

The elevator door chimed, and he pulled open the metal gate and stepped inside. 'Wait and see.' He tapped the side of his nose, closed the gate and pressed the button to take them down to the first floor.

To add to her annoyance, he recommenced the tuneless humming that had driven her crazy in the corridor. Kitty was torn between wanting to deliver a sharp dig with her elbow to his ribs, and not giving any sign that he was getting to her. She opted for the second option, folding her arms and pretending she couldn't see or hear him until they were inside her grandmother's suite.

As soon as the door closed, Kitty pounced. 'Okay, Inspector, what did you find?'

Matt took a seat at the bureau and waited for her to unlock the lid, his solid frame strangely incongruous in the dainty gilt chair that her grandmother used each day when dealing with her correspondence. 'I need a pencil.' He took out the sheet of paper he'd acquired in Mr Smith's room and started hunting in the pen tray.

Exasperated, Kitty smacked his fingers away before selecting a pencil and handing it to him. 'For the last time, Matt, what did you find out?'

'Let's just see what's written on this first and then I'll tell you.' Matt quickly and carefully shaded over the sheet of headed paper, revealing the indented message that had been pressed in from the missing top sheet. 'Good thing our man is heavy-handed.'

Kitty peered over his shoulder to read. '"Check out lower ferry dock".'

'Looks like he was giving someone some instructions.'

'That's not very surprising if he is a commercial traveller. He might be expecting some samples or something.' Except that was where the body of the Dutch man had been found, floating in the water.

'I also found several other very interesting items hidden in his bathroom. They were wrapped in oilskin and tucked inside the toilet cistern. I think you'll agree that isn't very innocent behaviour.'

'I don't understand, what did you find?' She felt sick.

'That our Mr Smith is also known as Mr Delguardo, Mr Avery and Mr Jones.'

Realisation dawned. 'Fake passports?'

Matt nodded. 'Along with a large amount of bank notes.'

'We need to report this to the police. Matt, this is bad.' She sank down onto the sofa and pressed her hands into her lap in a bid to stop them from shaking. 'It's like something from the cinema. Suppose he had something to do with that man who was killed?'

Matt shifted his weight in the chair, causing it to creak in protest. 'It's possible; a falling out amongst thieves, perhaps. I don't know if he's connected to the letters, or what he's doing here. You say he requested that particular room when he booked in?'

She nodded. 'I noticed it when I checked the booking notes this afternoon. He requested that room and said he'd be staying until this Saturday, but that he might extend his stay if his business went on for longer than he thought. He paid up front, in cash.' She shivered as she wondered what his business might be if it involved fake identities.

'So far he's not actually done anything illegal. Okay, so he has some fake passports and papers, but he hasn't tried to use them, at least not here, and if we hadn't been poking around inside his toilet cistern, we wouldn't have been any the wiser.' Matt picked up the pencil and drummed the tip against his teeth.

Kitty placed her head in her hands; she couldn't work out Matt's logic. 'I'm scared, Matt. Who is this man? We need to go to the police; clearly he doesn't have multiple fake passports hidden in a toilet cistern for any good purpose. Then there's the murder. It could have been him; he could be a murderer.'

'Okay, I know you're right. I just wish we could find out if the letters your grandmother received and our Mr Smith have a con-nection. We'd better come up with an excuse for what I was doing looking in the toilet cistern too.'

'What did make you look in there?' Kitty asked. It wasn't something she would have thought of doing and she wondered what Matt had done before his arrival at the Dolphin.

'Lucky hunch. Watched too many spy films when I was younger.' He moved his shoulders upwards in a nonchalant gesture.

Before she could ask him anything else, he was on the telephone to the local police. Kitty decided she would ask her grandmother a few things about Matt during her next telephone call. He appeared very knowledgeable about some very strange subjects.

*

Matt had seen the questions in Kitty's eyes and knew he hadn't fooled her. Fortunately, she was called away to the reception desk while he dealt with reporting their find to the police. He had to hope they wouldn't steam in mob-handed, otherwise Mr Smith, or whatever his real name was, would clam up. Or, even worse, disappear.

Kitty already appeared to be more concerned about the hotel's reputation and the possibility of spreading alarm to her other guests by having a patrol car and uniformed officers come to the Dolphin than what Mr Smith might be up to.

Fortunately, Mr Smith was intercepted in a side street as he was returning that evening, so the police presence at the hotel was minimalised. Matt was kept busy providing a statement to say what he had found in the room and Mr Smith and his bogus documents were spirited away to the police station.

Kitty tracked Matt down in the kitchen as soon as her shift on the reception desk had finished. He hurriedly finished off the last mouthful of the gammon and eggs that he'd persuaded the chef to cook for him.

'Well?' She caught hold of his arm and tugged him into a nearby store cupboard full of dried goods and mysterious jars. 'What happened? What did the police say?' She kept her voice low so they wouldn't be overheard by the kitchen staff. 'Who is Mr Smith? Do you know if he's connected with the letters, or the murder?' Questions tumbled from her lips faster than he could answer.

'Whoa, they haven't said anything to me. They need to question the man first and he might not tell them anything. Obviously, they are going to see if there's any connection between him and the Dutch man.'

Her grip tightened. 'What if they let him out? We have all the rest of his clothes and things here. He still has his room. He could be very upset and clearly he may be dangerous.'

Matt looked pointedly at where her hand had scrunched up the sleeve of his jacket. 'Well that's easily dealt with. Ask the maids to pack all his things into his case and lock it in one of the storerooms. If and when he needs to collect it, we can arrange for it to be dropped off. The chances are the police will want to go through his things anyway. He's not going to come back to the Dolphin.'

Kitty's grasp relaxed. 'I'm just glad Grams isn't here; she'd be horrified by all of this. I don't know what I'm going to tell her about Mrs Craven, she's going to be very upset. They've been friends for years.'

'I suggest not telling her anything just yet.' Unbeknown to Kitty, he would brief her grandmother himself later. He extricated himself and rubbed his arm where she'd been holding on to him.

She didn't appear to notice. 'I called the hospital earlier too, but they wouldn't even tell me if Mrs Craven was conscious.' She wrapped her arms across her body as if suddenly chilly even though the interior of the storeroom was warm and humid. Matt realised his mouth was dry and he ran the tip of his tongue across his lips trying to unglue them.

The faint rose scent of her perfume teased his senses and the pupils of her eyes were wide and dark with anxiety. A dull roaring noise started in his ears and the air around him closed in, choking him. Perspiration trickled down his spine and he had to use every inch of his iron self-control to stay on his feet. The walls of the storeroom appeared to move in towards him and, before he could stop himself, he pushed past Kitty and hurried out of the kitchen.

He pushed his way past the ovens and out of the back door before finishing up leaning against the wall next to the metal waste bins. He slumped against the brickwork and tried to gulp down the cooler outdoor air. He closed his eyes, trying to stop the dizziness that had taken over his body.

'Matt? Matt, where are you? Are you okay?' He heard a woman's voice call from the direction of the doorway.

He shook his head, trying to clear his mind of the images that had crowded into his head when he'd been in the storeroom. Images that sometimes haunted him in his sleep. That dreadful feeling of being suffocated and unable to breathe.

'Matt.' Someone touched his arm.

'Edith?' Her name slipped out before he could stop himself. The name he never said aloud any more.

'Who's Edith?'

He opened his eyes to see Kitty standing next to him, her slender fingers touching his arm, concern and bewilderment etched into her delicate features.

'Matt, what happened? You look terrible. Who's Edith?'

He sucked in another breath and straightened himself back up. 'Nothing. Nothing, it's all right. I just felt a little dizzy. Confined spaces.'

He could tell from the frown on her forehead and the look in her eyes that she wasn't buying into his lame excuse. Why had he mentioned his wife's name?

'Let's go for a walk; you look as if you could use some fresher air.' She wrinkled her small nose in the direction of the bins, and he allowed her to steer him round the side of the hotel towards the river.

As they rounded the side of the building, the breeze from the water cooled his skin and his heart began to settle back into its normal rhythm. 'Look, I'm fine, really. I just can't be in enclosed spaces.' He paused as they neared the locked side gate. 'Truly, I just needed to get some fresh air.'

Something that sounded like a snort came from Kitty as she pulled out the master keys and selected the one for the padlock. 'Yeah, right.'

He watched as she undid the lock. 'Oh.' She sighed as she pulled the key free.

'What's that?' He caught hold of her hand so he could take a closer look.

'Looks like oil, all over my fingers. I guess Mickey must have greased the lock.' Kitty shrugged and pulled out a handkerchief to clean her hand.

'Who uses this gate?'

'Not many people. All the deliveries come around the other side through the vehicle entrance. This gate is really just an emergency and alternative route.'

He followed her through to the other side and snapped the padlock closed shut again behind them. 'I'll check with Mickey tomorrow to see if he has done anything to the padlock recently and I think a new lock might be in order.'

Matt fell into step beside her as they made their way to the paved path running along the embankment next to the river. He matched his longer stride to her shorter steps as the wind ruffled his hair and cooled his skin. 'I'm sorry about earlier. I'm not good in confined spaces.'

She halted at the short stretch of railings near the upper ferry stop. 'I gathered.' She leaned her arms on the rails and looked out across the water.

Matt copied her actions, watching as a boat rowed by six oarsmen skimmed lightly over the river surface. 'It's a bit of a hangover from the war. Sometimes it takes me by surprise.'

'The war affected so many people, I suppose we all forget as time moves on and memories fade. It's so peaceful here now this evening it's hard to believe that there's all this madness going on. Threatening anonymous letters, fake passports, murder and old ladies being bashed over the head.' Kitty's voice wobbled. 'We need to look for more clues.'

'The police might tell us something once they uncover Mr Smith's real identity. Then we can try and see if he's connected with the letters or what happened to Mrs Craven. And of course if Mrs Craven regains consciousness, she might be able to tell us what happened.'

'Maybe.' Kitty picked at a piece of paint flaking off the railing. 'Perhaps the key to all this really is back in the past, something to do with what happened in the war. What do you think, Matt? Is it connected to my mother's disappearance back then?'

CHAPTER EIGHT

There was a moment's silence before Matt replied. 'Honestly, I don't know if it's connected to your mother's disappearance. I believe it's what your grandmother may think.'

Kitty stared at the river and watched as the rowing boat began to battle its way back upstream against the current. 'Grams spent a lot of time and money looking for my mother. She placed advertisements in the newspapers, offered a reward for information. All the trails and leads we had were dead ends. Every now and again there would be something that would give us fresh hope, but...' her voice tailed away as she blinked back the tears that threatened to escape down her cheeks.

'Before your grandmother left for Scotland, she said the last investigator she hired claimed to have found some kind of proof that your mother was dead.' Matt's tone was gentle.

Kitty fumbled in her pocket for her handkerchief. 'There wasn't any proof as such, but he said we needed to accept that it was the most likely outcome from all the leads he'd followed up. I think it was more the absence of any evidence of her being still alive. When she went missing the war was on, there was bombing, people were moving about. They know she bought a ticket to London but think she left the train earlier. Something must have made her change her plans. There were letters from people who claimed to have seen her in all kinds of places, but nothing could be substantiated.' She folded the cloth to avoid the oil from earlier and patted the skin dry under her eyes, trying not to make her eyes red.

'Do you have copies of all the searches?'

She nodded. 'Of course. They began when I was very young. My mother wasn't… well, she wasn't very conventional. She was involved in the women's suffrage movement. She had travelled a lot, kept company with actors and musicians, arty people. She was quite talented herself, I think. That's why Mrs Craven and some of the other old biddies didn't like her. It didn't help that my father couldn't be found, although Grams didn't really look for him. She said he was something of a rogue.' Kitty tucked the handkerchief back in her pocket. 'The files are stored in the hotel safe. Come on, I'll dig them out for you.'

They crossed the road side-by-side. Kitty was glad that Matt seemed to be more himself now. She wondered if anything else had made him behave so strangely in the kitchen and she longed to know who Edith was, and why he didn't want to talk about her.

'I don't remember seeing any files when your grandmother showed me the safe.' Matt frowned as he waited for her to enter the hotel ahead of him.

Kitty laughed. 'That's because she showed you the new safe. That's the one we store all the business things and guests' valuables in. I meant the old hotel safe. Grams keeps it for her own personal use. No one knows about it.'

He followed her to the elevator. 'I'm assuming it's in her suite?'

She nodded. 'Of course.'

'Miss Kitty!' The evening receptionist called her as she waited for the elevator to return. 'I've taken your grandmother's post up to her salon.'

'Oh, thank you.' She'd forgotten to check the pigeonhole where all her grandmother's personal post was placed. It must have been quite full for Mary to have taken it upstairs.

The frown lines on Matt's face had deepened as he entered the elevator, pulling the gate closed behind them and pressing the brass button for the next floor. 'You know, far too many people have easy access to wander in and out of yours and your grandmother's private rooms.'

'Most of our staff have worked here for years. Nearly all of them have lived locally for all of their lives and only a few staff are permitted to enter the rooms.' All of Kitty's most vivid memories were of living in the hotel, so she had never thought much about it. It had always been normal to consider the staff as a kind of extended family. Even as she denied what he'd said, she had a horrible feeling that he might have a point. Times had changed and perhaps the way they had always lived at the Dolphin needed to change too. Whoever had alerted the man in her grandmother's rooms had to be a staff member. The Mr Smith incident had also shaken her confidence.

'So, you would know exactly who could get into your room and your grandmother's suite?' Matt leaned on the wall of the elevator as they headed upstairs.

'Yes. Well, mostly. Didn't we already have a similar discussion about this when I told you my room had been searched?' Kitty strode out of the elevator as soon as the door opened and Matt slid back the gate.

She still found it hard to believe that the mysterious Mr Smith and the anonymous letters could have anything to do with her mother's disappearance. The war seemed such a long time ago now. When she had first left, her grandmother had assumed that Elowed had gone to visit some of her bohemian friends and had left Kitty behind so as not to unsettle her.

It hadn't seemed terribly odd at first that Elowed hadn't been in touch for a few days. She often took off for London or other parts of the country to stay with various people, none of whom were known to her grandmother. It had been the source of many arguments between them. It was only when the days had stretched into more than a week with no contact that the alarm had been raised and the police contacted.

'Where's the safe? Don't tell me it's behind that awful picture of the bowl of fruit over there.' Matt's voice broke into her thoughts.

'Fine, I won't.' She bit back a smile as he strode confidently forward to move the picture, only to discover a blank wall behind the frame.

'Very funny. Where is it?'

Kitty walked across the delicately patterned floral carpet to the window seat that ran the length of the sash window overlooking the river. She lifted off the padded seat cushion and ran her fingers under the edge of the sill until she felt a small notch in the wood. With a faint click the sill lifted, revealing a dark metal safe. Kitty extracted a tiny key from her master bunch and opened the lock.

Once open, she took out the large Manila envelope that occupied most of the space inside the safe.

'Here you are. This has everything the investigators did to try and find my mother. And what little they discovered about my father, although that wasn't much. Grams' main focus was on finding Mother.'

'Are there any pictures of her?'

Kitty nodded. 'Yes, a few, and I have some more in an album in my room if you need them.'

Matt took the file and sat on the sofa to study the contents while Kitty relocked the safe. She wondered what he hoped to find in a battered file of dusty old papers from the nineteen twenties. She had long given up on finding out what had happened to Elowed, her hope having diminished with every passing birthday, Christmas, school play, sports day, and prize-giving. Her father had left at the start of the war, two years before her mother's disappearance. All she knew about him was his name and that he was probably in America, and she wasn't sure exactly how she knew that.

To distract herself from her own thoughts, she turned her attention to the bundle of mail the receptionist had left on top of her grandmother's bureau. She swiftly sorted the post into advertising material, personal mail and official correspondence. The advertising material went straight into the wastepaper basket. The clearly personal post she clipped together for her grandmother to read on her return.

Kitty couldn't resist taking covert peeps at Matt, noticing the firm line of his jaw as she busied herself with her task. He appeared engrossed by the file, making notes from time to time on his notepad as he read.

'Anything jumping out at you?' she asked.

'Not really. They seem to have done quite a thorough job searching for her. It seems she bought a ticket for London but wasn't seen beyond Exeter. None of the other sightings were ever verified. As you said, it must have been difficult with people moving around during the war.'

She picked up the last of the letters. There was something familiar about the plain envelope and local postmark. 'Matt, I think this might be another one of the anonymous letters.'

He abandoned the file on the sofa and came to take it from her. Her fingers shook as she passed the envelope over. Matt sliced the letter open with her grandmother's paper knife and shook the contents onto the open bureau, being careful not to touch it. 'I doubt if there will be any fingerprints, but you never know.'

He opened the single sheet of paper out flat using the blade of the knife and a pen.

You have had enough time. You know what is due. It's time you gave back that which is not yours to keep.

'That makes absolutely no sense. Why can't these people, whoever they are, just come out and say what it is that we're supposed to have that isn't ours?' Kitty shook her head. 'And, even if I did know, then how would we be able to return whatever it is?'

'Kitty, are you sure your mother didn't leave anything behind?'

'Only me, and a bag of clothes.' She was aware that her voice held a note of false gaiety.

Matt rubbed his hand across his chin. 'And you can't think of anything a guest may have left behind that's gone unclaimed?'

Kitty laughed. 'False teeth, walking sticks, umbrellas and a set of golf clubs once but nothing of any value. No gems or gold bullion.'

'Well somebody thinks you have something that belongs to them, that's for sure. Though you're right, how you are supposed to give whatever it is to them I'm not certain.'

'The whole thing is completely mad. How am I supposed to return something I don't have, and don't know what it is, to people I don't have any way of contacting and who are obviously dangerous?' It was like being trapped in a penny dreadful novel. She rolled her head slightly, trying to ease the tension knots at the base of her skull.

'From this latest message, I'd say we're about to hear more from them.' Matt took an empty brown paper bag from the drawer of the bureau and eased the letter into it with the paper knife. 'I'll run this down to the police station. If you think of anything or if you hear any news that might shed any light on it, let me know.'

*

Matt left Kitty to eat a belated supper while he took the latest letter across town to the police station. The night had drawn in now and the air held a chill from the river. Matt shivered and tucked his hands in the pockets of his overcoat as he walked. The streets were quiet, with only the occasional dog walker out and about by the area known as the 'boat float', a small inshore marina near the town centre separated from the river by a road bridge.

His route took him past the dock for the lower ferry and he wondered why Mr Smith had given instructions to someone to go there. Had he gone himself to meet someone? Or to collect something? Was he connected to the body in the river? Usually it was a busy place during daylight, with the river ferry doing a brisk trade in both vehicles and foot passengers. He made a mental note to come back in the morning to talk to the ferry crew. Maybe they had seen or heard something.

The river flowed inky black; the silence only broken by the gurgling slap of the current against the side of the docked ferry. A familiar tingle between Matt's shoulder blades triggered a sense that he was no longer alone as he passed the closed-up green and yellow striped booth advertising Mr Farjeon's motor coach excursions to Dartmoor.

Years of training had taught Matt not to give any outward sign of awareness, but he listened carefully for clues, poised and ready for a possible threat as he slowly turned to continue towards the police station. He kept to the same pace as before, conscious that someone was following in the shadows behind him.

Matt stopped in front of a shop window as if studying the contents, whilst using the reflection of the darkened glass to try to see who his follower might be. He pretended an interest in the selection of fancy goods and listened. He thought he caught a glimpse of someone whisking swiftly out of sight, but they were too far away to give him more than a blurred impression of a dark coat with a flash of red.

He was almost at the doors of the station when he sensed his follower had gone. Clearly whoever it was had no wish to get too near the police.

The desk sergeant greeted Matt affably, remembering him from his earlier visit, and took the bagged letter from him.

'Your Mr Smith turned out to be a very interesting man, Captain Bryant. Wanted by police in four countries.'

'Really? Any connection to your murder victim?' Matt leaned against the counter while the paperwork was completed.

'He's refusing to talk at the moment but we think they were in the same line of work. They've remanded him in custody till the bigwigs from London get here to question him. Seems his real name is Gerald DeVries; he's something of a specialist in his field.'

Matt signed the forms acknowledging that he had received a receipt for the letter. 'And what is Mr DeVries's field?'

The sergeant took back his pen and closed his file. 'Gem cutting. Precious stones, diamonds, mostly.'

CHAPTER NINE

Mrs Treadwell didn't telephone and Matt's attempt to contact her on the number she'd given him went unanswered. Mrs Craven remained resolutely unconscious but stable at the cottage hospital and there was no more information forthcoming from the police.

Matt's enquiries at the lower ferry also drew a blank. No one had seen or heard anything. No one of Mr Smith's description had called there that they could recall, and no one had enquired about collecting any goods. He arranged to meet Kitty in her grandmother's suite for luncheon so he could update her.

'This is so frustrating. What are we going to do?' Kitty had her arms folded as she stood at the window.

'The only thing we can do – wait. Sooner or later they will contact you again. I think they are probably already watching us.' He told Kitty about his shadow from the previous night.

She rubbed the tops of her arms as if trying to physically remove contamination from her body. 'That is so eerie. Should we tell the police? What if they attack one of us?'

Matt swallowed at the signs of panic etched into her delicate features. Once upon a time, before Edith, he would have reassured her straight away. He would have made a joke and promised she'd be safe if she stayed by his side.

'We'll simply have to be careful. Don't leave the hotel without telling me. Have someone trustworthy with you whenever you go out.'

She left her post by the window to sit beside him on the couch. 'That's it? That's all we do?'

He couldn't meet her gaze. 'We wait. We behave absolutely normally, and we'll hear from them. It's the way blackmailers and villains always work.' He knew that all too well.

Kitty shivered. 'You sound as if you have plenty of experience with this kind of thing.'

*

For a moment she thought he wasn't going to answer her. A shadow fell across his face and she sensed his thoughts were a million miles away from the Dolphin Hotel.

'Matthew?' She placed a hand on his arm. His hand fisted and the muscles of his forearm bunched beneath her touch.

Taken by surprise at his reaction, she snatched her hand away.

'I'm sorry, Kitty, I think I'm a little jumpy after last night.'

'That makes two of us then.' She kept her tone light although irrationally his reaction had hurt her. As soon as her grandmother called, she intended to try to learn more about Matt's background. So many things about him didn't add up, and with the sinister turn of recent events, she needed to know if she could truly trust him. For all she knew, he could have been the one calling the mystery intruder on her grandmother's telephone.

After Matt had gone, Kitty picked up the file on her mother's disappearance that he had been studying so closely the previous evening. The familiar ache started in her chest as she stared at the faded envelope. It had been years since she'd read the contents. She'd only really looked at the file properly once before, when she was eighteen, shortly before she'd officially been launched into Dartmouth society.

She slid the contents of the file out into the space where Matt had been sitting moments earlier. Her mother's face gazed up at her from the top of the pile. The black and white photograph had faded with age, her mother stiff and formal in an old-fashioned dress, with the longer skirts and fussier hats that had been the order of the day.

The picture must have been taken shortly before she disappeared because she was wearing a bracelet made from papier mâché beads that Kitty had given her for Mother's Day a few weeks earlier. The setting seemed familiar and she guessed it had been taken locally.

'What happened, Mother? Where did you go?' A sudden breeze shook the window frame, sending a shiver along Kitty's spine.

She had been too young when her mother vanished to have many memories of her. Snatches of songs she must have sung to her, the scent of a particular perfume her mother had always worn, and jumbled scraps of disjointed scenes were all she had.

She knew that they had lived in London before her mother had returned to the Dolphin and somewhere in her mind, she seemed to think she had been on a ship. Kitty sighed as she read the meagre collection of facts and witness statements that various detectives had collected.

She had often wondered if part of the reason Mrs Craven disliked her was because of her physical resemblance to her mother. They shared the same blonde-brown hair and wide blue-grey eyes. That was all they shared, though. Elowed had been a free spirit, where Kitty was cautious and restrained. Elowed had flouted convention where Kitty was obedient and followed the rules.

She also knew that Mrs Craven suspected that Elowed had never married Kitty's father, although the file contained confirmation from Somerset House of her marriage in London to Edgar Underhay, gentleman.

Perhaps if her mother hadn't vanished, she would have been different, maybe Elowed herself would have changed, settled down and stayed at the Dolphin. Kitty stared at the photograph. Did her mother hold the clues to all the strange events that were happening now?

She flipped through the files. Elowed's bank account had been untouched, her passport still in her room when she'd disappeared. She hadn't packed a bag or taken any of her clothes with her. Not that they had discovered that until later. It seemed that one fine spring day she had walked out of the hotel, leaving Kitty with her grandmother, and had simply disappeared from the face of the earth.

Elowed's friends had all been quizzed – those that had come forward at least – pictures placed in the press, even a slot on the radio; nothing. Kitty's grandmother had hired three different investigators over the intervening years and all of them had drawn a blank. For a time, every unidentified female body that had turned up in the river had sparked both a hope and a fear that it was Elowed.

The police had listed her as a missing person but that was as far as it had gone. The war and the shortage of manpower had categorised the case as being of low priority. With her mother's history of taking off whenever she wanted, they had been reluctant to take the missing report seriously at all at first. It had only been later when Elowed had not reappeared that they had intensified their efforts to find her.

As for her father; if it weren't for the proof that there had been a marriage, then Kitty would have struggled to believe in his existence. There were no pictures or mementos, no correspondence. Maybe her mother had destroyed them if the marriage had been unhappy. Her grandmother had always been dismissive whenever Kitty had asked about him. She knew he hadn't enlisted to fight during the war but didn't know why. He remained a shadowy figure on the periphery of her life. She wondered if he were still alive and if he was, whether he ever thought about her.

Kitty stashed the documents back inside the envelope but left the photograph of her mother on top of the bureau. She really ought to frame it and place it in her room with the other picture she had of her. She took a seat at the window and stared out at the scene below. River life continued much as it had for many centuries, despite the drizzly afternoon. Pleasure craft had replaced many of the trade vessels which had once sailed up the river to unload their cargo. The ferries were busy plying their trade, both upper ferry and lower crossing the river, one at each end of the town, carrying cars, small vans, horse and carts and foot passengers. The ferries ran on huge chains which held them in place against the current. A plume of steam from Kingswear station on the opposite bank signalled the imminent departure of a steam train taking trippers off around the county.

She rested her head against the glass. She'd watched this scene play out a thousand times. Her grandmother always said that Elowed had been a restless spirit. Kitty sighed, remembering the times when she too had felt confined by the small town and sense of obligation placed on her shoulders. It was certainly weighing heavily on her now.

The telephone on the side table rang out, breaking her thoughts. 'Kitty?'

Her heart skipped when she heard her grandmother's voice. 'Grams, how are you? How is Aunt Livvy?'

'We're both fine. Livvy is asleep and I'm not so I thought I'd call you and make sure you were managing.'

'Grams, there's so much going on here.' Kitty told her everything that had happened, including the news about Mrs Craven.

'I knew you were keeping something from me when I called to say I'd arrived. I also have a number of missed calls from Matthew, judging by the pile of messages next to the telephone that the help has left for me. I assume this was why he was attempting to contact me?'

'Probably. He wanted to know more about Mother and the day she disappeared.' Kitty fought to keep her voice from wobbling, anxious not to give her grandmother any indication of how unsettled she felt.

'Hmm, it sounds as if he thinks this funny business is connected to Elowed after all, then. I wonder why he's changed his mind. I'll have to call him tomorrow; it's getting too late here now and I must confess I'm rather tired and in need of a rest myself.' Her grandmother sounded thoughtful.

'Grams, how much do you know about Matthew? He is okay, isn't he?'

There was the tiniest of pauses before her grandmother replied. 'Matthew is the son of an old friend of mine, General Bryant and his wife, Patience. He is completely trustworthy, although he has endured a great deal. He has an exemplary war record and is very well connected. He was wounded twice during the war and suffered a great personal tragedy. After the war he remained in the army before moving into a government post. I hired him to ensure you would have someone to support you while I was away.' There was a reproving note in her tone.

'Did something happen to him during the war?'

'He lost someone very dear to him.' Her grandmother's voice was hesitant, and Kitty guessed she was wondering how much she should tell her.

'He mentioned someone called Edith?'

'I'm not sure it's my place to tell you about Edith. It was a terrible tragedy. I'm sure if Matthew wishes to share that with you, he will.'

Kitty knew when to stop probing. 'I'm sorry, Grams. I love you, give my love to Aunt Livvy and go and get some sleep now.'

The telephone rang again as soon as she replaced the receiver.

'I just had a tip-off from the hospital. Mrs Craven has recovered consciousness.' The enthusiasm was back in Matt's voice.

'How is she? Did she say what happened to her? When can she have visitors?' Questions tumbled from her lips; finally it seemed they might get some answers.

'Hold your horses, the police are with her now.'

'Oh.' Her great, gusty sigh of frustration must have resonated over the telephone.

'My contact will get us whatever information she can, and we may be able to see Mrs C later this evening depending on her condition and if the police and matron allows it.'

A tiny spear of jealousy nudged her in the ribs. 'Who is your contact?' Visions of Matt flirting with some pretty little nurse flashed through her brain.

'A good detective never reveals his sources.' There was a note of amusement in the fake American accent he used.

Kitty was glad he wasn't there to see the flush which had heated her cheeks. Why should she care about how Matt got his information or from whom?

'By the way, I just got off the telephone from talking to Grams. She said she'll call you tomorrow.'

He mumbled something unintelligible into her ear.

'I told her about everything that had happened. I think she's quite tired from looking after Aunt Livvy.' She wished she didn't have the sense that she was being excluded from something. She wasn't even sure why she felt that way, but there was something going on, she just knew it.

'Can't be helped, I suppose. Hopefully I'll be able to catch up with her soon. Be ready by seven and we'll see what we can find out from Mrs Craven.'

Kitty hung up the receiver once more and picked up the file, ready to lock it away in the safe. The knock at the door made her start.

'Come in.' She had to stop jumping at every little thing.

Cora poked her head around the door. 'I brought you a cup of coffee. I thought you might want a drink about now. Reception said as you were in here.' The older woman entered the room bearing a small circular tray with a delicate china cup and saucer and a plate with some biscuits.

'Thank you, Cora.' Kitty cleared the papers to one side as the woman set the tray down on the table.

'That looks old, miss,' Cora observed as she passed the photo of Kitty's mother on top of the bureau.

'It is; this is a picture of my mother taken when I was young.' Kitty stared at the photograph.

'Yes, of course… I'm not sure but that looks as if it might have been taken at Cullever Steps.' Cora squinted at the picture.

'Where?'

Cora delved in her apron pocket and pulled out a small, black-rimmed pair of glasses. She placed them on her nose and took another good look at the photograph. 'Yes, I'd say that was Cullever Steps, just below Scarey Tor on Dartmoor. Mr Farjeon takes trippers there in his motor coach.'

'Golly, how can you tell?' To Kitty, the picture could have been taken anywhere. She had guessed it was probably Dartmoor but she couldn't have been so precise.

'The stepping stones in the background. There's a pool there too, look.' Cora handed the photograph back before taking off her glasses and returning them to her apron pocket. 'Good meeting place up there, popular with lovers. Lots of people used to go there before the war.'

Kitty blinked and nibbled her top lip as she tried to recall if her grandmother or anyone else had ever mentioned Cullever Steps before. 'Right, thank you, Cora. This must have been taken when I was a child, though. She's wearing a bracelet I made her.'

'I don't know how she would have got there then, unless someone took her up on a cart ride or something. A lot of the moor was closed off for military things as I recall but then, I could be wrong. It's a nice picture. Your mother looks happy there, doesn't she?'

Kitty gave the picture a last look before stowing it away again inside the folder. Something about Cora's expression when she looked at the photo made her want to hide it from prying eyes. 'Yes, I suppose she does.'

Cora tucked her tray under her arm, gave her a sympathetic smile, and left the room. As she closed the door, Kitty let out a sigh and sank back onto the sofa cushions. Cora may have provided the answer to one question but now there were a lot more. What had her mother been doing that day at Cullever Steps? How did she get there? Who had she been meeting? And who had taken the photograph?

CHAPTER TEN

Matt glanced at his wristwatch, ten past seven, Kitty was late. He was about to call her room when she arrived, breathless, in the lobby.

'Sorry, there was a crisis in the kitchen, and I needed to make arrangements for the start of the jazz evening tomorrow. Miss Delaware is something of a diva, but she is a star and we are very fortunate to have secured her.' She shrugged on her dark blue coat and reached behind the reception desk for her umbrella.

'Mr Potter is giving us a lift in his taxi. He's waiting in the rank. Even though it's not very far, it's a foul night, too wet to walk.' He opened the door for her and followed her outside into the rain. They hurried the few short steps from the front of the hotel to the taxi without speaking, the gusting wind rendering speech impossible.

Matt slipped into the rear seat of the cab next to Kitty and they set off on the brief journey through the town. She slid on the leather upholstery as the car lurched around a corner on the narrow street. Her leg brushed against his and he noticed her ease away from him, putting a few inches of space between them.

'Do you think we'll be able to see her?' Kitty broke the silence.

'We should be able to, they said she was feeling better, matron has given us special dispensation. Of course, she may not wish to see us.' The spring rain was drumming hard now on the metal roof of the car and the windows had begun to mist over, caused by the damp drying off their clothes. Matt rubbed his hands against the reassuring roughness of his twill trousers to remove the sweat building in his palms. The familiar buzzing started in his ears and he knew he couldn't bear it for much longer. He wound the handle to crack open the side window, sucking in the cold, damp air as it entered the car.

'Matthew?'

He was only dimly aware of Kitty taking his hand in hers. He closed his eyes tight shut and focused on his breathing, the way the self-help guides had told him. The rainwater was cold on his face and he gulped in lungfuls of the cool air as he tried to shut out the memories of the past that threatened to close in and overwhelm him.

At last the roaring in his ears began to subside and he opened his eyes to see Kitty staring at him, her face white with anxiety.

'Here, you ain't going to throw up in my cab, are you?' the driver asked, his gaze meeting Matt's in the rear-view mirror.

He shook his head.

'Matt?' There were unshed tears shining in Kitty's eyes and he became aware that he had her fingers in a vice-like grip.

'I'm fine.' His reassurance came out as a croak as he released her hand. He was aware of the driver's continued scrutiny via the rear-view mirror. 'I get a bit claustrophobic, remember.'

Kitty was flexing and releasing her fingers, presumably to try and restore her circulation.

'I'll drop you here.' The taxi jerked to a halt outside the front doors of the hospital.

'Cheers, mate, we appreciate this.' Matt paid him for the short trip. The building was a red brick cottage hospital sited right on the embankment.

The receptionist at the main desk pointed them in the direction of the private wing. Mrs Craven was located in a small, quiet room. The air smelled of soap and stale cabbage.

'I hope she'll be able to tell us what happened.'

'Me too.' The scent of the air and the clinical surroundings made Matt's skin itch and he wanted to finish the job and get out as soon as possible.

The elderly woman was propped up on a pile of pillows, her eyes closed, as they approached the bed. The papery whiteness of her skin was almost the same colour as her pillows.

A fierce-looking nurse in a dark uniform crackled up to them. 'Ten minutes, she tires easily.'

A crepe bandage covered most of Mrs Craven's hair, with just a few grey curls peeking out. Matt approached the bed with Kitty at his side. The heavy wooden door banged as it closed behind the nurse and Mrs Craven's eyelids fluttered open.

'You can come closer, I don't have anything catching,' she rasped.

Matt pulled up a chair and offered the seat to Kitty before getting one for himself.

'How are you feeling?' Kitty asked.

Mrs Craven waved a bony hand in the air. 'I'm alive, which at my age is something to be thankful for.'

'It was lucky I found you when I did or you might not have been,' Matt remarked.

The old lady fixed him with a stare. 'We had an appointment, young man, there was nothing lucky about it.'

'Mrs Craven, what happened?' Kitty leaned forward.

A faint frown puckered Mrs Craven's forehead. 'I went into the back garden to pull up some weeds. My gardener had missed a few. I wasn't outside for very long and I heard a noise near the house. At first I thought perhaps the breeze had blown the back door shut, but there wasn't any breeze.' She paused in her narrative as if trying to recall what had happened.

She motioned for Kitty to hand her a tumbler of water from the bedside locker. After taking a few sips she passed the glass back to Kitty and continued with her story. 'I couldn't see anything, so I carried on pulling out the mare's tail. I was conscious of the time and I wanted to get the job done before Captain Bryant arrived. With it being Gladys's day off I wanted to go back in, so I'd hear the door.' She moved her hand in Matt's direction. 'I'm not sure what made me look up again, I suppose the back door closing had made me uneasy.'

Matt wished the old woman would hurry up and spit out the facts. 'So, what happened next?' he prompted.

Kitty frowned at him and kicked his foot with the toe of her shoe.

'The door had opened again, just a crack, not very much, but enough for me to notice. I was still on my kneeler, so I went to stand up so I could go and see what it was. I thought it might be next door's cat, a beastly ginger striped thing that kills the birds.' She halted again and Matt noticed her face pale and her skinny, ringed fingers began clutching at the white hospital sheets. 'Anyway, at first I thought it might be the cat from next door but then I realised someone was standing to the side of me.'

'Did you get a good look at them?' Matt interrupted.

'Whoever it was wore dark trousers and a man's jacket.' Mrs Craven's voice faltered again, and Kitty offered her some more water. The elderly woman took a sip and gave the glass back. 'The sun was in my eyes, and she tried to disguise her voice, you know, to make it sound gruff and manly.'

'She?' Matt and Kitty spoke in unison.

Mrs Craven closed her eyes. 'It was a woman. At least it might have been a woman; he or she had this strange giggle.'

Matt could see she was tiring. 'Young or old?' he asked urgently.

'Elowed's age.'

Kitty stared at Matt. 'What did she say?'

Matt shook his head. 'We'd better go, I think we've exhausted her.' He rose from his seat and Kitty followed suit, pushing her chair back into place. He took a last backward glance at the small wizened figure on the bed, now sleeping peacefully. They had come tonight expecting to get some answers but were now leaving with even more questions.

Kitty frowned at him as they prepared to leave the ward. 'A woman? I don't understand, and what did she mean, *Elowed's age*?'

Matt shook his head; he couldn't think inside the clinical confines of the hospital. 'I don't know.'

They strolled together side-by-side to the front entrance. 'The rain has slowed off a little now.' Kitty unfurled her umbrella.

'Let's go for a drink somewhere.' Matt knew he needed to get out of the hospital, and away from the Dolphin Hotel.

Kitty hesitated for a moment then moved her umbrella to share the cover. 'Very well.'

During the short time they had been inside the hospital ward, the traffic had virtually disappeared and the storm had dwindled. Matt turned up the collar of his overcoat and dug his hands deep in his pockets as he walked beside Kitty, grateful for the scant protection of her umbrella.

Fortunately, the nearest respectable public house was only a couple of minutes away. 'Have a seat and I'll get the drinks. What would you like?' Matt asked.

'Gin please.' Kitty collapsed her umbrella and headed for a quiet corner table while Matt placed their order at the bar. Thankfully the pub was quiet as it was still early, and the foul weather seemed to have deterred people from going out. Her grandmother would not have approved of Kitty being seen in a public house in the town with a young man, no matter how respectable the place was.

He carried the drinks over to the table and took a seat next to her.

'Thank you, I feel like I really need this right now.' She took a large sip of her drink.

Matt raised his own glass and took a long pull of his pint. 'I know what you mean.'

'So, where do we go from here? This has thrown us all of a heap! I thought talking to Mrs Craven would give us some answers. Now

I feel more confused than ever. *A man or a woman…*' Kitty's voice tailed off and she shook her head as if trying to clear her thoughts.

'Why did she mention your mother? Did something about the person who attacked her remind her of Elowed or was it because you were in the room just now and she was getting tired?' Matt took another pull at his drink.

'I don't know. I didn't know if she meant my mother when she was my age or the age she would be now if she was still alive. Maybe it's like you said, she was just too tired to answer you properly and was confused.'

'Or perhaps her attacker reminded her of Elowed in some way.' Matt replaced his pint glass on the table.

'Did I tell you that Cora identified where that picture of Mother was taken? The old picture we found in the folder?' Kitty fiddled with the corner of the cardboard coaster under her wine glass.

'Who's Cora?' This was another surprise; he hadn't been aware that Kitty had confided in a staff member.

'She works at the hotel; she brought a cup of coffee upstairs as I was putting the folder away and she saw the picture. You met her the day you first arrived; she took you to meet my grandmother.' She folded another tiny pleat in the coaster edge.

'Where did she think it was taken?' After all this time he wasn't certain that knowing the location that Kitty's mother had visited would be of any value, but with the mystery deepening, any clue might help.

'Cullever Steps on Dartmoor, near Scarey Tor.'

'She was sure about it?' He was vaguely familiar with the name from various training routes in his army days of artillery practice.

Kitty nodded and took another sip of her gin. 'She said it used to be a courting spot. Mr Farjeon takes motor coach trips there. He has done for years.'

'Farjeon, the one with the green and yellow booth by the ferry crossing?'

'Yes, that's the one. You must have seen him around the town. A short man in a yellow and green blazer, wears a straw boater. He was the one who found the body in the river.'

'Hmm, interesting. How old is Cora? I take it she's local?'

'Yes, she's lived here all her life, I think. Grams took her on years ago when she struggled to get work. Her son, Colin, was a bit wild apparently and got sent away. I don't know what happened to her husband. She's been at the Dolphin for a long time now.'

'Did she know your mother?'

His question seemed to surprise Kitty; her eyes widened, and he could see her thinking. 'I suppose she must have but she never talks to me as if she knew her. Maybe Grams told her not to when I was small, so I didn't get upset, and she's kept that up.'

'Is she the same sort of age bracket as your mother?'

'You mean if my mother were alive?'

Matt nodded.

Kitty frowned. 'I never thought about it before. I suppose I could ask her. I would have thought she would have mentioned it before, though. I know a few people who knew Mother when she was young but most of them are Grams' friends.'

'Like Mrs C?'

'Yes.'

'If your mum grew up here, why is that? She must have had friends her own age, people she hung around with?'

Kitty took a large swallow of gin and shook her head. 'Mother wasn't exactly conventional, and Grams thought she was in with the wrong crowd, so she sent her away to school outside Dartmouth. I don't know if Grams really knew who her friends were. Mother was quite bohemian.' Her expression grew sad.

'No diary anywhere or any clues for us to trace anyone?'

'The various investigators all asked that. No, nothing. They couldn't even trace where my father was likely to be. I think Grams mentioned once that she thought he was in America, but I could be mistaken. He's as much a mystery as my mother.'

Matt's tone softened when he noticed the sorrow in her eyes. 'Do you ever wonder about him?'

Kitty tossed back the last of her drink. 'Not any more. I used to when I was young, but I have no memories of him at all. He could have come forward at any time when all the publicity was out there when Mother vanished. If he comes now, he'll be twenty-three years too late.'

CHAPTER ELEVEN

The barkeeper leaned over the counter. 'Excuse me, Miss Underhay, happen you'd best go back to the Dolphin.'

Foreboding gripped her. 'What's the matter?'

'Sirens. The bloke who's just come in the public bar reckons as there's smoke coming from the hotel and people out on the embankment.'

Kitty was out of her seat before the bartender had finished speaking. Matt handed her coat to her. Her heart pounded against the wall of her chest as she sprinted along the wet embankment. The acrid stench of smoke grew stronger the nearer she got to the hotel and the eerie wail of the fire siren echoed along the gloomy rain-soaked streets.

The fire engine was blocking the end of the street in front of the hotel. A gaggle of her guests accompanied by members of her staff stood in the fire evacuation zone.

'Kitty, wait.' Matt caught hold of her arm as she moved towards the fire engine. At least the flames of her imagination weren't leaping from the windows.

'I need to find out what's happening, and my staff and guests…' She waved a hand in the direction of the group on the pavement.

'Go and talk to the fire crew while I check up on the guests.' He gave her arm a gentle squeeze and headed over to the crowd.

She continued towards the fire engine. It only took a few seconds to locate the fire officer in charge.

'Are you the proprietor, miss?'

Kitty nodded, her gaze still anxiously scanning the exterior of the hotel for any signs of damage. 'What happened? Is anyone hurt? Is there much damage?' If the hotel had suffered much damage her grandmother would be heartbroken, *she* would be heartbroken. She noticed that the crew were recoiling a large hosepipe which had been attached to a hydrant.

The fire officer turned and gave a few more instructions to his crew before returning his attention to Kitty.

'The damage is confined to the rear of the premises. No one was hurt, miss. It's mostly smoke. The rain we had earlier stopped the fire from getting a proper hold.'

Kitty noticed the guests and her staff being addressed by another of the fire officers.

'What happened, though? When can my guests go back inside?'

'The premises are safe for people to return. If you'd like to come with me, I can show you the cause of the blaze.' He set off along the path at the side of the hotel. Kitty quickly spoke to her guests then followed at his heels, aware that Matt had joined her.

As they passed through the normally locked side gate and rounded the corner, the damage was obvious. The kitchen waste bins stood scorched and blackened near the rear of the hotel. A mixture of steam and smoke arising from the melted metal with a strong stench of burning hung like a pall in the air. A uniformed police officer stood to the side talking to one of the kitchen staff.

'I don't understand. What happened?' Kitty coughed and frowned as she tried to comprehend the scene before her.

'The kitchen waste bins appear to have been deliberately moved to a point close to the building but out of view of the staff, and then set alight using an accelerant. The contents inside the bins would have been dry enough to light.' The fire officer indicated the remains of the metal chains which usually kept the refuse containers in the assigned area.

Matt stepped forward and peered at the links. 'Someone seems to have had a bolt cutter on these.'

Before the fire officer could respond, the policeman came over to join them. 'Miss Underhay?'

'Yes.'

'This is a serious business, miss. I'm sure the fire officer has told you that the blaze was started deliberately?'

Kitty nodded. 'The bins are always secured away from the buildings. It looks as if someone has cut the chains, but I don't understand how they could have accessed this area. The gate is always locked.'

Much to her dismay, she noticed Walter Cribbs of the *Torbay Herald* making notes as he tried to eavesdrop on the conversation. Her grandmother would not be happy with negative publicity and ever since Christmas, when Kitty had turned down his advances, he had been looking for an opportunity for revenge. This was all she needed with Miss Delaware and her band due to arrive in the morning.

The policeman nodded and scribbled some notes in his pocketbook. 'Where were you this evening, Miss Underhay?'

'Why do you need to know Kitty's whereabouts?' Matt asked.

The policeman raised an eyebrow. 'I'm sorry, sir, you are?'

'Matthew Bryant, Miss Underhay's security officer.'

The policeman appeared to make another note in his book. 'I'm trying to establish if anyone saw or heard anything earlier this evening.'

'We were out, visiting someone at the hospital. We stopped for a drink and were about to return when we were told about the fire.' Kitty could still barely take in the events of the evening. A soft drizzle started, leaving a fine film of water clinging to her hair and face.

'You were in the kitchens earlier this evening, though, miss?'

'Yes, my chef was having problems with the grill, I needed to call a man to look at it.'

'If I could have a word with you, officer?' Matt took the policeman to one side, leaving Kitty with the fireman. She moved a few steps away from Walter Cribbs and his busy pen.

'Everything is secure now, Miss Underhay. We have all the evidence we need for our report.'

'Thank you for coming so quickly. I don't know what would have happened if you hadn't been able to put the fire out so fast.' She shivered as she took in the soot deposits and black scorch marks on the rear red brick wall of the hotel, dangerously close to the storerooms.

'We'll be in touch and if you require the information for your insurance company, the station will have a report for you.'

'Thank you.' Kitty hugged her coat closer to her as she joined Matt and the police officer.

Matt shook hands with the policeman as she approached. 'Is everything all right?' she asked.

'Captain Bryant has been very helpful. We'll be in touch if there are any developments.' The officer stowed his notebook away in his top pocket and took his leave.

Kitty folded her arms. 'What was that about?'

Matt shrugged. 'He was simply checking out who was where and when.'

She could tell from the way he didn't meet her gaze that there was more to the conversation that he wasn't sharing with her.

'And?' she asked as he went to turn away from her.

His gaze found hers. 'And nothing. We should go inside; this rain is getting worse again.'

She caught hold of his sleeve as he moved to walk inside the hotel. 'I asked a question, Matthew.'

'Come with me.'

She followed him through the kitchen, past the questioning eyes of her kitchen staff. He headed up the back stairs towards the landing and their rooms. Kitty hesitated for a second when he pulled his room key from the pocket of his trousers and opened the door.

'After you.' Matt stood to one side of the open door and waited for her to enter. She knew he had noticed her pause and it amused him.

Folding her arms across her chest, she marched through the door. She placed her umbrella in the corner of the room and hung her wet coat and hat on the hook on the back of the door before taking a seat.

'Well, *Captain* Bryant?' She deliberately emphasised the 'captain'.

He took off his own dripping hat and coat and added them to the peg next to hers. 'The war ended a long time ago. I prefer plain "Mister", although I admit I find my rank useful when dealing with the authorities.'

She wondered what had happened to him during the war, how he had been wounded and what exactly his post war government job had been. Her grandmother had said his service record was perfect, but many men had gone to war and come home as different people. Matt certainly appeared to have demons he was still fighting, like his fear of enclosed spaces.

He reached into the pocket of his overcoat and removed a small object. 'Do you recognise these at all?'

She stared at the broken pair of black-framed spectacles. 'Cora has a pair like those, she keeps them in her apron pocket. She's dreadfully shortsighted. She had them earlier when she looked at my mother's picture.'

'Mickey spotted her earlier this evening and thought she appeared to be behaving furtively. I asked him to keep his eyes open for anything that appeared out of the ordinary. These were next to the bin where the fire started.'

She stared at him. 'You're suggesting that Cora had a hand in this?'

'I think we need to speak to her.'

'Cora has always been a loyal employee. I've known her for years, since I was a child. I don't understand.'

'Cora was the one who identified the place on the moor. Do you think she was telling you the truth or is it some kind of wild goose chase to get you out of the way for some reason?' Matt asked.

'I don't know, why would she mention where she thought the picture had been taken? I would never have guessed Cora would be involved in any of this. The very idea makes me feel sick.'

'What do you want to do about it?'

Kitty stared at him. 'I don't understand.' It was hard enough trying to believe the evidence of her own eyes without thinking what she should do next.

'Do we question her ourselves? Hand her over to the police to question? Do you want to dismiss her? Or do you want to set a trap and see what happens?' Matt waited for her to reply.

'Finding her glasses is hardly a presumption of guilt. She could have noticed something herself and been investigating. She's terribly nosey. What do you suggest we do?' She knew from the look on his face that he was several steps ahead of her and he clearly already had his own ideas on what should happen.

His eyes narrowed as he considered. 'It's a tricky one. Technically, all we have are her glasses at the scene and Mickey's assertion that she was behaving oddly out near the bins shortly before the fire started.'

'Unless someone opened the gate from this side with a staff key, no one could open it from the other side.' Kitty hoped Cora had merely gone out to the bins for some innocent reason.

'Someone had oiled that lock recently, and it wasn't Mickey.'

'I can't believe Cora would attempt to burn down the hotel. It doesn't make sense. She relies on her employment here and certainly has no reason to bear a grudge of any kind.'

Matt jumped up and began to pace about the room. 'I agree. She has had other opportunities to set fires. This was something designed to frighten you rather than do any actual harm. Whoever set the fire knew the rain would make a lot of smoke without the fire being able to take a proper hold. Someone wants you out of the hotel for a while, almost as a distraction. The question is who and why.'

'The jazz evenings begin tomorrow. Do you think whoever this person is wanted to spoil the events? A rival hotelier perhaps?'

Matt glanced at his watch. 'I don't know. It's getting late. I think we need to talk to Cora tomorrow and I think I also need to talk to Mr Farjeon. His booth is near the lower ferry and he's been linked to Dartmoor with his tours. It seems too much of a coincidence that his name has popped up a few times now.'

Kitty rose and collected her umbrella. 'Miss Delaware arrives at lunchtime. I shall be tied up with arrangements for the evening for most of the day. The launch of the new summer visitor season is a big event, the local people look forward to it as much as the guests.'

Matt handed over her hat and coat. 'I've asked Mickey to let me know when Cora arrives for work. I'll talk to her and see what she has to say.'

'I do believe my poor hat is beyond saving thanks to all the rain.' She grimaced as she twisted the limp, felt brim between her fingers. 'Walter Cribbs from the *Herald* was buzzing around outside so I expect the fire will be in the newspaper. I hope we can get to the bottom of all this nonsense before anything else happens.'

Matt opened the door for her. 'Or before anyone else is hurt.'

CHAPTER TWELVE

Kitty expected Matt to contact her when Cora arrived for her shift, but it was time for luncheon, and she'd heard nothing. Unusually, she hadn't seen Cora all morning either. She left Mary in charge of the reception desk and headed for the dining room, intending to ask one of the staff if they had seen either Matt or Cora. She passed Mickey in the corridor, carrying his tool bag.

'Mickey, have you seen Mr Bryant this morning?'

The older man touched his cap as she approached. 'No, Miss Kitty. I did hear as how he'd been called to the police station, though. Probably be about that bother last night I expect.'

'Oh, thank you. Have you seen Cora today?' She wondered what had happened to her. Usually Cora would have brought a cup of tea for her mid-morning, but she hadn't appeared.

The maintenance man shook his head. 'No, Miss Kitty, her hasn't come to work.'

Kitty continued on her way, deep in thought. It was most unlike Cora not to come to work, and especially without sending a message. The implications of her absence made her feel quite ill and her appetite for the steak pudding that was on the day's luncheon menu was considerably diminished. Only the knowledge that she had Miss Delaware's imminent arrival to prepare for and a long evening ahead of her forced her to eat.

The rain of the previous evening had given way to a fresh, bright day. Miss Delaware's burgundy Rolls Royce Phantom Continental drew a small crowd as it temporarily blocked the street in front of the hotel. The statuesque personage of Miss Delaware herself emerging from the car drew audible gasps from the gathered people.

Kitty hurried out to meet her star entertainer, curious to greet her in the flesh. Miss Vivien Delaware had to be at least six feet tall, not including her rather marvellous hat. Her skin was the colour of dark chocolate and she was swathed from head-to-toe in magnificent white fox fur stoles.

'My dear child, let me look at you. The last time I saw you, you were an itty-bitty baby in your mama's arms.'

Kitty was swallowed up in the furs as Miss Delaware swooped to embrace her. Exotic perfume surrounded her senses. She struggled to make sense of the woman's statement.

'I'm sorry. I don't recall…' Kitty stammered.

'Of course not, honey. I mean I am pretty unforgettable, but you were just a babe in arms back then.' Vivien released her and stood back to look at her. 'I can't believe it, Eddy and Ella's little girl all grown up. You are just the very image of your mama.'

There was a strange buzzing in Kitty's ears as she stared back at this remarkable woman. 'You knew my parents?'

Vivien had turned her head to supervise her chauffeur and Albert, the porter, who were struggling to unload her luggage from the car. 'Sure thing, honey. That's why I agreed to come here. As soon as I saw the address and your name on the bottom of that letter, I said to my agent, Bobby, I just got to do that little pre-season slot before we go back to America.'

Vivien turned her attention back to Kitty in time to see her swaying on her heels. 'Baby girl, are you all right?'

Kitty was vaguely aware of a strong arm supporting her and leading her inside the hotel and Vivien calling for water.

'Breathe, honey. Are you all right? Don't you go passing out on me, you hear?' She had a soft American accent as smooth as honey.

Kitty managed to nod as Vivien steered her onto a nearby chair, while someone pushed a tumbler of water into her hand.

'Take a sip now.'

'Did you say you knew my father and mother?' She knew she'd already asked the question, but Vivien's response had been so unexpected it made her quite faint.

'Sure thing, honey. I last saw your mama before she caught the boat home. I waved her off at the dockside. Your pa was staying behind in New York as he had some kind of business to fix up. Nineteen fourteen, I think it was, right before the start of the war. You must have been what, four? Three? You had those great big eyes.' Vivien's dark brown eyes were filled with concern. 'Is something wrong?'

'I've never met anyone before who knew my parents when they were together.' Kitty's teeth chattered on the edge of the glass. 'My mother disappeared when I was six, only a couple of years after you last saw her, and I don't remember my father at all.'

'Oh, my goodness.' Vivien leaned back in her seat, before calling out to Albert. 'Be careful with that bag.'

Kitty took a deep breath and tried to give poor Albert a reassuring smile as he hauled Miss Delaware's baggage to the elevator. The remainder of her staff beat tactful retreats at her apparent recovery. 'When did you last see my father? Do you know where he is?' The whole thing was surreal.

'Do you know, honey, it's the strangest thing, I hadn't seen Eddie Underhay for over twenty years. We lost touch with moving around so much, but then a few weeks ago, who should I see at the club? Your pa. Older and, I don't want to upset you, looking a little worse for the wear. I didn't notice him at first, he was closeted up with some guy in the shadows. Looked like they were having an intense conversation. By the time my set finished, the man had disappeared.'

'My father was in London? But you're sure it was him?' It was impossible. No one had been able to locate her father for years.

'Uh-huh. I'd have thought he'd have stuck around to say hello or something, but he'd gone. I checked with the doormen to see if he'd left me a note or a message, but nothing. I thought since he came to my club, he would've made contact. You feeling better, sweetie? I'm so sorry, I had no idea about your parents or that I'd upset you so much.'

'I'm fine, really. It was just such a shock. I wasn't even sure my father was still alive. He never came forward when my mother disappeared. I've no photographs or letters, nothing.' Her pulse seemed to be resuming its normal rate now the startling news had begun to sink in. Surely Miss Delaware must have been mistaken.

'I expect he wasn't in England at the time so I guess he wouldn't know, especially if you say he hadn't seen your ma since she came back here. He has dual citizenship I think; his mother was from Boston, and he always spent most of his time in the US. I'm so sorry about your mother, Elowed was one of a kind, and she was a good friend to me.'

'Thank you.' If what she'd just heard was true, then where was her father now? Why hadn't he come to see her? Surely he knew where she was, even if she had not been able to find him.

Kitty asked Mary to show Miss Delaware to her room and to provide her with refreshments. She needed a little time to gather her thoughts. She had hundreds of questions she wanted to ask, but right now she simply needed to think about what she had just learned. Her father was alive, and had been in London so recently. She needed to talk to Matt as soon as he returned, then later she would need to call her grandmother.

*

'Thank you for attending, Captain Bryant. Mrs Cora Wakes's only known relative is her son, Colin, and we are having some difficulties locating him. It didn't seem right to ask Miss Underhay.'

Matt nodded and waited for the mortuary assistant to uncover the woman's face. This was the part he had been dreading. Memories of other dead faces, bloated and swollen, flashed back into his mind. He took a deep breath and tried to fix his mind on Cora, alive, in the hotel. 'Yes, I can confirm that is Cora Wakes.'

The assistant re-covered Cora's face and Matt slowly released the breath he had been holding, glad the ordeal was over. He was thankful that Kitty had been spared the onerous task of identifying her late employee.

'You say she was found in the river?'

The sergeant grunted an affirmation as Matt followed him from the room. 'Yes, sir, near the lower ferry. Normally you'd have expected the tide to have took her out and round the bay this time of year but she got caught up in the reeds, probably took there by the backwash off one of the boats. Same as the other gentleman.'

'Accident?' Matt drew a cigarette from his case as soon as they were outside the building and offered one to the sergeant.

'Police doctor reckons not. Large wound on the back of her head. No water in her lungs. She would have been dead before she hit the water.' The officer accepted the cigarette and the two men strolled a short distance together.

'Murder?'

'Her still had her purse in her coat pocket, so it doesn't look as if she were robbed.' The sergeant's expression was grave.

'Nasty business.'

'Very bad.'

'Do you have any more leads on the other murder?' Matt asked.

The sergeant sighed. 'Beyond identifying him, we don't know very much more than that. They've sent an inspector up from London to deal with your Mr DeVries, and I reckon he likes him for the murder. A nasty piece of work by all accounts.'

'Perhaps he was simply in the wrong place at the wrong time. I hope you catch the culprit soon.'

'Thank you, sir. I expect Miss Underhay and Mrs Treadwell will be upset, Mrs Wakes has been at the Dolphin for a good many years. What is this town coming to?'

Matt blew out a narrow stream of smoke. 'Yes, I'm sure they will be. What was Mr DeVries's line of business exactly?' He would have welcomed a chat with the mysterious 'Mr Smith', if only to rule him out of involvement in the anonymous letters.

'He's an expert in his field but on the shady side. Specialist gem cutter. Whisper is, he was here to do a cutting job. And that Mr Blaas, the man we fetched out the river, is a gem buyer.'

Matt stubbed out his cigarette and let out a low whistle. 'No idea what the cutting job could be, I suppose? No ladies been relieved of their jewels hereabouts lately?' He knew there were several country houses in the area as well as the well-heeled guests at the grand hotels in Torquay.

'No, sir, it's a puzzle and no mistake. At least we know he weren't the one murdering Mrs Wakes, him being locked up and all.' The sergeant extinguished his own cigarette.

'No news on who attacked Mrs Craven either? Same modus operandi?'

'Ar well, sir, who knows. Inspector Greville is doing the looking into things.' The sergeant's expression changed slightly, and his gaze shifted so he was no longer meeting Matt's eyes. Matt wondered if Mrs Craven's ramblings about Elowed had made the police suspect Kitty, especially with the anonymous letters.

He held out his hand to shake the sergeant's. 'Well, good luck. I'm sure you'll do everything to catch the man or men responsible.'

'Yes, sir, and thank you again. Not a nice task on a bright spring day.' The man bade farewell, leaving Matt to meander along deep in thought.

'Captain Bryant!' A breathless shout from behind him broke into his reverie. He paused on the pavement as a short man in his mid-twenties wearing thick-lensed spectacles caught up to him.

'Whew, nearly missed you, sir. Walter Cribbs, *Torbay Herald*.' He proffered a slightly dog-eared card.

Matt took the card to be polite. Much as he disliked and distrusted the press, he had no wish to make an enemy. 'I believe you were at the Dolphin Hotel last night to report on the vandalism?'

The reporter's eyes gleamed behind his glasses as his breathing steadied to a less wheezy rhythm. 'Yes indeed, a shocking business. Miss Underhay must be very relieved no one was hurt.'

'Indeed. Let's hope they catch the culprit soon.'

'The crime rate in Dartmouth appears to have increased dramatically since you arrived, Captain Bryant. A wanted man staying at the Dolphin, a fire, Mrs Craven viciously attacked in her own home, and now an employee of the Dolphin found drowned, believed murdered.'

A faint sneer framed Walter Cribbs's mouth and Matt experienced a sudden desire to remove it with his fists. Instead he remained calm. 'Yes, I had no idea the town was so dangerous. That must be why Mrs Treadwell asked me to work for her, to ensure her guests' safety and privacy.'

'I'm given to understand that Miss Underhay may be implicated in the attack on Mrs Craven?' The reporter had produced a notepad and his pencil was hovering over the page.

'Then you are misinformed. Miss Underhay is very concerned for Mrs Craven's recovery as the lady has been suffering from confusion since the assault. Mrs Craven is a dear friend of her grandmother.' He had guessed correctly that Mrs C had been waffling on about Elowed and now the police were investigating Kitty's alibi. It was clearly ridiculous that Kitty could be involved.

'And the body of Cora Wakes, drowned in mysterious circumstances shortly after the fire?'

Matt snorted. 'Are you insinuating that Miss Underhay is in the habit of trying to burn down her own hotel on a rainy night and that she killed Cora Wakes because she saw her do it? I think you've been watching too many films at the cinema, my friend.'

Walter returned his notepad and pencil to his coat pocket. 'You can't blame a bloke for trying. Usually the most exciting thing I get to report on is Jeb Carter being fined for being drunk and disorderly again. I have to ask the questions. Miss Underhay and I are very close, and I can't be seen to show favouritism.'

From the way Kitty had spoken about Walter, this was evidently untrue. 'Will you be attending the jazz evening tonight? Miss Delaware and her band were a huge success in London, I believe?'

'A reporter's work is never done, the public must have the news. I expect I shall see you and Miss Underhay there. I'm sure Kitty will be expecting me.' Walter tipped the brim of his hat before scuttling off down the street.

On his way back to the hotel, Matt decided to call at Hubert Farjeon's yellow and green striped booth near the ferry site. The little wood-panelled building was shaped like a fairy-tale castle turret complete with pointed roof and a pennant on top.

The booth was closed but he spent a few minutes looking at the bills advertising Mr Farjeon's motor coach tours. Every Wednesday it seemed he took parties to Torquay to try the refined delights of the glorious beaches and sophisticated promenades. On Fridays there was a whole day tour to Dartmoor to see the glorious wildness of the moors and to sample a delicious Devon cream tea. There were several other tours described with so much hyperbole that Matt wondered if Mr Farjeon employed Walter Cribbs to write his advertising copy.

He noticed a uniformed officer searching along the grassed area of the embankment near the ferry and wondered if that was where the authorities thought Cora had entered the water. It certainly seemed to be the same place that the other man had been found. He would have liked to ask questions but decided he needed to return to the Dolphin to tell Kitty that Inspector Greville might be calling on her.

CHAPTER THIRTEEN

Kitty was struggling to finish dressing when there was a knock on the door of her room. 'Who is it?' She wiggled her dark blue satin sleeveless dress into place over her hips and looked on her dressing table for her necklace.

'It's Matt, are you decent?'

'Are you determined to ruin what's left of my reputation?' She flew across the room to haul him inside before anyone came along the corridor and saw him there. 'Where have you been all day? I have so much to tell you.'

Without waiting for his reply, she handed him her necklace and turned her back, bowing her head forward, exposing the fashionable low-cut back of her dress. 'Could you fasten the clasp on this for me, please? I have no maid tonight as everyone is busy downstairs and I need to get to the ballroom for the start of Miss Delaware's performance.'

'Kitty, I need to talk to you.' His fingers were cool against the skin at the nape of her neck as he fumbled with the tiny clasp of her necklace.

'Is it about the body in the river? Such horrid news. One of the guests told one of the girls this morning and it's been the buzz of the day. They said it was the same place where that other poor man was found. Mickey said you'd been called to the police station and then Cora didn't come to work.' She straightened her head as his fingers moved away from her neck, leaving behind the faintest sizzle of electricity.

'Kitty, the body in the river...' He stopped speaking as she turned to look at him.

'Who was it?' She suspected she already knew the answer but dreaded the confirmation. The very idea made her sick. The gossip had said it was a woman, and Cora was missing. She hadn't wanted to believe there might be a connection.

'The police asked me to officially confirm her identity. Obviously, they knew who it was already, but protocol has to be followed. I'm so sorry, Kitty.'

'Cora.' Although she had already guessed it might be the case, it was still shocking to have it confirmed.

Matt nodded. 'They're trying to trace her son, Colin. He's not been seen at his address for a few weeks.'

'Accident? Or suicide? What happened to her?' It was hard to believe Cora was dead. She was part of the furniture at the Dolphin, poking around in everyone's business, feeding people tea and biscuits. Trying to be first to find out any titbits of news and passing the gossip whether a person wanted to hear it or not.

'It looks like murder. The police doctor says she was hit over the head before she fell into the water.'

Kitty gasped and placed her hand over her mouth. Hearing her fears made real made bile rise into the back of her throat. 'What's happening around here, Matt?'

She watched as he paced about the room. 'I don't know. I wish I did but whatever is happening it's far more dangerous than either your grandmother or I thought it would be.'

Kitty sank down onto the chaise longue at the foot of her bed. 'I knew Grams was keeping something more from me.'

'Only that she was afraid for your safety. She was convinced the letters were to do with your mother, but she was reticent on the subject of your father. With these events happening, I wonder when we'll hear from the anonymous letter writer again and if the letters will become more specific.'

'You think we will get more, now Cora is dead?'

Matt nodded. 'Oh yes, I'm sure of it. There has to be some connection; I don't believe in coincidence.'

'Miss Delaware told me she saw my father in her club in London the other week.' She didn't think she would ever see Matt struck dumb, but it seemed she had succeeded. 'She knew my parents when they were together it seems, and she says she recognised him.' She quickly filled Matt in on all she'd learned that afternoon.

'Kitty, be very careful. Again, this can't simply be coincidental.' He didn't look happy. 'We'll call your grandmother in the morning. She needs to know what Miss Delaware has told you about your father, and about what's happened to Cora.'

'Do you think what she said was true? My father is alive and in London?'

'I don't know. She may be telling the truth. We can try and find out more over the next few days. I think it's time your grandmother told us everything she knows.'

She caught sight of the time on his wristwatch. 'I have to go downstairs. I'm late.' She jumped to her feet.

'I'll be down shortly. I need to change.'

He slipped out of her room and she finished her toilette before locking the door and heading towards the ballroom. She took a deep breath as she descended the broad oak staircase, her satin skirts swishing against her legs.

The hum of conversation mingled with the music from the Dolphin's small house band to greet her as she entered the ball-room. Cigarette smoke hung in a pale blue fuzz over the white linen-covered tabletops and the huge glass chandeliers glittered with electric light. Some couples were already on the dance floor, others seated at the tables. Jewellery sparkled on the ladies' gowns and hair ornaments and the gentlemen were formal in dark dinner suits. Evening entertainment at the Dolphin was free to guests and at a small ticket price for visitors. A satisfying number of tickets had been sold for the opening night and the hotel was fully booked.

She spotted Walter Cribbs lurking behind one of the potted palms and swiftly headed in the opposite direction. She had no wish for an encounter with him. Miss Delaware was due to make her entrance within a few minutes with her musicians and it seemed that all of Dartmouth society was there to see her.

Kitty moved through the crowds, nodding and smiling in acknowledgement to those she knew. It appeared that news of Miss Delaware's arrival had spread around the bay like wildfire. There were several parties that she guessed must have motored from Torquay. There were also lots of faces she didn't recognise.

She made it to the small, low-set stage just as the band were finishing the last song of their set and Miss Delaware's musicians prepared in the wings to take over. The crowd applauded and the couples on the dance floor resumed their seats as Kitty entered the stage to take to the microphone.

'Welcome lords, ladies and gentlemen to the Dolphin Hotel. We are delighted and honoured to have as our guest entertainer for the next two weeks the wonderful Miss Vivien Delaware and her band. Miss Delaware has recently completed a residency at The Cat's Miaow club in London and is a huge star in her native city of Chicago in America. We are so fortunate to have her here. I'm sure you'll all make her very welcome, Miss Vivien Delaware.'

Kitty stepped off the stage to rapturous applause as Vivien strode out in a daringly cut, new style gold silk evening gown. She nodded her head to acknowledge Kitty's introduction before launching into 'Night and Day', a huge hit from the previous year and a guaranteed crowd-pleaser.

'Champagne?' A glass was pressed into her hand and she turned her head to discover Matt standing at her side, resplendent in a black double-breasted dinner suit. His unruly hair for once was tidy and she caught a glimpse of gold cufflinks as he adjusted his bow tie.

'You scrub up very nicely, Mr Bryant,' Kitty murmured, 'and very quickly.' She took a sip of her drink and continued to survey the room.

'You too, Miss Underhay.' His deep voice so close to her ear called a blush to her cheek.

'Vivien is terribly good, isn't she?'

'Excellent. You were lucky to get someone of her stature. How did you come to book her?'

Kitty frowned. 'I'm not really sure. I remember thinking she probably wouldn't want to come as we obviously can't pay London rates, but I think I heard she'd been a little unwell and had been advised to take sea air, so I thought I'd try. I only secured the booking a few weeks ago after our original booking let us down.'

'And you can't recall who told you about her?'

She glanced up at him. 'I think I received a flyer from the theatrical booking agency we use. I wanted someone different from our regular entertainers and it was a little last minute. Do you know, I rather think Cora told me she'd read about Vivien in a stage newspaper so I wrote to her agent.' Her eyes widened. 'You think it might have been some kind of set-up to get her here?'

Matthew raised his own glass and took a sip. 'It's curious, don't you think?'

Vivien moved seamlessly on to her next song. Matt took Kitty's glass from her hand and placed it next to his on a nearby table. 'May I have the pleasure of a dance, Miss Underhay?'

Before she could protest, he swept her out onto the crowded dance floor. 'What are you doing?'

'Walter Cribbs was heading in our direction.' Matt expertly guided her into a less populated space.

'Ugh, that wretched man. I expect he has a photographer with him too. People pay the newspaper for print copies of themselves all dressed up on an evening out.' Even as she spoke, she could see the photographer taking a picture of Sir Roderick Nightingale, the local magistrate, with his wife and daughter.

'Still, all good publicity and fodder for the society column. Mr Cribbs was keen to impress upon me your close friendship,' Matt remarked. 'Better smile and look as if you're enjoying yourself.'

She gasped indignantly at Walter Cribbs's nerve. The gentle heat of Matt's hand through the flimsy navy satin of her dress as he guided her around the dance floor made her feel a little giddy as they moved together in time to the music and she relaxed into the rhythm.

She wasn't sure if she was glad or sorry when he finally released her at the side of the dance floor when the song ended.

'I see our drinks are gone. I'll get some more.' Matt vanished into the crowd.

'Miss Underhay, what a triumph this all is. Your dear grandmother must be delighted.'

Mr Farjeon stood before her. In place of his usual striped blazer and straw boater he wore a rather old-fashioned black dinner suit which appeared to have seen better days and bore a faint scent of mothballs. He was a stiff little man in his late sixties, with grey hair and a moustache.

'Thank you, Mr Farjeon, you're most kind. My grandmother is away at present and I know she will be very disappointed if she doesn't return in time to hear Miss Delaware sing.'

The man gave a tiny bow. 'Better news for her than the unfortunate fire, and of course, Mrs Wakes's terrible accident.'

'Goodness, news travels swiftly in our small town. Luckily the fire did little damage, but as you say, poor Cora's death is quite shocking. I heard you made the awful discovery of the earlier murder?'

Mr Farjeon became serious. 'Indeed, it was most distressing. I saw something moving in the water. I was quite cross at first thinking someone had deposited rubbish or an animal carcass. I used a boatman's pole to try to manoeuvre it to the bank. Forgive me, Miss Underhay, when I say the shock of those dead eyes looking into mine—' He broke off and wiped his upper lip with a slightly grubby handkerchief.

Kitty was relieved to see Matt arriving with fresh drinks.

'Mr Farjeon, may I present Captain Bryant, the new security manager here at the Dolphin.'

Matt's eyebrows rose by the tiniest fraction at her use of his military title. He extended his hand to Mr Farjeon. 'Delighted to meet you, sir. I understand you have a motor coach touring business?'

Mr Farjeon smoothed his moustache. 'Ah, yes, you may have seen my little booth. Day trips to visit the delights of our glorious countryside aboard the Daisy-belle.'

'It sounds delightful. Have you had the business for long?'

'Quite some years now. I had to stop for a time during the war. Fuel shortages and of course the military. It's taken some time to build things back up and the public expect so much these days.'

'Mr Farjeon and I were discussing poor Cora and of course that other unfortunate.' Kitty took a fortifying sip of champagne. She guessed that Mr Farjeon had suffered financial hardships over the last decade, hence his rather shabby appearance.

'Yes, I was saying to Miss Underhay, what a tragedy. Especially so soon after the other. The police were examining the area near my booth. I believe they may have recovered the unfortunate lady's handbag from the riverbank. Most distressing, the whole thing.' He shook his head sorrowfully. Kitty exchanged a glance with Matt.

'Poor lady. I think that the police are trying to trace her son.'

Mr Farjeon gave Matt a sharp look. 'Indeed, I was unaware... dear, dear. Colin Wakes was always something of a disappointment to poor Cora, I believe. He took after his father, drink and petty crime.'

'The police think she met with her end shortly before midnight.' Matt's tone was smooth.

'You live near your booth, Mr Farjeon, did you see or hear anything untoward?' Kitty asked.

'I, dear lady? No, not at all. Not in either case. I would have been secure in my bed by then. I'm not as young as I was, you know. You must excuse me; I see the mayor beckoning me.' He nodded to them both and made his escape.

'Another curiosity,' Matt remarked. 'That was a rather swift exit.'

'Hmm, do you think he did see or hear something?'

'I don't know, but he's a slippery customer all right. It would seem though that he couldn't have been involved with your mother's trip to Dartmoor if he wasn't operating his motor coach then.'

Kitty drained the last of her champagne. 'It certainly sounds that way; it could all be a red herring, I suppose, nothing to do with anything. I must go and mingle, and also check up on my staff. I believe Miss Delaware has another couple of songs before her first break.'

She walked towards the bar and saw that her staff all appeared to be coping with the throng of people waiting for drinks. Waitresses circulated the tables and the cold supper, included in the price of the ticket for visitors, was being set out in the side room.

Happy that all was going to plan she made her way around the side of the room, greeting people she knew and acknowledging others.

'Congratulations on a fine event, Miss Underhay.'

Kitty didn't recognise the speaker. He must be a visitor as he certainly wasn't one of the hotel guests. A smartly dressed older gentleman, he had greying hair and an undefinable trace of an accent. 'Thank you, sir. I hope you are enjoying your evening.'

She gave her stock answer and moved on but something about the man drew her gaze back to him and she discovered him staring at her in a very disconcerting way. By the time she had found Matt however, the stranger had gone.

CHAPTER FOURTEEN

Kitty was sorting out the receipts and accounts from the jazz evening in her grandmother's salon the next day when Inspector Greville paid her a call.

A tall, thin lugubrious man in his fifties, with a sad moustache, he removed his hat as he entered the salon. 'Miss Underhay, Inspector Greville.' He offered her his card.

'Please come in, Inspector, and take a seat. I've asked for some tea to be sent up and for Captain Bryant to join us. Do you have news yet about whoever attacked poor Cora?' She took a seat on the sofa and waited for his response. Matt had alerted her to the possibility of a call from the inspector and felt it wise to use his military title. She supposed from the inspector's age and appearance that he too was probably a former military man.

Inspector Greville appeared to be considering his response before answering her question. 'We have a number of lines of enquiry at present, Miss Underhay. We are trying to establish a timeline of events of who saw Mrs Wakes and when.'

There was a knock at the door and a young red-headed maid in a smart black uniform entered with a tea tray, followed by Matt.

'Thank you, Alice. You may go.' She dismissed the maid as Matt shook hands with the inspector.

'How can I assist you?' Kitty asked as she set out the cups, ready to pour.

'Thank you, miss.' The officer accepted his cup and took a sip. 'I'm just attempting to tie up a few loose ends, so to speak.'

'Of course.' Kitty passed a cup to Matt.

'Your grandmother, Mrs Treadwell, reported some anonymous letters which made her fearful for your safety and that of the hotel?'

'Yes, the letters were very vague, but they concerned her. She employed Captain Bryant to look after security here and I understand the police have made additional patrols.' Kitty drank some of her tea.

'Hmm, no more letters recently?'

'Nothing hinting at arson, Inspector, or murder.'

'I've handed the letters over to the local constable,' Matt interjected.

The inspector set his cup back on the saucer before drawing a notebook from the breast pocket of his coat. 'There are some points of similarity between the attack on Mrs Craven, the murder of Mr Blaas, and the murder of Mrs Wakes.'

'So, I believe.' Kitty waited for him to continue. She wondered if Blaas was a Dutch surname, the same as DeVries.

'Mrs Craven is an elderly lady, and clearly the nature of her injury has caused her some confusion.' He surveyed Kitty from under heavy-lidded eyes and she couldn't tell what he might be thinking. 'Mrs Craven has described the person who attacked her as possibly being female but dressed as a man. It was the person's slight stature and high-pitched giggle that appeared to confuse her.'

'Yes, she mentioned this to us when we visited her at the hospital. She did appear very muddled.' She proffered a plate of biscuits. 'Rather extraordinarily, she mentioned my mother's name.'

A faint reddish tinge appeared on the inspector's cheeks. 'Yes, miss, I believe your mother was reported missing some years ago?'

'In nineteen sixteen. I was six. The war was on and my mother was known to be somewhat bohemian. She was a keen supporter of the women's suffrage movement and there was a shortage of manpower. I don't think her disappearance was viewed as a cause for concern for some while. However, no one has seen her since then and all investigations have led to the sad conclusion that she is almost certainly dead.' Kitty placed the biscuits back on the tray.

'I see. And you have no idea why Mrs Craven would think she had seen your mother?' The inspector appeared uncomfortable.

'None. She disliked my mother, and in her confusion, she may have associated someone she disliked with an unpleasant event. It may also be that because I was in the room, and I'm told I resemble my mother, that she became confused.' She took a sip of her tea. Matt stayed silent.

'I understand from Captain Bryant that you were working here at the hotel on the afternoon when Mrs Craven was attacked?'

Kitty raised an eyebrow. 'I think that if you ask my staff you'll find I have the perfect alibi, Inspector. Captain Bryant himself saw me here as he left to go and visit her. I have no reason to go around assaulting my grandmother's friends and certainly couldn't have gone to her house and attacked her to return in time to pretend I had never left.' She watched as he made some notes in his book.

'When did you last see Mrs Wakes?'

She considered the question. 'I glimpsed her in the hotel foyer shortly before I left with Captain Bryant to visit Mrs Craven at the hospital. Cora should have finished her shift at four o'clock but a staff member hadn't come to work so she had offered to stay until eight to help out in the dining room. That wasn't unusual, Cora was often short of money and liked to take up extra hours. I also think she was somewhat lonely, hence her interest in other people's affairs.'

'You didn't notice anything unusual about her manner?'

'On the contrary, she seemed pleased with herself. I assumed it was because the extra money would be welcome to her and it was a foul night so she could stay in the dry.'

The inspector duly noted Kitty's replies in his book.

'Is Miss Underhay in the clear now? She couldn't have conked Cora over the head and pushed her in the river either as she was here at the hotel after the fire dealing with guests.' Matt leaned back on the sofa.

'Miss Underhay's responses have been very helpful. One has to tie up loose ends and as I mentioned, find a timeline. Miss Underhay's answers confirm the evidence given by your maintenance man.'

'Of course, Mickey saw her after we'd left for the hospital.' Kitty picked up the teapot and topped up his cup.

'Mr Farjeon told me that your men discovered Mrs Wakes's handbag not far from his booth in the long grass near the embankment. The same point where Mr Blaas met his end?'

The inspector turned his gaze to Matt. 'Yes, we believe that may be where she entered the water.'

'Her bag was on the bank, but her purse was in her coat pocket; did you not find that rather suggestive?'

Kitty frowned at Matt and wondered what he meant.

'You mean she may have taken out her purse to pay for something, or in the expectation of receiving money, and didn't return it to her bag?'

'Was there much in her purse?' Kitty asked.

The inspector drained his cup and eyed them both, as if judging if he could trust them with the information he was about to impart. 'There was a five pound note.'

Kitty's mind raced. 'Cora wouldn't have had that kind of money on her person. She was always short of funds because she supported her son, Colin. He was frequently unemployed and often asked his mother for money. How very odd.'

'Indeed, miss.' The inspector rose and collected his hat from the side table. 'Thank you for the tea, Miss Underhay. You have my card, should you think of anything which could assist the enquiry.'

'Inspector, the man who was staying here, Mr Smith – or rather, Mr DeVries – is he involved with the death of the other man?'

Greville turned his hat around in his hands as if unsure of how much he should say. 'The men were connected, but we don't believe he was involved in the murder.'

'I see, thank you.' She couldn't help feeling a little relieved that whatever crimes Mr Smith may have committed, at least he had not murdered Mr Blaas.

'I'll come with you and see you out.' Matt escorted Inspector Greville from the salon.

*

'You believe Cora had gone to meet someone to collect that money?' Kitty asked as soon as he returned to the salon.

'I'm not sure.' He felt her gaze resting on him as he paced about the room. 'Inspector Greville is making enquiries at the bank.'

'The bank?'

'Cora's son, Colin, hasn't been seen at his address for several weeks. Cora was nothing if not a doting mother. If she had gone to receive money from someone, they wouldn't have killed her and left the money behind.'

'Oh. You think Cora was expecting to meet Colin and the money was for him?'

'Could be. I think the money may be from her savings.'

'Do you think he might have been involved with the fire?'

Matt could see Kitty's mind racing.

'Cora may have been intending to give him money so he could get away. Why would he set a fire, though?'

'Perhaps so he could search within the hotel without interruption for whatever it is that someone is looking for?' Matt suggested.

'Oh, this is all so complicated. Do you think Colin is behind those letters?'

'It's a possibility; he would know about your mother and her disappearance. Now, we need to call your grandmother before we meet Miss Delaware and her agent for luncheon.'

'I think you should tell her about the fire and Cora before I ask her about Vivien and my father.'

'Coward.' He took a seat at the bureau and dialled. Mrs Treadwell was understandably shocked by news of the arson attack and she sounded genuinely upset over Cora. He passed the receiver to Kitty.

'Darling, are you all right? Such dreadful news. Poor Cora, do they think that ne'er-do-well son was involved?'

'I don't know if Colin is a suspect, the inspector didn't give much away. It does look bad for him, though. They still haven't made an arrest for the other murder. By the way, Miss Delaware's first night was a terrific success, despite everything. People came from miles to hear her. It's such a shame that something so terrible has happened to spoil things.'

'People are sensation-hunters, sad to say; I doubt something so awful as poor Cora's demise will put them off. I'm glad Miss Delaware went down well.' Matt could hear Mrs Treadwell's replies quite clearly.

'Did Mother ever mention a friend called Vivien?' Kitty asked.

'Your mother? I don't know, darling. Not that I can recall. She had many friends, as you know, but never said much about them. She knew I disapproved. Why?'

'Miss Delaware claims to know my parents. She says she met them when they were together, living in America. She says she knew me when I was an infant before mother bought me to the Dolphin.'

There was a moment of silence.

'How very unexpected.'

'Miss Delaware also says she saw my father in London a few weeks ago in the club where she was performing. She is confident that it was him.' Kitty's voice shook slightly.

Mrs Treadwell's gasp was so loud that Matt heard it. 'That's impossible. No one has seen Edgar in England for years. Not since he left for America at the start of the war.'

'When did you last see him, Grams?'

Matt raised his brow. To the best of his knowledge Mrs Treadwell had always denied ever meeting Elowed's husband, yet Kitty clearly now had reason to believe differently.

'In nineteen fourteen, at the start of the Great War. Your mother had returned to England with you. Edgar followed a few weeks later. Then Elowed sent a telegram to me from London saying Edgar was returning to America. She asked me for a loan to tide her over until he settled some business affairs.'

He could see Kitty's fingers turning white as she tightened her grip on the telephone receiver.

'I caught the train to see your mother and you. Edgar was only present at the house briefly. I wanted to remind him of his patriotic duty to serve his country. Young men all over the country were queuing up to enlist, I was ashamed that a son-in-law of mine would not be amongst them. Your father, however, had other ideas. His mother was from Boston and he has dual nationality; he had no intention of serving even if the war would be over by Christmas.'

'You never told me any of this. You always said you'd never met him.'

'No. I didn't want you to think of your father as a coward and to bear that shame. I only met Edgar a couple of times in total and that was the last time I saw him. Your mother was always reticent about where they had met and what line of business he was in. She was of age when they married so of course I could do nothing to prevent it. It was bad enough that you lost your mother, I couldn't bring myself to discuss your father and his shortcomings. I regret to say that your father was not the kind of gentleman I would have wished your mother to have married. I'm sorry, Kitty, I should have told you, but you had lost your mother and somehow the time never appeared right.'

No wonder Mrs Treadwell had not wished to discuss Kitty's father. A draft dodger and a coward. Cold fury coiled in Matt's stomach. The man must be a complete scoundrel to abandon his wife and child and flee overseas to avoid enlisting. Then to fail to return after the war to even find out what had happened to them was appalling.

'Oh, Grams, do you think all this unpleasantness is tied up with what happened when Mother went missing?' A tear rolled down Kitty's cheek and Matt swallowed hard. This had to be dreadful news for her.

'I don't know. I can't understand it. Why now? After all this time? Your mother only left you a few things. And yet someone must believe we have something of value.'

'I know. There was nothing that anyone could possibly find of any worth. Certainly nothing that could cause all this intrigue.'

'As soon as poor Livvy is well enough to travel I've insisted I shall bring her back to convalesce. Do say you forgive me for not telling you about your father, darling, I only wanted to protect you.'

'Of course I forgive you. It will be wonderful, Grams, to see you and Aunt Livvy. I've missed you so much.'

Kitty made small talk with her grandmother for a few more minutes before ending the call. She replaced the receiver before retrieving her handkerchief from her pocket and dabbing her eyes and nose.

He waited until she had composed herself. 'What do you have of your mother's?'

'An old locket, some photographs. A few of her scarves, her fur stole, and my clock.'

'A clock?'

Kitty smiled. 'Apparently, when my parents were first married, they toured Europe on honeymoon and Mother bought this darling, funny little wooden cuckoo clock. You must have seen them, the ones with the weights underneath and a little cuckoo sounding out the hour. I've always loved it and it's hung on my wall for years.'

'What happened to the rest of the things?'

'You saw the letters – well, some of them. My grandmother couldn't bear to keep Mother's things around, but she thought I might want them one day. She had everything packed up and they were stored in the hotel until the refurbishment a few years ago. There are only a couple of boxes.'

'So where are they now?'

Kitty shrugged. 'I'm not sure. We had to move them. I rather think Mrs Craven may have them. The storeroom roof had a leak and Grams was worried about damp.' Her eyes widened. 'Do you think that's what they were looking for? My mother's things? But there is nothing of any value in those boxes. Just some old clothes and personal effects. Really, I should have thrown them out.'

Matt wondered if that were true. 'Well, someone must think there is something in there.' He would dearly love to know what it was and why it was worth killing for.

Kitty sighed. 'I wanted to ask Grams more about my father, what he looked like, but she sounded so upset about keeping the truth from me for so long. I sometimes forget she's an elderly lady.' She gave a wan smile.

'We had better leave for the dining room, Miss Delaware doesn't seem like a lady you would wish to keep waiting. Perhaps she may be able to tell you more.'

CHAPTER FIFTEEN

Vivien Delaware was seated at a table overlooking the river. Her two-piece costume was chic and up-to-date in a soft lavender shade. Her matching hat was pert and in the latest style but her jewellery appeared somewhat loud for daytime. A short, rotund, rosy-cheeked man with a straggly beard, wearing a rather ostentatious checked suit, sat next to her.

'Kitty honey, come and meet my agent, Bobby. He was held up in London on business and only arrived here this morning.' Miss Delaware stood to embrace Kitty, whilst her agent also stood to greet them both.

'It's nice to meet you. May I present Captain Matthew Bryant, he is head of security here at the Dolphin Hotel.'

For a brief second something shifted in Vivien Delaware's expression and Matt sensed wariness enter the atmosphere. The bright spring sunshine highlighted the fine lines on her complexion, and he wondered how old Vivien actually was.

'Vivien always neglects to say that I'm her husband as well as her agent.' Bobby resumed his seat as Matt pulled out a chair for Kitty.

'Your little town provided a warm welcome last night. It's always a pleasure singing for an appreciative audience.' Vivien held out her glass for her husband to top up her champagne. Matt noticed she'd ignored Bobby's remark about her not mentioning that they were married, and her fingers were bare of a wedding band. Bobby finished pouring champagne all round and stood the bottle back in the ice bucket.

'Yes, it went very well, lots of people came from all over the place. I'm glad you decided to take up our offer.'

Kitty's reply gave Matt the opening he needed. 'It must be quite a change for you after London. How long were you at The Cat's Miaow club?'

Vivien leaned back in her seat and sipped her drink. 'Three months. My doctor felt the city air was starting to affect my vocal cords and darling Kitty's offer came at the perfect time. She said she'd been let down at the last minute and we had a little free time before returning home. I was looking forward to seeing the Dolphin and Kitty.'

Matt noticed Bobby appear slightly confused by Vivien's statement, his expression altering slightly.

'I'm sorry to hear you've been unwell,' Kitty said.

Vivien waved her hand dismissively. 'Oh, it's nothing really, darling, you know how doctors do fuss so. I'm sure the air here will do me a power of good.'

'Do you return to the US when your season here is completed?' Matt asked Bobby.

'Yes, back to Chicago. Vivien has a six-month residency at a very fashionable club there.'

'It must be difficult with prohibition still in place?'

Bobby laughed. 'Word is that it will be repealed before the end of the year and Chicago is hardly a dry city, if you know what I mean.'

The waiter arrived with the first course, stopping the conversation temporarily.

'Did you know my parents too?' Kitty asked Bobby as soon as the waiter had moved out of earshot.

'No, honey. I only married Vivien ten years ago.' He smiled at her.

'Your ma was the image of you, same big eyes and blonde hair.' Vivien's gaze rested on Kitty.

'What does my father look like? You know I've never actually seen him? I could pass him in the street and not recognise him. That's rather sad, don't you think?'

'Oh, sweetie.' Vivien dropped her soup spoon back in her dish and placed her hand against her breast. 'I so feel for you. Edgar was a good-looking fella when he met your mother. Dressed well, always had a diamond tiepin. Blue eyes and a moustache.' Vivien sighed, she appeared to be remembering the past.

'Do you know why he wouldn't come and see me? Or visit Mother?' Kitty toyed with the bread roll on her side plate, rolling bits of bread into tiny balls.

Matt sucked in a breath and waited for Vivien's reply.

'Darling, Edgar Underhay is, or was, a very charming man. I know he visited you and your mother in London at the start of the war but then he came back to America. I ran across him a couple of years later in Chicago. He was keeping some very suspect company. Eddie always wanted easy money, gambling and high stakes. I believe he gambles professionally.' She broke off her narration to lean across the table and take Kitty's hand. 'I don't want to upset you, darling. I do think he intended coming back to see you and your mother, but he mentioned that your grandmother didn't approve of the match and of course the war made things very difficult. Edgar was not the kind of man suited for the military. I don't know where he's been the last few years but the Edgar Underhay I saw at The Cat's Miaow was not the smart, dapper gentleman I knew from before the war.'

Kitty blinked and nodded. 'I understand, Vivien, and thank you for being so honest.'

Vivien shook her head. 'He always said he was coming for you and Elowed. He always said your mother held his two biggest treasures.' She shrugged her shoulders, making the diamante jewels on her lapel brooch throw tiny rainbows onto the tablecloth.

The waiter returned and cleared the soup bowls, giving Kitty time to compose herself.

'And you're sure it was Edgar Underhay? Although he had changed somewhat in appearance?' Matt asked.

Vivien released Kitty's hand and looked him in the eyes. 'Yes, it was Edgar. He was older, slightly shabbier. The diamond tiepin and the swagger had gone but it was definitely him. I'd know him anywhere.'

'Do you think he might come to see me now?'

Matt couldn't tell from Kitty's tone if she was excited or a little afraid of the prospect of meeting her father.

The waiter brought the second course and set it in front of them.

'I don't know, honey. I'm surprised he hasn't tried to send word to you or your mother,' Vivien said. 'He must know where you are. He has some kind of connection not far from here I think.' Her brow wrinkled.

'Unless he's found out about Elowed disappearing and thinks he's been gone too long,' Matt murmured.

He still wasn't sure about Vivien's story and he wondered if she might be sounding out Kitty in preparation for Edgar's return. He couldn't tell from Kitty's face how she felt about the possibility of seeing her father again after so long an absence. The bit about treasure hadn't passed him by either and he was certain Kitty would have picked up on it too. What was this so-called treasure that suddenly everyone appeared to want? Maybe enough to kill for.

*

After luncheon Kitty went back to her grandmother's suite. She called the hospital to enquire if Mrs Craven was any better and learned she had been transferred to a private nursing home in Torquay to convalesce. Vivien's information had left her restless and confused. Was her father really in England? Why didn't he want to see her? Was he in some kind of trouble? Vivien's description had been that of a man who had lived a slightly disreputable life and had now fallen on hard times. She was no fool, she'd heard about Chicago, the speakeasies and the gangsters. The newspapers often carried lurid descriptions of some of the more disturbing incidents.

Matt had gone to talk to Mickey about extra security precautions for the hotel, so Kitty decided to take some air along the embankment. She left a note at the front desk for Matt and set off at a leisurely pace, enjoying the breeze on her face and the welcome sights and sounds of normal life all around her.

She nodded hello to some of the people she knew as she walked and paused to admire a baby in a perambulator. Pleasure craft made their way along the river, some carrying trippers out to see the castle at the mouth of the estuary. The sounds of chat and laughter reached her from the people on deck. Other boats chugged upstream with the sunlight sparkling on the white wash. It was hard to believe that poor Cora had met such a terrible end here, in such a peaceful spot. A shiver danced along her spine at the thought.

She had reached the boat float. The other big hotel in town was situated right opposite, near the shops and tearooms.

'Good afternoon, Miss Underhay.' The gentleman speaking to her raised his hat and she recognised him as the stranger who had spoken to her the previous evening. His appearance was clean but slightly worn like so many who had suffered a downturn in fortune since the Great War.

'Good afternoon.' She went to continue with her walk but to her surprise he addressed her again. 'I hope you don't mind my enquiry, but I am an old acquaintance of your grandmother, Mrs Treadwell, may I ask after her health?'

A prickle of unease tickled the nape of her neck. 'My grandmother is well, thank you. She is away at present, visiting family.'

'And your mother?'

Kitty swayed on her feet.

'I beg your pardon. You appear distressed.' The stranger took hold of her arm and guided her to a nearby bench.

Kitty sat and took a deep breath to recover her wits. 'I'm sorry, sir, clearly you cannot have seen my grandmother for some time. My mother disappeared many years ago and we are unsure of her whereabouts. It has been a number of years since anyone asked after her.'

She thought she heard him murmur, 'So it is true.'

'Forgive me, Miss Underhay, I did not mean to cause you distress. I have been abroad for some time for my health and have only recently returned to the area. I had hoped to see your grandmother at the musical soirée last night.'

'It is understandable then that you wouldn't know what had happened, Mr…?'

She waited for him to give his name. Her curiosity was greatly piqued by the identity of this stranger, especially after Vivien's description of her father. This man would be the right age, had a faint accent and had been abroad. Her heart raced at the possibility but yet she felt no connection to him.

'Mr Kelly.' His eyes locked with hers. 'Are you sure you are quite recovered, Miss Underhay?'

'Yes, thank you.' She stood and adjusted her skirts, brushing off a few flakes of paint from the bench seat. 'Are you staying in the area for long, Mr Kelly? My grandmother hopes to return soon and I'm sure she would like to renew an old acquaintance.'

'Alas, I'm uncertain about how long I can stay, but I hope I shall see you again before I leave.' He touched his hat and before she knew it, he had disappeared from sight somewhere into the high street.

'Bother.' Kitty stared after the direction in which he'd vanished for a few minutes. Who was he? The hesitation when she had asked his name meant she was pretty certain he really wasn't called Kelly. She hardly dared entertain the thought, but was that her father? He had matched Vivien's admittedly loose description. Or perhaps it was someone more sinister, attempting to find information about this mysterious treasure. There had never been any mention of treasure before and the comment had been so vague her father may have been referring to herself and Elowed.

The encounter had left her feeling even more unsettled, and without Matt at her side, vulnerable. She wondered if she should have told Inspector Greville about the attempt to push her into the road.

'My dear Miss Underhay.' The unwelcome sound of Walter Cribbs's voice sent her spirits plummeting. She hoped he was not about to attempt any renewal of the unwelcome advances he'd made towards her at Christmas.

'Mr Cribbs.'

The reporter moved in front of her, effectively blocking her from returning back towards the hotel unless she physically stepped around him. Sunlight glinted on his round, black-framed spectacles.

'Any news from the police on the arson attack on the Dolphin? Or on the investigation of the murders of Cora Wakes and Mr Blaas?'

Kitty eyed him with distaste. 'Mr Cribbs, surely those questions would be better put to Inspector Greville?'

He ignored her and carried on. 'Colin Wakes is still missing and now a source has informed me that you have received threatening letters?' His notebook and pencil were ready to take down her replies.

'I think your source is misinformed, Mr Cribbs, and I have no idea about who the police may be looking for. Now, if you don't mind, I need to return to work.' She made to walk forward, hoping he would move out of her way.

'What about the rumours of treasure?' Walter's face was uncomfortably close to hers and she noticed a small pimple on the side of his nose.

'Treasure?' Kitty did her best to appear baffled and to prevent herself from recoiling at his proximity. Another mention of treasure coming out of the blue. Where had these rumours begun?

An unpleasant smile spread across Walter's face. 'Treasure. A fabulous jewel, entrusted to your mother.'

Nausea rose in her stomach. 'I know nothing of any such nonsense. My mother left nothing of any value. She has been missing for seventeen years. What is all this nonsense about a jewel?'

Walter drew back a little. 'Forgive my questioning, Miss Underhay. But my source suggests that the jewel is real and various parties are searching for it.'

Kitty spotted Matt approaching and relief swept through her. 'Matthew.'

Walter glanced over his shoulder and a flicker of annoyance appeared to cross his face.

'Is Mr Cribbs bothering you, Kitty?'

'Just doing my job.' Walter returned his notebook and pencil to the pocket of his jacket.

'He appears to believe that my mother had some fabulous jewel in her possession and that this is connected with what happened to poor Cora and that other man.' Kitty glared at Walter.

Matt raised his eyebrows and stared at Walter who now appeared less confident with Matt looming over him.

'What would give you such an extraordinary idea?' Matt asked.

'Two expert jewel cutters in Dartmouth, one of them dead and rumours of a long lost jewel worth twenty thousand pounds. You know a newsman's sources must remain confidential,' Walter blustered.

Matt leaned in closer to Walter. 'I'm sure Inspector Greville would like to speak to your sources. I suggest you hand over any information you may have to the police and stop bothering Miss Underhay. Twenty thousand pounds, my foot. Your informant must be mad or drunk.' He leaned back.

'I'm just doing my job, there's no need to get nasty.' Walter's voice came out as a squeak and he nodded to Kitty and scurried off.

CHAPTER SIXTEEN

'Ugh, that man is such a creep.' Kitty shuddered. 'He reminds me of one of those little black beetles, scuttling around the place, always creeping out from some damp or dirty corner.'

'I know what you mean.' Matt scowled. 'It bothers me more that this rumour of some treasure or gem appears to be spreading all over Dartmouth. Twenty thousand pounds. That is ridiculous. Where did this nonsense start, I wonder?' He fell into step beside her and they strolled back together towards the hotel. Kitty found his presence reassuring after all the upsets of the day.

'Who do you suppose his informant is?'

'Could be any one of a number of people. Someone at the police station who saw the last letter, Vivien Delaware and her husband, even Cora.'

'I met someone else whilst I was out.' She told him of her encounter with the mysterious Mr Kelly.

He shot a glance at her. 'You think he may be your father?'

Kitty's footsteps faltered. 'I don't know. I suppose I have to entertain the possibility.' Having confessed the idea aloud she felt a little better. She knew Matt wouldn't ridicule or pooh-pooh the possibility. She started to move again.

'Be careful, Kitty. I agree you can't rule out that he may be Edgar Underhay, but equally he could be an opportunist or a conman or even someone in league with Vivien and her husband.'

'In other words; trust no one.' A short time ago she had struggled to trust Matt. When her whole life had been constructed around uncertainty, she had no difficulty in being suspicious.

'Exactly.'

Kitty didn't see the mysterious Mr Kelly at Miss Delaware's next performance, although Walter Cribbs made an appearance. She successfully avoided him all evening although she thought she saw Hubert Farjeon whispering to him in a corner of the ballroom.

Matt had been making discreet enquiries to try to trace Mr Kelly but so far, he wasn't known at any of the lodging houses or hotels. Thankfully there had also been no further letters or notes, although her heart skipped a beat every time she checked the post.

Bobby was at the reception desk collecting messages the next day when Inspector Greville arrived in the foyer. The lobby was quiet, with her guests mainly being gone for the day.

'Inspector Greville, you have news?' She noticed Bobby freeze momentarily as she greeted the policeman.

'Are you free for a moment, Miss Underhay?' He eyed Bobby who appeared now to be leisurely reading his post at the end of the desk.

'Of course, I'll ask one of the girls to cover for me.' She rang the bell and handed over to one of the maids. 'Could you get Alice to bring a tray of tea to my grandmother's suite please, and ask Mr Bryant to join us. Come upstairs to the salon, Inspector.'

She led the way to the elevator, pulling open the metal gate. Inspector Greville followed her inside, removing his hat as he entered. Kitty entered her grandmother's salon and took a seat. Matt and the tea tray arrived to join them within minutes.

'Has there been a development, Inspector?' Matt asked as soon as the maid had left the room.

Inspector Greville stroked his moustache thoughtfully. 'Mrs Craven's house was ransacked last night. It was the maid's half day off and she had attended the pictures with her young man. He walked her home and when they arrived at the house the lights were on downstairs. Naturally, they were alarmed but when they entered, the thieves had already left.'

Kitty gasped. 'Oh, how frightful. Was much taken? Any damage done?' Her mind raced even as she asked the questions. The burglary had to be linked somehow to the other crimes or why else would the inspector be calling? She had a horrid feeling that she knew exactly what the thieves had been looking for.

'Miss Underhay, I believe Mrs Craven was storing two boxes for your grandmother that contained your mother's possessions?' Although he posed it as a question, Kitty knew he already knew the answer.

'Yes, when the hotel was undergoing renovations a few years ago, Mrs Craven kindly offered to store them for my grandmother. She didn't want them around but at the same time couldn't bring herself to dispose of them either.'

The inspector nodded. 'May I ask what the boxes contained?'

Kitty sighed. 'Clothes, a few books, nothing of any significance or value. My grandmother only kept them because she thought I might want something to remember my mother by if she didn't return. She found it so upsetting having them at the hotel, she wanted them out of sight. I think she was afraid having them around might distress me.'

'There was no jewellery or ornaments of any kind concealed within the boxes?'

'No, Inspector, not so far as I know.'

Matt cleared his throat. 'I take it that the thieves were looking for Kitty's mother's possessions?'

Inspector Greville took a sip of tea. 'Nothing was stolen. The silverware and pictures were left untouched. A few small items of jewellery that hadn't been locked in the safe were also left behind. The cash in the kitchen which was used to pay household expenses was also undisturbed. Only the boxes were searched.'

'This is ridiculous.' Kitty sprang to her feet and paced the few short steps to her grandmother's bureau. 'My mother left nothing of value, nothing.'

'And yet my constables tell me there are several rumours sweeping the town that a priceless gem was entrusted to your mother for safekeeping and that someone has now returned to collect it. There are suggestions that she may have been harmed because she refused to reveal where it was stashed.'

Kitty sank back into her seat. 'But who would have given her such a thing? And why would they look for it now, after all these years?'

The inspector had placed his cup back on the table. He leaned forward and templed his fingers together, his gaze fixed on her face. 'We are led to believe that your father, Edgar Underhay, acquired a very valuable uncut ruby from some gentlemen in Chicago before the war and entrusted it to your mother on the understanding that he would recover it at some point in the future.'

'You use the word "acquired", Inspector?' Matt asked.

The corners of the policeman's mouth twitched upwards. 'We are not sure that it was acquired legitimately, something to do with a poker game. This was not advisable as the gentleman who had claims on the stone is quite well-known in certain circles in Chicago. He let it be known that he expected it to be returned.'

A gasp escaped Kitty. A Chicago gangster and a stolen gem. The whole thing was preposterous, except Cora was dead and someone had searched both the hotel and Mrs Craven's home. 'But why now? Why after all this time?'

The grim smile on the inspector's lips grew tighter. 'All the main parties concerned have only recently been released from prison and are keen to recover the gem.'

'Was my father in prison?' Kitty asked.

'He is certainly known to the authorities but no, I don't believe he has been imprisoned recently. However, the officer I spoke to in Chicago believed he has sustained some major financial losses lately. I appreciate that Edgar has not been a part of your life, Miss

Underhay, but he is now a person of interest in my investigations, and if he should be in touch with you, please let me know.'

Matt whistled. 'You've no doubt heard also, Inspector, that there have been reported sightings of Edgar Underhay in London.'

'All of which adds credibility to the rumours, no doubt. Miss Underhay, I will be asking my men to keep a close watch on the hotel and strongly advise you not to leave the premises alone until this matter is resolved.'

'I'm sure Kitty will be very careful.' Matt gave her a meaningful look and colour crept into her cheeks as she remembered her stroll by the river the previous day. 'You may wish to trace a Mr Kelly. I've had no success so far, but he has approached Kitty twice now, and we suspect he may have some kind of connection to whatever is going on. He claimed an acquaintance with her grandmother but seemed unaware of Kitty's mother's disappearance.'

'Thank you. I agree, that would appear strange. We're also still looking for Colin Wakes. Again, there are rumours that he has been seen locally. Should he contact you, or you hear anything, please let me know.'

Matt showed Inspector Greville out and returned to the office.

'Suppose this Mr Kelly is my father?' The words burst from Kitty and she pressed her palms together to stop her hands from trembling. 'You could have put him in real danger if there are mobsters running around Dartmouth killing people and looking for something I don't have.' A sob escaped her.

Matt hunkered down in front of her and captured her hands in his. 'Kitty, we don't know who this man is. He may be a murderer. You are in danger because of him, you don't owe him any loyalty.' He squeezed her fingers.

'I honestly don't know what to think. First, I believe my father is probably dead or in America, then he's in London, now he may be here in Dartmouth but he's apparently both a coward of the worst kind and very possibly a convicted felon and a gambler.' She shook her head as a tear escaped to trickle down her cheek.

'This will all get sorted out soon. Inspector Greville is a good man, and I will be with you until he has apprehended the person responsible, whether or not that is your father.' Matt drew a handkerchief from his pocket and offered it to her, trying not to think about how he was now offering her the very reassurances he'd told himself not to.

Kitty dabbed away the tear, comforted by his proximity and his kindness. His gaze locked with hers and her heart skipped a beat.

He straightened up and turned away. 'Try and get some rest, Kitty. I'll be downstairs. I need to check on a few things.'

Before she could say anything, he left, and she wondered if she had imagined the expression she'd seen in his eyes when he'd comforted her.

*

Matt was thoughtful as he strolled down the broad, polished oak staircase to the ground floor. His reaction to Kitty's proximity disturbed him. After Edith's death he had never anticipated that he might feel something for another woman again.

As he was about to descend the final few steps, he spotted two people deep in conversation, which held him to his place for a moment. The tall, elegant, flamboyant figure of Vivien Delaware appeared to be engaged in a tête-à-tête with the stubby, straw-boatered Hubert Farjeon. A most unlikely pairing.

The couple passed the bottom of the staircase without glancing in his direction. Thinking swiftly, he slipped down the final few steps and dodged quickly into the back office behind the desk, leaving the door slightly ajar. Fortunately, the girl on reception was preoccupied with a new arrival and her lapdog and didn't notice his actions.

'Really, Mr Farjeon, I have no idea what you mean. I know nothing of the matter.' Vivien's voice carried to his hiding place. She sounded indignant but also slightly shaken and Matt wondered what the precursor to her reply had been.

He risked a quick peek through the gap between the door and the frame to see Miss Delaware marching away, pulling on her gloves as she walked.

Hubert merely appeared thoughtful as he strolled past Matt's hiding place and out of the hotel.

Matt was about to emerge into the lobby when he realised that he hadn't been the only voyeur of the little scene. Bobby was standing in the shadows near the elevator and he didn't look very happy with Hubert Farjeon. In fact, Matt thought he looked downright murderous.

CHAPTER SEVENTEEN

Miss Delaware seldom appeared downstairs before midday, preferring to breakfast in her room as her show finished quite late. Matt was therefore surprised to encounter her outside the hotel at a little before ten the day after he'd witnessed her meeting with Hubert Farjeon.

'Captain Bryant, Matt.' She placed a gloved hand on his arm. 'May I speak with you in private?'

He tried to hide his surprise and offered her his arm. 'Shall we take the morning air? Will your husband be joining us?'

They strolled along the embankment as if admiring the view along the river. The walkway was still quiet with few people about. On the water, the boat men were preparing their vessels. 'Bobby has some business matters to attend to. I had one of my heads so I came out to get some air.'

'How can I help you, Miss Delaware?' He was sure she had been loitering, hoping to catch him. He had no doubt that her maid or one of the hotel staff would have told her of his habit of going for a morning stroll after breakfast.

'Oh, do call me Vivien, please, honey. Miss Delaware makes me feel so old.'

'Very well, Vivien.' He waited for her to continue.

'You appear very close to Kitty. She's such a sweet little thing and I don't want to see her get hurt.'

Matt frowned; the hairs at the nape of his neck were prickling and he knew something was off kilter. 'In what way do you mean?'

'Listen, Edgar Underhay is here in Dartmouth. I saw him yesterday. I know about the jewel he left with Kitty's mother and I'm sure he must be here to try and recover it.'

Matt stopped. 'Is that what Hubert Farjeon was discussing with you yesterday?'

Vivien released his arm, a look of fury crossing her face. 'That unpleasant little chancer. He was fishing for information, hinting he knew something about that woman who was found in the river.'

They paused for a moment, looking out at the dark water rushing along just a few feet from where they stood.

'Did he say what he knew?' Matt asked.

'No, just a load of unpleasant hints.' Vivien held her chin high.

'He was trying to blackmail you?'

She snorted. 'Hell no, what with? Like I said, the man was fishing for something, like he thought I might know something. Absurd.'

Matt was not convinced by her denial. Hubert may have been fishing for information but her demeanour when he mentioned blackmail had been telling. 'You said you knew about the jewel?'

She darted a quick glance at him. 'That's why I'm worried for Kitty. She needs to put that thing in a safe place. There are people who will stop at nothing to get their hands on it. That chunk of rock was Eddie's insurance and I'd say he wants it back now. His coming here is pointing right at Kitty.'

'Is that *chunk of rock*, as you call it, the real reason why you took this engagement?'

Her gaze shifted from his. 'That would be ridiculous. I was curious to see Eddie and Elowed's girl. I hoped to renew my friendship with Elowed. I would have expected her to have gotten rid of that gem a long time ago if Edgar hadn't been back for it.'

Perhaps it was the army training, but Matt just knew that she was lying. 'Did you ever see the jewel?'

'It didn't look like much, just a chunk of rock. It hadn't been cut. Edgar showed it to me once when he'd had a few, just before Elowed and Kitty sailed. He won it in a poker game.'

'And seeing him in the club in London, you guessed why he was here and where he would be headed. What makes you think Elowed didn't have it with her when she disappeared?' Matt knew his tone was scornful. 'I think you should return to the hotel.'

Vivien faced him, her eyes blazing. 'You can think what you like, Mr Bryant, but Kitty's life may be in danger over that jewel. Edgar isn't the only person to want to get his hands on it, and there are people who want to get their hands on Eddie and they may try to use Kitty to do that.'

'Thank you for the warning.' Matt tipped the brim of his hat to her and strode away towards the town. He made straight for the police station; he wanted to speak to Inspector Greville as soon as possible.

He was shown into a small, rather dark back room containing a desk and a couple of chairs that the inspector appeared to be using as an office. 'Captain Bryant, good morning.'

Matt told the inspector of his conversation with Vivien Delaware.

'I take it you don't believe her motivation for speaking with you?' Greville asked.

'No, sir, I think she may have been trying to establish if Kitty had found the stone or had contact with her father. Although I do believe she is correct to think that Kitty might be in danger.'

The inspector leaned back in his chair, tapping the end of his pencil on the desk as he thought. 'I've increased the patrols and Miss Underhay appears to be a sensible young woman. I've men searching the area making house enquiries to try and trace this Mr Kelly and also to try and find Colin Wakes. That wretched reporter appears to be everywhere though, asking questions. I'd like to know who told him about the jewel, although I suppose it could have come from a number of sources.'

'Walter Cribbs. Yes, I suppose this is a big news story. He certainly seems very well informed.'

'Humph.' The inspector didn't appear impressed. 'Miss Underhay and her grandmother know nothing about this supposed jewel?'

'No, sir. At least Kitty definitely doesn't. I'm not sure about her grandmother. I always get the feeling she may not have told me everything.'

'I see, and you say Miss Delaware was in conversation with Mr Farjeon and he hinted that he knew something about Cora's death?'

'Yes, sir.'

'In that case I think we need to speak to our friend Hubert and see what he has to tell us.'

Greville had barely finished speaking when the telephone rang. 'What? I see, yes, on our way.' He placed the receiver back on the handset.

'It seems we are too late, Captain Bryant. Mr Farjeon has been found dead, murdered inside his booth.'

Matt scrambled to his feet and joined the inspector as they headed back towards the riverbank. It took a matter of minutes to reach the green and yellow turret-shaped booth where Hubert Farjeon sold tickets for his motor coach tours.

A small knot of interested bystanders had gathered nearby, kept at bay by a sturdy, ruddy-cheeked constable. Matt tagged along with the inspector as he approached the small booth.

'Where is he?'

'Inside, sir. Sergeant said to leave everything till you got here. The doctor is on his way.'

The booth was still shuttered with the door slightly ajar.

'Who found him?' The inspector surveyed the scene.

'The errand boy from the grocers. Mr Farjeon had ordered some bread, cheese and fruit. It was a regular order and the lad came down, knocked on the door, it swung open and he found Mr Farjeon dead inside.' The constable pointed to a young boy sitting, white-faced, on a nearby doorstep talking to the sergeant.

Inspector Greville nodded and opened the door to the booth carefully with a gloved hand. Matt followed behind him as the constable shielded the scene from the bystanders with his body.

Matt did his best not to recoil from the sight that greeted him. Hubert Farjeon lay sprawled half-off the high wooden chair he used for taking ticket sales. The sticky metallic scent of blood reached Matt and it was all he could do not to gag. It brought back too many memories, images of other scenes with that terrible scent. Faces of friends and comrades flashed through his mind.

Hubert looked startled, as if he had not expected his assailant to strike him down, but the dull black hilt of a large knife buried in his chest told its own story.

Matt was relieved when the inspector closed the door again. 'The doctor should be here in a moment. Constable, please move these people on, after you've checked if any of them saw or heard anything suspicious and taken their details.'

Relieved he no longer had to look at Hubert's body, Matt sucked in a lungful of air. He had seen too many bodies, too much death. The bystanders were grumbling as the constable shooed them away. Amongst them was the black-coated figure of Walter Cribbs scribbling away in his notebook as he talked to the people.

The doctor's car drew up and the inspector accompanied him into the booth. Matt stayed outside and lit a cigarette. He would wait until the corpse had been removed before asking the inspector about the doctor's thoughts.

A hearse drew up behind the doctor's car and a few minutes later the undertakers were given the nod to remove the late Hubert Farjeon from his booth.

Greville joined him. 'Doctor Carter puts the time of death no earlier than about two hours ago. That ties in with the time Hubert normally reached his booth every morning.'

Matt finished his cigarette, dropping the stub and grinding it out with his toe. 'I thought so, the blood was still viscous.'

'No clues from the knife. Looks like a common or garden kitchen knife. The kind they sell at the local store. The boy didn't see or hear anything suspicious. He said the ferry hadn't come over when he arrived with the food for Farjeon's lunch.'

The sound of the hearse door slamming signalled that Hubert Farjeon had been removed.

'There didn't appear to be any signs of a struggle. It looks as if Farjeon let his murderer into the booth.'

'Suggesting it was either someone he knew, or someone he was expecting,' Matt said. He wondered where Vivien had been before she had waylaid him. Even more importantly, where was Bobby?

'There appeared to be no papers or documents other than the ticket pouch for the tour company. No signs of anything being taken or of a search being made.' The inspector stroked his moustache. 'This is a most serious turn of events. I'm going to Mr Farjeon's lodgings to see if there is anything there which could shed any light on his death. Captain Bryant, I suggest you return to the Dolphin and stay with Miss Underhay. The killer is getting bolder, and if this man, Kelly, attempts to contact her, I need to know immediately.'

'Of course, sir.'

Matt cut through the town to return to the Dolphin. The scent of blood was still in his nostrils and he found it hard to reconcile the normal everyday hustle and bustle of the town with the horror he had just witnessed. Coming so soon after seeing Cora's bloated features, all the buried horrors of the war were pushing to the front of his mind.

He knew he couldn't return to the hotel in this frame of mind. He needed some time and space to think. He retraced his steps until he reached St Saviours church. Finding the huge carved medieval door standing open, he stepped inside and took a seat at the back of the church. The interior of the church was old, the woodwork carved and painted in reds and golds. He was dimly aware of the curious gaze of the cleaner, mopping the entrance. Closing his eyes, he allowed the sanctuary of the ancient space to enfold and calm him.

Gradually the smell of death that seemed to have followed him from the booth was replaced by the lavender aroma of the beeswax polish being diligently applied to the pews. He wasn't certain how long he had been there, but the cleaner had almost finished her chores. At least now his hands had stopped shaking and his heart rate and breathing were back to normal.

Matt smiled apologetically and slipped a donation into the offerings box as he left the church. He wasn't a religious man, not any more. The war had seen to that, but he found the space inside the church soothing to his nerves. With luck, it might mitigate the nightmares that he knew would inevitably haunt him in his sleep later.

CHAPTER EIGHTEEN

Matt took his time walking back to the hotel. He needed more space to fully recover from seeing Hubert Farjeon's body inside the booth. The time inside the church had helped but he wasn't ready yet to talk to Kitty. His feelings for her when he had comforted her the other day had caught him by surprise.

Without thinking, he had spoken to her the way he and Edith had used to talk to each other. He paused on the embankment and stared out across the water. He and Edith had been so young when they had married, but so happy. The war had accelerated their courtship and marriage and the arrival of baby Betty had set the seal on their happiness, until the day it had all been taken away. He'd never thought he might one day be open to having that same kind of love and companionship again.

'Captain Bryant,' Mickey, the maintenance man, called him as soon as he entered the lobby. It looked as if he had been loitering, waiting for his return.

'What's the matter, Mick?' He'd asked Mickey to look out for anything he thought might be unusual or suspicious around the hotel.

'I think there's something funny going on round the back of the hotel.' Mick's tanned and grizzled features contorted in a frown.

Matt guessed the elderly man was struggling to explain what he thought was wrong. 'Better show me what you mean.'

He followed Mickey through the hotel, along the service corridor and out through the busy kitchen past the chefs and pot-boy into the yard where the fire had occurred. The soot had been scrubbed away from the bricks and the yard floor washed.

'I been keeping my eyes open like you asked, Captain. Come over here, sir.' He took Matt across to the old wooden gate that sealed one of the smugglers' tunnels in the cliff face. 'Have a look at that lock.'

Matt could see what he meant. The padlock looked shinier than before and there was a thin film of oil around the top. It contrasted with the faded, blistered paintwork of the door, still bearing soot marks from the fire. 'Have you got the key for this, Mickey?'

The old man fished a huge ring of keys from his belt and sorted through the bunch. 'I reckon it might be this one.' He inserted the key into the lock. The key turned easily and he unclipped the padlock. 'Ain't nobody supposed to have been in here for about five years now, at least.'

Matt watched as Mickey opened the door. On a small ledge inside the tunnel was a glass storm lantern. Mickey lifted it out, peered and sniffed. 'Been primed and used recently.'

Matt produced his cigarette lighter and ignited the wick. Mickey held the lantern in front of him and they ventured into the tunnel. Sweat trickled down Matt's back as he entered into the confined space. Today seemed to be the day that he was confronting all his demons at once. More horrific memories of being buried in mud in the trenches flooded into his mind, the constant fear of being buried alive, entombed beneath the boards used for shoring up the sides and the layers of heavy, glutinous soil. To his relief, after about twenty yards the tunnel opened out into a larger space that looked as if it might once have been a natural cave.

'They smugglers used to store some barrels here back in the old days.' Mickey lifted the lantern up so they could look around. The yellow light flickered and played over the rough, red rock face. In the corner Matt spotted a bundle of what looked like cloth.

'Over here, Mick.'

Mickey followed him with the light. The bundle comprised of some blankets, a small bag containing a change of clothes, a packet of sandwiches wrapped in greaseproof paper, a tin mug and a bottle of beer. Melted stubs of candles stood on a ledge nearby.

'Somebody been sleeping in here,' Mickey said.

'But who, and how did they get the key to access this area?' Matt checked around the cave and the exit tunnel which led further into the cliff. 'Where does this come out, Mick?'

'Below yon castle, but you have to wait for low water. Come high tide, the entrance floods. ''Tis dangerous.'

'How many people know about it?'

Mickey shrugged, the movement making the lantern light bob and weave. 'Dunno, 'tis mainly the older ones now I suppose. In the war no one could get near it, like, and Mrs Treadwell has kept this end locked for years, especially since Miss Elowed went missing.'

Matt knew the castle dated back to the thirteen hundreds so there had to be other passageways connected with it and probably with the church of St Petroc, which stood beside the castle. 'We'd better get out of here.'

Mickey grunted his assent and the two men made their way back out into the sunlight. Matt automatically reached for his cigarettes as soon as he was free of the cramped, dark confines of the tunnel. His hand trembled as he lit up.

'Put the lantern back, Mickey, and relock the door. I'll alert Inspector Greville and see if he will set a watch to catch whoever is using the tunnel. Are there any other ways in or out that you know of?'

'There used to be a regular warren of tunnels. Some was dead ends, and some have caved in over the years or the entrances have been lost with the building works for the town. I don't remember there being one still open to this one, other than that one by the castle and you need a boat for that.'

'I'd better tell Miss Underhay what's going on.'

Mickey nodded. 'I'll keep my eyes open till they puts one of they police on to watch.'

Matt thanked him and set off back inside the hotel. Whoever was using the tunnel was well set-up and had to have been given access to a key. The obvious suspect was Colin Wakes, but why would he be hiding in the tunnel? His mother's house would be empty, and he had no reason to evade the law. At least no reason as far as Matt knew. Colin may have a dodgy past, but he wasn't in trouble this time, or was he?

He stopped off at the reception desk to write a note to Inspector Greville before giving one of the kitchen porters a few coins to take it to the police house.

Kitty was in the ballroom, standing at one of the tables with Mrs Homer, the head of the housekeeping staff. 'I've been trying to sort out the curtains, table linen and the décor, ready for next Saturday's masked ball. It's Vivien's finale before she returns to America, and then I've a troupe of acrobats coming for two weeks to entertain the guests.' Her cheeks were flushed and she had a small streak of dust on one cheek. She added another bundle into the housekeeper's arms and dismissed her. 'Where have you been all morning? Mickey was looking for you.'

'It's all right, he found me.' Something in his tone must have warned her that something was wrong.

'What is it? Has something else happened?' The colour drained from her face.

'Hubert Farjeon was found murdered this morning.'

'How? Where?' She sank down on one of the small gilt chairs.

'Stabbed, in his booth. Inspector Greville is down there now.'

He saw her swallow. 'Does he have any idea who may have done it? Or why?'

'He's still looking for Colin Wakes and this Mr Kelly, if only to clear them of any involvement.' He knew she must be worried in case her father was somehow implicated in this latest tragedy.

She nodded. 'Yes, I suppose so. It's so awful, Matt. Poor Mr Farjeon.'

'Kitty, there's something else.' He told her of his and Mickey's discovery in the tunnel.

'It could be Colin. Cora could have given him a key and kept him supplied with food from the kitchen. He could be the one that set the fire. It has to be someone local and he would be the obvious suspect. But why? None of this makes sense. It's so horrible to think about what is happening at the hotel, I miss Grams so much right now. It's frightening, Matt. That's two people close to me murdered, and if you hadn't rescued me from that coal truck, it could have been my fate too.'

'I've sent a message to Inspector Greville. Mickey is keeping an eye on the door until they get a policeman in place to keep watch.'

Kitty shivered and rubbed the tops of her arms. 'Someone just walked over my grave. I've got goosebumps. I hope they catch whoever is responsible for this soon. Do you think Hubert did know something about who killed Cora?'

Matt rubbed his chin. 'I don't know. Greville is checking his lodgings, but clearly someone must have believed he knew something or else why kill him?'

'And it might be to do with this gem that I know nothing at all about and don't have.' Kitty shuddered. 'Horrid, absolutely horrid.' She buried her face in her hands.

'Come on, let's go and get some lunch. If you're a good girl I might treat you to a cream scone later.' He deliberately kept his tone light and teasing, hoping it would lift her spirits. He decided not to share Vivien's information with her just yet. She was already concerned about her father; she didn't need to worry even more.

She accompanied him along the corridor towards the dining room. 'I'll join you shortly. I need to freshen up.' She waved her dusty hands at him and grinned.

'I'll see you there.'

Bobby was in his usual spot, loitering in reception near the elevator, his gaudy checked suit visible in the shadows. Matt approached him from behind. 'Vivien not with you?' he asked, clapping a friendly hand on the man's shoulder.

The rotund little man jumped into the air in surprise. 'No, not yet. I'm er, just waiting for her. You know how she likes her beauty sleep.'

'Oh, she was out and about quite early this morning. I met her taking the air.'

Bobby appeared flustered, small beads of sweat forming on his hairline. 'Ah, yes, I was busy this morning, business, you know.'

'Of course. I'm curious, do you manage any other acts or does Miss Delaware keep you busy?'

Bobby produced a large yellow silk handkerchief and began to mop his brow and around his neck. 'Goodness me, hot today, isn't it? Oh, I have a few other acts, you know, as well as Vivien to look out for. Contracts to check, you know.'

'Must be a difficult life, living out of a suitcase, travelling about?'

Bobby seemed to relax a little. 'Yes, it can be, but it's more difficult in America. The colour bar, you know.' He waved his hands vaguely.

Matt suspected that Bobby and Vivien would encounter a great deal of prejudice and obstacles were their marriage to be widely known. 'I expect that's why Miss Delaware retains her own name?'

'I try to get contracts overseas where I can. London is easier, and Paris, of course.'

'But this time you are returning to America?' Matt asked.

Bobby fidgeted, shifting uneasily from foot to foot. 'Business calls. I have my other acts to manage and this is a longstanding obligation.'

The penny dropped for Matt. 'An obligation to the kind of people you can't refuse?'

Bobby's lips quirked. 'You could say it would be better to be obliging.'

CHAPTER NINETEEN

Bobby melted away as soon as Kitty appeared, the dust smudge on her cheek gone and her lipstick renewed.

'I thought you would have gone into lunch?'

'I ran into Bobby. We were chatting.'

'Oh?' She raised a perfectly arched eyebrow.

'Let's go and eat and I'll tell you all about it.'

In the dining room, Matt took the seat opposite Kitty. The room was fairly quiet, with many guests out for the day, so there was a low level of chatter in the room. They had just finished the first course when a maid came scurrying into the dining room and straight to their table. 'Oh, miss, I'm so sorry to disturb you, but you need to come right away, miss.' The girl kept her voice low and cast a nervous gaze around the room, as if afraid any of the other diners might hear her.

'What's wrong, Alice?' Kitty set her glass back on the table.

'Your room, miss.' The girl looked distressed, her fingers worrying at the sides of her apron.

Matt jumped to his feet. 'You'd better show us what's happened.'

Kitty joined him as they hurried up the staircase, the maid explaining breathlessly as they walked. 'I went to clean your room, miss, and the door was open.'

The maid's cleaning cart was outside the door to Kitty's room. Matt could see that the lock on the door had been forced, splintering the wood.

'Was anyone up here when you arrived?'

'No, sir, it were all quiet.' The maid's expression was a mix of excitement and fear.

Kitty gasped aloud when she looked into her room. 'What on earth?' Everything was disturbed; all the drawers were out of her chest, the contents strewn across the floor. Her clothes were torn from the hangers and dumped. Even the mattress on her bed was skewed, as if someone had looked beneath it. The lock on the drawer of her bedside cabinet had also been broken and the scanty contents of her jewel box tipped carelessly out.

'Clearly no ordinary robbery,' Matt murmured.

'I'm so sorry, Miss Underhay.' The maid hovered uncertainly in the doorway as Kitty made her way carefully into her room.

'Leave us for a minute, while Miss Underhay checks to see if anything has been taken.' Matt fumbled in his jacket pocket for a notebook and pen. 'Please can you take this message to Inspector Greville. Alfie, the kitchen boy, knows where to find him.'

The young maid took the note and vanished.

'Who could have done this?' Kitty stared around the room. 'Oh!' She let out an anguished cry and bent to retrieve an object from the floor. 'Matt, my mother's darling little clock, it's broken.' She placed the carved wooden cuckoo clock down carefully on the bed.

Dark wood, with a typical Black Forest carved bear and tree decorating the front, the clock was nothing special other than the sentimental associations it held for Kitty. The fretwork on the top had been broken, the hands had come off and he could see the weights that hung from the chains below the clock had been damaged, probably when the thief had tossed it away.

'What's that?' He peered more closely at one of the weights. He had assumed they were made of wood, like the clock, but the fall had revealed they were painted papier mâché designed to resemble fir cones.

Kitty looked more closely. 'There's something inside the weight.' She picked up the clock and pulled at the damaged covering. Instead of the more usual lead, something else appeared: a dark red, rough rock that glittered as the light from the window caught its surface. The size of a small pigeon egg, the gem nestled in her palm.

'It was here all the time,' Kitty whispered.

Voices could be heard approaching in the corridor so Kitty quickly slipped the jewel into the pocket of her cardigan and covered the clock with one of her dresses.

Inspector Greville was at the doorway accompanied by Alice, the young red-haired maid who had been dispatched with the note.

'Is anything missing, Miss Underhay?'

Kitty shook her head. 'Not as far as I can see, Inspector. My jewellery is scattered about, but all appears to be here. I have nothing else of any value in my room.'

'No witnesses? No one heard or saw anything suspicious?'

'No, sir. This is a quiet time of day. Most of the guests are gone for the day or are taking luncheon in the dining room. This floor isn't used by guests, so apart from the staff when they come to clean or return laundry, no one would be here.'

The inspector nodded. 'You think it's someone familiar with the layout and routine of the hotel?'

'It would appear so.' Matt was frustrated with himself. He should have realised that as the people searching for the ruby became increasingly desperate, they would try Kitty's room once more. They should have come and searched again themselves, even though Kitty had clearly been unaware of the ruby's hiding place.

'And only this room was searched? No damage to your room, Mr Bryant? Or that of Mrs Treadwell?' The inspector asked. 'What order were the rooms cleaned?'

'I did Mr Bryant's room first, it being further along the corridor and Mrs Treadwell's rooms is on the first floor. There was nothing.' The maid spoke quickly, as if anxious that she should not be blamed for the happenings of the day.

Matt caught Kitty's gaze and she gave a barely imperceptible shake of her head, warning him not to tell the policeman of the discovery of the ruby.

Inspector Greville examined the broken door lock and damaged door jamb. 'Most likely a crowbar or lever of some kind.'

'Yes, we increased security so perhaps they couldn't obtain the key. Or of course, it could be someone different,' Matt observed, thinking through the implications of this new development.

'Shall we go down to my grandmother's suite?' Kitty said. 'Can Alice begin to clean up my room?'

'I don't see why not. There seems to be little more information that can be gathered here.'

Matt stayed for a moment to give the maid some instructions as Kitty and the inspector walked back along the corridor and down to Mrs Treadwell's suite. He caught them up outside the door as Kitty produced the key to let them into the suite.

Matt was relieved to see that everything in her grandmother's rooms appeared untouched. Kitty sat next to him on the sofa, after calling down to reception for a tea tray.

'Did you find anything of interest at Hubert Farjeon's lodgings?' Matt asked, once the tea had arrived and the maid dismissed.

Inspector Greville stroked his moustache thoughtfully, before helping himself to a biscuit. 'Nothing very conclusive. No indications that he had heard or seen anyone in particular in connection with the murder of Cora Wakes.'

'But?' Matt asked, certain the inspector was holding something back.

'I believe Mr Farjeon may have been attempting to convince certain people that he knew they were involved with Cora's death and possibly that he had seen something when Mr Blaas was killed. A most dangerous game to play with a murderer.'

'Blackmail,' breathed Kitty.

'He clearly hit the target with one of his victims. The question is, which one?'

'We suspect that one of them was Vivien Delaware, and she was out and about unusually early this morning. Her husband, Bobby, also doesn't appear to have an alibi.' Matt took a sip of tea.

'Mr Farjeon could have seen Colin Wakes too, if it transpires that Colin is the person sleeping in the old smugglers' tunnel. He knew Colin and didn't think well of him,' Kitty added.

'There is still no trace of this Mr Kelly or of Edgar Underhay and no definite confirmation that they are one and the same person.' Inspector Greville looked at Matt. 'Indeed, we only have Miss Delaware's assertion that Edgar Underhay is possibly in Dartmouth or even in England at all.' He helped himself to a biscuit.

'I take it you wish to interview Miss Delaware and her husband?'

'May I ask you for the use of your grandmother's suite, Miss Underhay? It would be more conducive to obtaining a good result I feel, rather than asking them to come to the police station.'

'Of course, Inspector. I would only ask that you remember that Miss Delaware is my guest and I need her for the masked ball next Saturday. The Dolphin has invested heavily in Miss Delaware to launch our summer season.'

Matt noticed Kitty's hand stray towards the pocket of her cardigan.

'Certainly, miss. I will be entirely cordial until there is some conclusive evidence against her. And for your peace of mind, I have a man stationed out of sight at the back of the hotel observing the entrance to the tunnels. I'm hopeful we will apprehend whoever is sleeping in there very soon.'

Kitty smiled. 'Thank you, Inspector, that does make me feel safer. I'll call downstairs and ask if Miss Delaware and her husband are free to see you and I'll arrange for some more tea to be sent up.' She looked meaningfully at the empty biscuit plate.

'Thank you, Miss Underhay, that's very thoughtful of you. Captain Bryant, could I trouble you to stay for the interviews? My resources are somewhat stretched at present and having another person present would be most helpful.'

Matt saw the spark of annoyance in Kitty's eyes at being excluded, however she merely smiled once more, collected the tray and left the suite.

*

Kitty made her way down the stairs to the back office behind the reception desk. The ruby in her pocket nestled against her hip. She tried to think through the ramifications of its discovery. What should she do with it? If anyone found out she had it, her life would be in danger – although after everything that had happened today, she was probably already in peril. She couldn't see that giving it to the police would solve anything either, but she couldn't keep something that was stolen. Perhaps she should have given it to the inspector, but everything had happened so quickly. It was also the only link she had that might enable her to discover what had happened in the past with her father and mother.

She took over from the girl on the reception desk so she could go for a tea break. It was better to be occupied so her mind wouldn't keep dwelling on the day's events. She was unsurprised when the telephone rang, and her grandmother was on the line. 'Darling, I just had a call from one of the gels. Is it true? Has Hubert Farjeon been murdered?'

'Yes, Grams. They found him in his booth this morning. Matt was with the inspector when the alarm was raised.' She might have guessed one of her grandmother's friends would call her. Even with the ringleader, Mrs Craven, out of action, the rest of the town's matrons were still on patrol.

'What are the police doing about it? Are you safe?'

'Inspector Greville is here now, Grams, talking to suspects. Please don't worry, we are all quite safe.'

'I do hope they're not guests. The hotel does not want a reputation for harbouring murderers.' Her grandmother sounded indignant.

'Grams, it is quite scary here at the moment but nothing that can affect the guests.' She couldn't tell her grandmother about the burglary in her room or the intruder in the tunnels.

'Where is Captain Bryant?' her grandmother demanded.

'He's with the inspector. I promise he is keeping an eye on me.'

'Oh, my dear, I've never known anything like it. Get Matthew to telephone me as soon as he is free. Have you received any more letters or heard anything further about your father?'

Kitty sighed. 'No, Grams, nothing. I promise I'll ask Matt to update you on everything once he's finished with the inspector.'

'I have some good news for you at least, Livvy and I are coming back soon. She is seeing the doctor tomorrow and I'm very hopeful he will say she is fit to travel.'

Kitty's spirits lifted. 'That would be lovely, Grams. I can't wait to see you both. Do you think you may be here in time for the masked ball next Saturday?'

'I'm not sure, my dear. It depends on Livvy. We shall have to break the journey as I fear being in the car too long might be too much for her. We shall do our best, though. Promise me you will do as Matt asks and stay safe, Kitty.'

'I will, Grams, don't worry.' Speaking to her grandmother had lifted her mood. Perhaps when she returned, she would know what the best thing would be to do with the ruby. Though she was tempted, she had held back from saying anything on the telephone for fear of being overheard.

No sooner had she replaced the handset than her mood was sent spiralling downwards at speed by the unwelcome sight of Walter Cribbs on the other side of the reception desk.

CHAPTER TWENTY

'Mr Cribbs.' She struggled not to wrinkle her nose in distaste, trying to maintain her professional manner.

'The lovely Miss Underhay.' Walter appeared very pleased with himself.

'How may I assist you, Mr Cribbs?'

'Walter, please, we've known each other long enough to dispense with formalities, surely.'

'Are you here to report on the upcoming masked ball?' Kitty enquired.

'I am always delighted to report events at the Dolphin, Kitty, but with the terrible murder of Mr Farjeon earlier today, I am merely following up leads.'

Kitty knew she was going to regret asking but did it anyway. 'And why would that bring you to the Dolphin Hotel?'

An ingratiating smirk spread across Walter's face, revealing yellow uneven teeth. 'Just a hunch. Inspector Greville keeps returning here so it has me wondering whether there's a link between the murders and the Dolphin. Oh, and of course the rumours of the fabulous jewel.'

'Inspector Greville must have other business besides the murders, and rumours of a jewel are just rumours. I fear you are wasting your time, Mr Cribbs, and I'll thank you not to print libellous material in your rag.'

Walter's smirk grew bigger. 'Really, then what about the story of how your room was burgled earlier today?'

Who had he been talking to? Gossip always spread like wildfire in a small town and Alice, the young maid who had discovered the break-in, would easily be persuaded to talk.

'Dartmouth must be becoming a veritable hotbed of crime. Does nothing happen in Torquay or Newton Abbott lately?'

'Was anything of value taken during the robbery? Do you think the thief was searching for the jewel? Why is there a policeman in the hotel kitchen?' Walter pushed his face closer to hers. His notepad and pencil were poised to scribble down her responses.

'I have nothing to say, Mr Cribbs. You really are wasting your time. Nothing of any value has been stolen. Once again, there is no jewel. We have very good security at the hotel and the officer in the kitchen is taking statements about the fire.' Kitty tried to keep her tone light, refusing to give him the satisfaction of trying to rattle her nerves. She would need to have a talk with the staff and remind them not to be talking out of turn.

Walter slid his notepad back into his pocket, giving her what she supposed he thought was a winning smile. 'Maybe we should talk about the masked ball instead. It promises to be quite an event. I shall of course be covering it for the society column. I do hope you'll keep a dance or two free for me.'

Kitty thought Hell would probably freeze over before that happened. 'I doubt I'll have time for dancing. There is a lot of work to ensure the success of such big events.'

Walter tittered, the high-pitched sound grating on her. 'All work and no play will make Kitty a dull girl.'

'I'm sure you'll be working hard too,' she remarked. 'The worthy people of Dartmouth like to see their names in print at prestigious events. I'm sure the *Herald* doesn't pay you to go dancing.'

'Some of the luminaries of Dartmouth are lucky they don't feature in the court column.' Walter sounded sulky.

'Ah, Mr Cribbs, how very fortuitous.' Inspector Greville loomed up behind Walter. 'I wonder if I might have a word?'

Kitty had the satisfaction of seeing Walter look a little uncomfortable, the smirk he'd worn since arriving suddenly vanishing from his face.

'Anything to oblige the law, Inspector Greville.'

'How did you hear of the demise of Mr Farjeon? You were at the scene remarkably swiftly.'

Walter fidgeted beneath the inspector's gaze. 'A newsman's sources are normally sacred, but in this case, I happened to be passing when the delivery lad shot out of the booth and ran into me.'

'I see, and where were you going when you were just passing?' His eyes suddenly took on a flinty look and Kitty was glad that she wasn't on the receiving end of that stare.

'I was on my way to pick up some provisions. It can be a long day when you're out and about chasing up stories.' Walter's voice held a whiney note.

'Alone?'

'Here, what's this about? I came out of my lodgings and walked towards Farjeon's booth. I was going to ask him a few questions, but it looked all shut up, so I thought I'd go and get some food from the shop first and see if he was there on the way back. I'd just got near to the booth when the young boy shot out wailing like a banshee.'

Inspector Greville raised an eyebrow. 'The lad went for help, so what did you do while you were alone with the body?'

Kitty's eyes widened.

'Nothing, I didn't do nothing. What would I do with old Hubert? I stuck my head in and seen he was dead. All that blood fair turned my stomach, so I come out to take some air and then the lad come back with your constable and he told me to sling my hook.'

'You didn't search the booth? Or remove any papers?'

'No, I told you. It was enough to give anyone the heebie-jeebies seeing Hubert there with that knife in his guts.'

The inspector coughed and Walter suddenly appeared to recall that Kitty was present.

'Did anyone join you? Or did you see anyone before the lad returned with the constable?'

Sweat beads formed on Walter's brow. 'No, I don't know. People started gathering as I reckon they heard the boy wailing and yelling his way up the street.'

Kitty attention was drawn to a dark brown mark on Walter's cuff as he waved his arms during his narration. There was another stain on the edge of his jacket. Bile churned in her stomach as she realised that Walter must have been right inside the booth to get blood on his clothes.

His cuff didn't go unnoticed by Inspector Greville either. 'You appear to have blood on your shirt and the edge of your jacket, Mr Cribbs.'

The tips of Walter's ears turned pink. 'That was probably done when the boy cannoned into me. I didn't touch nothing in that booth.'

'What questions did you intend to ask Mr Farjeon?'

'He'd said something to me about how he thought he knew something about who killed Cora Wakes. He kept hinting so I thought I'd try and find out if he was telling the truth. I thought some money might persuade him to tell me what he knew. He was fond of money, was Hubert.'

'And where did you hear the rumour about a valuable jewel?'

'Gossip, in the local public house and a few coins here and there in the right palms.'

The inspector's expression looked stonier than ever at Walter's confession of how he obtained his new stories. 'You didn't feel you should come forward to the police with any of this information?'

'It's a big story. I can sell this stuff to the nationals and make some money, maybe get a byline, or even my ticket to London and the big time.' Walter shuffled his feet.

'If I find out you've compromised a crime scene, Mr Cribbs, or hampered my investigations in any way, I shall be speaking to your employer,' Greville warned. 'You may go for now, but I may need to speak with you again.'

Walter bolted from the hotel at a less than dignified scuttle.

'Ugh, that man.' Kitty gave vent to her feelings with a shudder and saw Inspector Greville hide a smile in his moustache.

'I agree, Miss Underhay. Unfortunately, in my experience, it appears to be the nature of certain journalists.' He bade her and Matt farewell and followed Walter Cribbs out of the hotel.

'How much did you hear?' Kitty asked. She hadn't noticed Matt join the little group; she had been too busy watching Walter. She wanted to ask him what Vivien and Bobby had said to the inspector.

'Enough. Why didn't you give the inspector the ruby?'

'I couldn't, not yet. I need some time to think things through.'

Matt's face was pale in the fading light. She switched on the green shaded desk light, creating a golden pool of light in the wood-panelled lobby. 'The clouds have gathered outside; it seems to be dark early this evening.'

A family party came in to collect their room keys and she was distracted for a moment dealing with her guests.

'Matt, is everything all right?' Something in his demeanour told her something was wrong.

'I'm sorry. It's been a very difficult day. I wish you had given him that stone.'

His response was unexpected. She was used to the confident Captain Bryant. She suddenly recalled what he'd shared with her about the war, and how in the taxi he had opened the window to cope with the confined space. A warm emotion washed over her.

'I'm sorry, it was, I don't know, instinct to keep it. You shouldn't have gone into that tunnel with Mickey.' She kept her voice low so no one passing might overhear her.

A dull flush coloured his cheeks and his spine stiffened. 'It was my duty to check it out. Your grandmother has employed me to do a job.'

'I know. I'm sorry, I was only thinking of you. After seeing Hubert and formally identifying Cora, it can't have been pleasant.'

His shoulders drooped slightly. 'I'm sorry. You're right, the events of the past week or so have affected me more than I thought they would.'

'Is there anything I can do?' She reached across the counter and touched his arm in further unspoken support.

He moved his arm away as if her fingers had burned him. His gaze met hers and she struggled to read the maelstrom of emotions revealed there. 'I'm going to ask you to lock me in my room tonight and to keep the key. If you hear noises do not come to me. Sometimes when I'm exposed to events such as these, the nightmares come back.'

A faint gasp at his request escaped her. His expression was bleak. 'I will be perfectly fine, there is nothing anyone can do, by tomorrow I will be as before.'

'I understand.'

Many men had returned home from the battlefields carrying scars that went far deeper than those visible on their skin. She had had guests at the hotel who had come to convalesce, their wives hoping the quiet peace of the resort would help to heal their shattered minds. Some of those men had also suffered terrifying dreams or had walked out in the night, one into the cold, inky river.

Matt had only hinted at the trauma he had suffered. He had risen to the rank of Captain and her grandmother had said he had a distinguished war record. It seemed that he was still paying the price for his service.

That evening, Kitty did as Matt asked and locked him into his room, keeping the key to his door with her. The maids had managed to restore order to her own bedroom, but with the lock smashed, she had decided to sleep in her grandmother's suite until Mickey could make repairs.

She arranged with Matt to unlock his door at eight the next morning. Once in her grandmother's suite, she secured the door and slid a table in front before opening the ancient secret safe that was hidden in the window seat. She held the stone closer to the light. Even in its uncut state she could see the blood-red lustre and her heartbeat speeded up. Shaking herself mentally, Kitty wrapped the ruby inside a clean, white lace-edged handkerchief and placed it below the papers relating to her mother's disappearance. Matt was still most unhappy that she hadn't handed it over to Inspector Greville or told him about it.

Once all was secure, she took a seat on the cushion at the window and stared out at the river. A fine mist covered the water and there were a few people out on the street tonight walking their dogs or heading for the town's hostelries. She shivered and pulled her cardigan more closely around her. Suddenly she missed her mother and grandmother very much. She had no idea what she should do about the ruby. Who was the rightful owner? Was it her father, if he had won it in a poker game? It surely couldn't be worth quite so much money as Walter Cribbs had said. And as she pondered, Kitty's mind kept wandering to Matt, hoping that he was okay.

She expected to sleep badly after all that had happened, especially with her concerns for Matt playing on her mind. Instead, she woke with a start when the maid bringing her morning tea rapped at the door, jiggling the lock and asking anxiously if she was all right.

Kitty slipped out of bed and pulled on her dressing gown before sliding the table back from the door. Alice stood wide-eyed in front of her, a tray of tea on her trolley. 'Begging your pardon, Miss Underhay, but the door wouldn't open.'

'The lock sticks sometimes. Thank you for the tea.' She took the tray and returned inside.

CHAPTER TWENTY-ONE

Matt woke that morning to discover his sheets in a crumpled sweaty heap. He sat up and looked cautiously around the room. Apart from an overturned side table, nothing was smashed or destroyed. He heaved a sigh of relief. He hadn't wanted to scare Kitty but when the night terrors came upon him, he couldn't remember what happened during those hours. He would wake to find items destroyed, his feet cut and bleeding and parts of his body bruised or aching.

When he had first returned from the front at the end of the war, they had been worse. More violent and frequent. He would dream about Edith, baby Betty, and the Zeppelins, and wake screaming with rage and grief. Only a few people knew his secrets, about the dreams, the soul-sucking terror of being trapped in a small space and about what had happened to Edith.

He had remained in the army for several years after the end of the war, travelling around England and Europe working for the government. But he had been unable to settle in one place, the memories pursuing him like unwelcome ghosts, until he had finally been decommissioned a few months ago. He had accepted this job to please his parents, mainly his mother, who believed that time spent quietly by the sea might help him to settle. He hadn't expected to be thrown into a confusing mystery of murders.

There was a light tapping at his door. 'Matt? It's Kitty, are you all right? Do you want me to slide the key under your door?'

'Yes, thank you, everything is fine.'

He watched as the key appeared in his room, sliding along the polished boards to stop at the edge of the rug.

'I'll see you later, after breakfast.'

'Okay.' He wondered what she'd done with the ruby. At least Kitty had a cool head, and he appreciated how she had been seemingly unfazed by his request for help last night. Hopefully she'd locked it away in the secret safe in her grandmother's suite. He wished she would agree to hand it over to the police, although he could sympathise with why she had held on to it.

Outside in the corridor he heard Mickey talking to someone and guessed it must be the carpenter come to fix Kitty's door. He assumed that whoever had been sleeping in the tunnel hadn't returned as no one had alerted him. If it was the person who had broken into Kitty's room, then perhaps they had given up and decided to leave now there was a police presence. Much as he hoped that might be true though, he couldn't quite see it.

After breakfast, he found Kitty hard at work finalising the plans for the masked ball.

'Do you have a mask ready for the ball?' she asked.

'Mickey found me one out of the storerooms. He said there were some left in there from the New Year ball.'

'Good. I'm hoping this goes well as it's Vivien's last performance here.'

'Are she and Bobby leaving straight away?'

'No, they are staying on for a couple of days to visit Torquay and to see some of the countryside before they head for Plymouth to board the ship. I rather wish I hadn't agreed to that now with everything that's happened.' Kitty pushed the pile of paper she had been working on to one side and sighed. 'I'm having trouble concentrating today. I still have a policeman in my kitchen annoying my chef, and the carpenter is working on my door.'

'Come on then, take a break.' He smiled at her.

'What kind of break?' Her tone held a note of suspicion.

'I want to look at access to the tunnel from below the castle. Mickey said there used to be an entrance there.'

Kitty laughed. 'There are probably quite a few entrances, the castle grounds used to be much larger than they are now. There are even rumours that there were tunnels in a secret crypt below the church. But I am not getting on a boat, it's choppy today.'

'You don't have to; we can visit the tearooms at the castle and check it out from there.' The tearooms had reopened after the war and enjoyed a brisk trade with day trippers.

'True. I won't say no to cake and tea. We can always talk to Pete, the castle caretaker, too, if he's around. He lives in the castle so he would know if anything odd had been happening.' Kitty collected her hat and handbag. 'I haven't been for tea at the castle for ages.'

The rain of the previous evening had left the day feeling fresh but sunny as they strolled along the embankment away from the town, past the old customs house towards the castle. The walk led uphill away from town around Warfleet Bay past the old lime kilns. The streets were narrow with steep alleyways climbing between the houses into the hills. There appeared to be plenty of other couples with the same idea as they walked to the small entrance leading into the tearoom.

Matt studied the tearoom with interest. It was larger than he'd expected, nestled as it was inside the sturdy ancient stone walls of the castle. The tearoom occupied the top floor of the turret with the entrance opening onto the upper level where the castle was built into the hillside. Dark oak tables were covered with lace-edged cloths. The walls were whitewashed and a few black and white framed photographs of views of the coast hung on the walls. Outside, there were a few tables positioned to take advantage of the view of the river. They took a seat at one of the smaller tables inside and gave their order to the young waitress, smart in her black dress and white cap and apron.

'Is this what you were expecting?' Kitty drew off her gloves and placed them neatly on top of her handbag.

Matt looked around. 'I don't know. I really want to take a look around to see if the tunnel might be visible from the far side of the castle.'

Kitty shrugged. 'I expect not, it's below water at high tide and well hidden. There are more tunnels near Kingswear Castle tower on the opposite side of the river. Lots of them are lost now or unusable. During the war everything was closed off.'

The waitress returned with their order and, as the girl made to move away, Kitty stopped her. 'Do you know if Pete, the caretaker, is here today?'

'I dunno, miss, I'll ask for you. Is there a problem, miss?' The girl looked worried.

'No, no problem at all. I just need some information and I know he has a wealth of knowledge about the castle.'

A relieved smile lit the girl's face. 'I'll go ask, miss.'

'Pete lives in as caretaker. He's a veteran like you. He helped man the defences here during the war. He knows my grandmother well.'

A few minutes later, an older man with a slight limp appeared at the table. 'Miss Underhay, how can I help you? Is your grandmother well?'

'Quite well, thank you, Pete. Captain Bryant here was enquiring about the tunnels that lead from the castle, I think they link with the one at the rear of the Dolphin.'

Matt noticed he was back to being Captain Bryant again. Pete scratched his head, pushing his cap slightly to the side as he did so. 'They tunnels is mostly lost, miss. There is one that still works.'

'The one from the sea?' Matt asked.

'Yes, sir, that one I think is still open. It did have a metal grid over it, but I think it may have been lost in a storm last spring.'

'Do you know of any others?' Matt asked.

Pete screwed his face up in thought. 'There used to be some as opened up in the hills just outside the castle boundary, but I heard as the farmer had closed them in.'

'I don't suppose you've seen or heard any boats lately, near where the tunnel opening would be, have you?' Kitty asked.

'Can't say as I have, miss. Do you think someone is back smuggling again? Or spying?' Pete's gaze sharpened.

'No. My grandmother has a door closing off the tunnel at our end, which she keeps locked and it looks as if someone has been trying to get inside.' Kitty told a half-truth.

'T'would probably be children messing about.'

'I'm sure you're right, Pete. I just wanted to check. If you do hear or see anything odd though, please send a message to Captain Bryant at the Dolphin.'

Pete nodded. 'That I will, Miss Underhay.' He shook hands with Kitty and Matt and left.

'You realise he thinks I'm on some covert military detail?' Matt eyed Kitty as she took a sip of tea.

'No doubt, but Pete is a good, honest soul and a patriot.'

After finishing their tea, they strolled out onto the top of the castle to look over at the sea.

'The tide is in so you can't see the tunnel.' Kitty shaded her eyes with her hand.

'How old were you during the war, Kitty?' Matt asked.

'I was four when it started. My mother disappeared when I was six. You must have been young yourself?'

He was silent for a moment trying not to remember. 'Not as young as you, but too young, fourteen almost fifteen.'

'What happened, Matt? Who is Edith?'

He shook his head. 'I'm sorry, Kitty. I can't talk about her, not here, not yet.'

She placed a gloved hand on his arm. 'Come, we should get back to the hotel.'

The walk back to the hotel was silent. Matt was lost in his own thoughts and Kitty appeared content to allow him to be quiet.

The Dolphin's wide half-timbered frontage dominated the street scene. The carved, wooden grey-painted dolphin sign creaked gently in the breeze from the river high above their heads. The glass in the diamond leaded panes twinkled in the sunshine.

Matt stole a peep at Kitty. He wondered if running the hotel would have been her choice had she been free to make it. Maybe Elowed had run away from her destiny after all, although he feared that Kitty and her grandmother's instincts were correct and that Elowed was long dead. If Elowed had planned to get away, why leave the ruby behind, and her daughter?

'Post, Miss Underhay.' The girl at the reception desk passed a small bundle of letters to Kitty as she entered the lobby. He waited as she flicked through the pile, instinct telling him to stay close. He saw her frown at one particular envelope.

'Kitty?'

She glanced at him 'I think I should open this upstairs.'

He joined her as they hurried up the wide polished oak staircase to the first floor. Kitty unlocked the door to her grandmother's suite and crossed to the bureau. She dropped the other letters down before pulling off her gloves and taking up a small gilded paperknife.

'I don't recognise the writing and it has been hand-delivered.' She waved the envelope at him so he could see there was no stamp. She carefully slit the top of the envelope open and drew out the thin sheet of paper from inside.

Immediately he could see it was unlike the other anonymous one-line letters. This one had a full page of writing and what appeared to be a small photograph enclosed in its folds.

Kitty sank down onto the sofa, the photograph tumbling onto her lap as her eyes scanned the letter.

'What is it?' Matt asked.

'It's so strange. I don't know what to say.' Her eyes glistened with unshed tears as she picked up the photograph from her lap. She blinked as she studied it and shook her head fiercely as if to clear her thoughts. She passed the picture to him.

'My mother.'

He studied the photograph. It had clearly been taken some time ago and was battered and creased. Elowed appeared a similar age to Kitty now. It was a formal studio portrait with Elowed seated in front of what appeared to be a photographer's backdrop of a classical Greek scene with columns. In her hands was a large bouquet of lilies. He flipped it over. On the back was written, '*My beautiful bride on our wedding*'.

'The letter is from Edgar?' He passed the photograph back to Kitty.

She nodded. 'It would seem so. He enclosed the picture to prove himself genuine.'

Matt waited for her to continue. He longed to take the letter and read what Edgar Underhay had to say to the child he had abandoned, but he waited for Kitty to compose herself.

Kitty dabbed her eyes with a small lace-edged handkerchief before picking up the letter once more and reading it aloud to Matt.

'*My dear daughter, I hope I might still claim to call you this despite our long separation. I was deeply shocked when I learned only recently of the loss of your mother. I must ask you to believe me when I say I knew nothing of this, or the circumstances surrounding her disappearance. I had believed her to be safe with you at your grandmother's hotel. I realise that you may find my correspondence unwelcome, especially after so much time has passed. I have only lately returned to England, having been in America for several years. I had reason to believe correspondence would have been unwelcome so, to my shame, I did not write to you.*

'*I enclose a photograph of your mother to prove my authenticity. It is one which I have carried with me since our wedding. I understand that you may not wish to see me or hear from me, but I greatly fear that my coming to Dartmouth may have inadvertently placed you in some danger. This is why I have not yet come forward openly to meet you in person as I had first intended. Your mother had in her keeping something of mine of great value and I have been double-crossed by a person whom I trusted in my endeavours to regain it and to reconnect with you. My dear, I beg you to keep safe and to engage with someone who you can trust to protect you.*

'*I do not know if you have discovered the jewel. If you have, then please ensure it is locked up safely and in secret. I hope to try to contact you in person to explain myself further, but I dare not place either you or, to be frank, myself, in any more danger.*

'*If you do not wish to see or hear more from me then I will understand, but I cannot emphasise enough how serious the situation is in which I find myself, and in which I have inadvertently placed you. If you will agree to further communication, I ask you to place a vase of red roses in the window of your grandmother's room visible from the street and I will contact you.*

'*Please take care my dear child, I could not bear to think of you coming to any harm through some fault of mine.*

'*Your father, Edgar Underhay.*'

Kitty's voice cracked as she read the last line. 'What do I do now, Matt?'

CHAPTER TWENTY-TWO

Matt paced about the room, thinking hard about the contents of Kitty's letter.

'Well that's a turn up for the books, old girl.' The phrase slipped out.

Kitty was busy rereading the missive once more. 'I don't know what to do. I don't know what to do about this letter, or about the ruby.' She dropped the letter and picked up the photograph once more.

'You look very much like your mother,' Matt remarked.

She touched the corner of the battered image with a tender fingertip.

'I don't know. What do you want to do, Kitty?' He waited for her reply. He knew what they should do: hand everything over to Inspector Greville, including the blasted ruby, but it wasn't his call to make. All he could do was try to keep Kitty safe.

'If I give the letter and ruby to Inspector Greville, my father could well be in more danger. For that matter, so could I. The ruby is my first tangible link to my parents, and might be the key to my mother's disappearance.' Her tone was troubled.

'Kitty, I know it is a difficult thing to think, but you must face facts. We don't know who killed Mr Blaas, Cora or Hubert Farjeon. And I admit, I am worried about the interest this person has in you.'

She sighed and placed the letter and photograph on the bureau. 'I know my father is a rogue and a coward. His own words more or less admit to that, but I cannot think him capable of violence.'

'You wish to place the roses in the window?' Matt asked.

She nodded slowly. 'I wish to solve this puzzle. I wish to actually see my father face-to-face. He must have had that photograph with him all these years. I want to hear from him why he stayed away.'

'I understand.' And in a strange way he did. He wanted to find out who had killed Blaas, Cora and Hubert, and hopefully assist Inspector Greville in bringing them to justice. But he also understood the longing to fill an empty space in a heart left by someone who was missing.

'I shall send out for some red roses and then we shall wait to see what happens,' Kitty stood and unlocked the bureau, slipping the letter and photograph inside. 'We say nothing of this to Inspector Greville, not yet.' Her worried gaze met Matt's.

'Very well, if you are certain. You know I have concerns about this, though. I made a promise to your grandmother to keep you safe and that did not include looking after a priceless ruby.'

A slight smile lifted the corners of Kitty's lips. 'I know and I promise I shall not be reckless.'

Matt wished he could believe her.

She followed her father's instructions and placed a large vase of flowers on a small side table in the bay window of her grandmother's suite, sending Matt outside to check that it was visible from the street.

'And now we wait,' she said.

'It will be dark in a few hours. I don't expect he will contact you again today. If he is as concerned as he said about your safety, and his own, I'm expecting it to be a fleeting meet-up when you probably least expect it.'

Kitty sighed. 'I expect you're right.'

The evening was a busy one. Vivien Delaware had proved to be a huge success during her engagement at the hotel and it was late by the time the last of the guests had retired to their beds and the visitors had all departed the hotel.

Vivien appeared to be in no mood to chat with either Kitty or Matt and she, Bobby and the musicians all left the ballroom as soon as their performance was finished. Matt accompanied Kitty to the lobby to ascertain that the night porter was at his station and observing for anything untoward.

'Is the poor constable still on duty in the kitchen?' Kitty asked in a low tone, out of earshot of the night porter.

'Yes. Greville is leaving someone here for a few days.' Matt personally felt happier knowing there was some kind of police presence in the hotel. Kitty had to be safer with the extra security.

'I'm going to pop into the kitchen and get some hot milk to take upstairs.'

'If you make it cocoa then I'll join you.' Matt smiled at her.

They made their way along the corridor companionably, quietly warning the constable stationed in the gloom next to the large pantry door that they were coming to make drinks. Kitty offered to make the constable some cocoa too. She left the main light turned off, relying on light from the corridor to see by.

She had barely had time to tip some milk into the pan when Matt took hold of her arm, stilling the movement.

'Look!' The constable rose from his seat and they looked towards the door in the cliff face, all of them scarcely daring to breathe.

The door had opened a fraction; someone was inside the tunnel. The constable swore they hadn't entered via the door, but were clearly about to exit that way. Matt touched the constable's sleeve and gestured towards the rear door to the kitchen which stood unlatched.

He and the police officer edged slowly and carefully towards the door. Kitty followed them. In the moonlight they watched the tunnel door open further and a shadowy face peep out.

Matt held his breath. The next move was crucial. If the man were to see them, or if they moved too soon, he could dart back inside and be gone. A cold shiver danced along his spine at the thought of possibly having to enter the tunnels again, especially in the dark.

For what felt like an eternity, nothing happened. Then the door to the tunnel opened wider and the slight figure of a man emerged. The man glanced about as if to check the coast was clear and then darted towards the gate. Before Matt could prevent him, the constable let out a blast on his whistle and charged through the back door of the kitchen.

The man they were chasing startled and ran back into the tunnels. Matt groaned aloud and, cursing under his breath, he followed the broad shoulders of the constable as he charged after their quarry.

'Matt!' Kitty raced behind him, her heels clicking on the paving stones. 'Take this.'

He paused to accept the large metal torch she handed him. 'Stay here. Go inside and telephone Greville.' He shouted the instruction to her as he switched on the torch and followed the constable inside the cliff face.

Darkness enveloped him as soon as he entered the tunnel and the door swung shut behind him. He was thankful for Kitty's quick thinking as the yellow light of the torch lit his way as he followed the constable along the narrow tunnel. Up ahead in the dark he heard the rapid, scrabbling footsteps of the man they were hunting.

Soon they were in the cave where he and Mickey had discovered the blankets. He swung the torch around looking for any other exits but only saw the one that Mickey had said led to the sea below the castle.

This time Matt led the way, with the policeman behind him. He listened as he went forward for any sounds of their quarry. The air smelt damp and briny and his heart pounded hard against the wall of his chest as they ventured deeper into the cliff.

Just as Matt was beginning to feel the walls of the tunnel closing around him, it suddenly widened out and forked. Matt breathed a sigh as he tried to fight the terror in his mind by considering the options before them. One branch of the tunnel led downwards and the other, much smaller, swerved away up and to the right. The fugitive had a head start and Matt played the torch around the ground and walls searching for clues as to the direction he might have taken.

'I can't hear him,' the constable said.

Matt could barely hear anything beyond the sound of his own blood rushing in his ears. 'I doubt he came in by boat, let's try this way.' He took the path leading upward, and against every survival instinct he possessed, led the way further into the complex.

As they worked their way along, the tunnel grew narrower and Matt found his shoulders scraping against the side of the passage. Up ahead he thought he could hear the man they were chasing.

'Sir, I can't get no further.' Matt glanced behind him to see the policeman's burly frame prohibited him from making further progress. He swallowed.

'Can you go back, check on Miss Underhay and tell any others where I've gone?'

'Yes, sir, I have some matches in my pocket to light the way.'

The police officer began to work his way backwards down the tunnel. Matt took a deep breath and continued on his way. He forced himself to concentrate on the task at hand, to push aside the horrific memories taunting him at the edge of his mind. Memories of Flanders mud, heavy and sticky, falling, pressing against the wall of his chest, filling his nose and mouth. The rocky walls began to give way to soil, damp and earthy-smelling, long pale roots, white in the torch light, dangled from the ceiling and brushed against his hair.

Every now and then he thought he heard scrabbling sounds from up ahead and he hoped it was his quarry. A shower of dirt and small stones rattled down on his face and he almost dropped the torch. He wanted to be sick, surely the tunnel had to open out soon.

Even as the thought crossed his mind, the space closed in even further so he was forced to drop onto his stomach and crawl. By the torch light he could see leaves ahead of him, smell green air and could feel the cool of the night on his face. He wriggled forward, hoping the man he had been pursuing wasn't hiding just ahead, about to attack.

Finally, he emerged through what seemed to be the entrance to a badger's sett into the vast open slopes of a field just outside the castle walls. His eyes took a moment to adjust to the moonlight as he looked around for the man he had been following. A hedgerow lay in shadow and he shone the torch, trying to see if his quarry might be lying hidden there, but there was no sign.

Matt sank down on his knees on the grass, so thankful to be outside the tunnels and alive. He supposed it would be a long and difficult walk back into the town through the woods, but he simply couldn't face returning to the Dolphin the way he had emerged.

Slowly, he began to follow the hedgerow line, taking care over the uneven ground beneath his feet, until he came to a gate and made his way towards the small stone-built Devon longhouse. His approach set the farm dogs barking and in response a light came on inside the building.

*

Kitty had telephoned the police station as soon as Matt had disappeared inside the tunnel. She waited anxiously in the kitchen for any signs of either Matt or the constable emerging back into the yard.

Her patience was rewarded after about half an hour when the police officer came out.

'What happened? Where is Captain Bryant?'

Her heart raced. The constable's uniform was torn and dirty. She led him to the kitchen and put on the kettle, trying to calm herself by keeping busy and being purposeful.

'Captain Bryant is still in pursuit, miss. The tunnel was too narrow for me to get through, so he carried on by himself. He asked me to return and stay with you, miss.' The policeman sank down on a kitchen chair, clearly shaken by the pursuit. 'It's dark as pitch in those tunnels, can't see a hand in front of you.'

'I've telephoned the police station, your colleagues should be here soon. Did you see the man at all? Where did you go?' At least Matt had the torch with him, but that thought was of little comfort.

The constable told her about the journey through the tunnel and their theory that the man had escaped via the land route.

'Matt could be anywhere. He could be in mortal danger!' She knew the tunnel would be his worst nightmare, and to go on alone after the fugitive was brave beyond belief. He would suffer terribly from the adventure. For two pins she would set off along the tunnels herself if she thought she could help.

'Miss Underhay. Constable Jones. Would you care to tell me what has been happening?' Inspector Greville entered the room, escorted by the night porter.

CHAPTER TWENTY-THREE

Exhaustion washed over Kitty, draining her of any remaining energy she had when the telephone call finally came to say that Matt was safe. Inspector Greville sent a car to collect him from High Castle Farm.

By the time he arrived back at the hotel, the first pinky-coloured streaks of dawn were staining the sky and the birds had begun to sing.

'Captain Bryant, I understand you were lucky Farmer Dykes didn't discharge his shotgun at you,' Inspector Greville remarked as Matt entered the hotel lobby, looking tired and dishevelled. Dirt clung to his suit and he had a scratch mark on his left cheek.

'I think he thought I was a fox after the hens at first. It was a close thing to convince him I was not a tramp about to rob his household.' He sank down on a nearby chair. Kitty passed him the tumbler of whisky she had prepared for him.

'No sign of your quarry?'

Matt shook his head. 'No, sir, he obviously knew those tunnels and the lay of the land well. By the time I managed to get into the field he was gone.'

Greville sighed deeply. 'I think we can most probably assume our man is Colin Wakes. It has to be someone local to know the layout of those tunnels so well. Did you get a good look at him? Constable Jones said he couldn't see clearly in the moonlight.'

'Only a glance, I'm afraid. Constable Jones and I were some distance away and it was quite dark. He is a thin man, shorter than average, thin face and narrow moustache, that's all I can tell you, sir.' He swallowed a gulp of whisky.

The inspector glanced at his watch. 'That certainly fits Wakes's description. For now though, I think we should all get some rest, it's been a long night. We will carry on the search for Colin Wakes as there must be some reason why he is so anxious to avoid coming into contact with the police and is lurking about inside the old smugglers' tunnels.' He donned his hat and bade them all a good morning.

The night porter set about his morning duties, leaving Kitty alone with Matt in the lobby.

'How are you?' she asked, keeping her voice low.

'Glad to be away from the tunnels.' He grimaced as he spoke.

Kitty bit back a yawn. 'I'm sorry, I need to get some sleep. Can I get you anything else?'

He finished his whisky. 'No, thank you for the drink.'

'Will you be all right?' she asked as he stood to ascend the stairs with her. She hoped his ordeal wouldn't trigger another bout of night terrors.

'I'll survive.' He gave her a brief smile and she had to be content with his response.

*

Preparations for Vivien's final performance and the masked ball took up the next few days and Kitty threw herself into it to distract herself from frustration with the lack of progress in the case. The police continued their efforts, but Colin Wakes appeared to have vanished. Kitty kept expecting to receive further contact from her father, but nothing happened, although she continued to keep the vase of roses in full view. Her grandmother and her great aunt had set off from Scotland but wouldn't arrive until after the ball as Livvy had been told she must have frequent stops on the journey.

Vivien and Bobby continued to keep a low profile. Kitty only saw them when Vivien appeared to give her nightly performances.

Much to Kitty's frustration, Matt continued to monitor her every move, both inside the hotel and whenever she went out, often finding excuses to accompany her.

'I'm starting to feel as if we're an old married couple,' she complained as he insisted on walking with her to the post office.

His eyebrow quirked and the corner of his mouth lifted. 'Then I'm sure you'll agree I'd make you a most attentive husband.'

She scowled as he strolled along beside her as if he had all the time in the world. She wondered if he had ever been a husband, if that was the personal tragedy that had marked his life. Perhaps the mysterious Edith.

'I need to call at the market for a few things.' She set off towards the ancient, covered Butterwalk which lay away from the river behind the main streets.

'I don't think I've seen the market,' Matt remarked and fell into step beside her as they passed under the overhanging upper stories of the buildings supported by stone columns, past the shop windows. The market was small but busy with stalls laden with all kinds of goods. Vegetables, fish, ironmongery and haberdashery all jostled for position and for customers.

She completed her purchases, stowing the packages in the large wicker basket she carried over one arm and they were about to walk back to the hotel when Matt touched her elbow. 'Look there.'

She glanced in the direction he indicated. To her surprise, Bobby was deep in conversation with Walter Cribbs. Matt drew her to the side of the footpath so they weren't blocking the way. As they watched, Bobby drew a brown Manila envelope from inside the breast of his jacket and passed it to Walter before hurrying away.

'Well, wasn't that strange?' Matt remarked.

'What do you think was in that envelope?' Kitty asked.

Matt shrugged. 'Money? Information? Walter Cribbs is such a sly character, anything is possible.'

'Do you think he may have taken something from Hubert Farjeon's booth that he is blackmailing Bobby and Vivien over? He admitted he went in there and we are fairly certain he lied to Inspector Greville.'

'Bobby and Vivien both seemed quite shaken up when Greville interviewed them. If anybody is under suspicion, I would have thought it would be Bobby. Vivien draws crowds wherever she goes due to her appearance so she can hardly have managed to murder Cora or Hubert without someone seeing her. Bobby, on the other hand, who knows?'

Kitty frowned as she pondered the information. 'Why, though? What motive would they have? They weren't here either when Mr Blaas was killed.'

'I have been thinking about this, and I believe Vivien and Bobby are here under instructions to try and retrieve that ruby. Bobby admitted that their next singing engagement was back in Chicago and it sounded as if it was for a mob-owned club. Or they could be after it for themselves, of course.'

'I suppose that makes a horrid kind of sense. If they recognised my father in London they could have told someone who they knew was looking for him. It's not so far from London to here by train or motor vehicle and Bobby arrived later than Vivien.'

'Exactly,' Matt said.

'I'll be glad when the masked ball is over. A few more days and they'll be gone back to America. I wish now I hadn't said they could stay for the extra couple of days before they are due to board their ship.'

'It's strange that the transfer of the envelope wasn't the other way around,' Matt said.

'Oh yes, I see what you mean. Walter has already admitted that he pays for information, so you would think it would be Walter paying Bobby.' It was strange. A shudder ran down her spine. Walter was so untrustworthy, and the way he always looked at her made her blood run cold. When he had made unwelcome advances at the Christmas ball, under the mistletoe, she had been forced to physically stamp on his foot to elude his clutches.

As they arrived on the embankment, she couldn't help but glance up the river towards Hubert Farjeon's booth, which remained cordoned off.

'I understand Inspector Greville is not amused that it has become a must-see site for the more ghoulish of the day trippers.' Matt drew her arm through his and turned her gently towards the Dolphin. 'I believe the mayor is pressing the council to remove it as soon as possible.'

'That would be a good thing. Hubert Farjeon had no family as far as I know so there is no one to take on his company or to drive the motor coach. It's horribly sad.' Kitty shivered at the thought of strangers peering at the gay little booth where Hubert had met such a terrible end.

'Miss Delaware is also out for a stroll this afternoon, I see.'

Vivien was indeed out for a promenade along the embankment. She was elegantly dressed as usual in a pale fawn costume; a fox fur stole around her shoulders and one of her hats bedecked with a tall feather. Trailing behind her at a short distance, their mouths agape at such a sight, were three small urchins.

'Good afternoon.' Matt raised his hat as she drew closer to them.

Vivien nodded her head regally in response, making the feather in her hat dip and the urchins giggle. 'I don't suppose you have seen Bobby anywhere? He was supposed to escort me to the castle tearooms.'

'We passed him earlier in town near the Butterwalk. I expect he'll be here soon,' Kitty said. If Vivien wanted to go to the tearooms she was walking in the wrong direction. Vivien wasn't really attired for a walk either, unless she and Bobby intended to take a car to the castle, as rounding Warfleet Bay on foot involved an uphill hike.

'Thank you, honey. He did mention something about going to the post office.' Vivien drew her stole a little closer around her shoulders, her eyes unfriendly.

'Perhaps running into Walter Cribbs delayed him,' Matt said smoothly.

Vivien blinked, her scarlet lips pressing together with a snap. 'Walter Cribbs? Oh, the reporter guy. Bobby always deals with the press for me, arranging interviews and such.'

Matt smiled. 'I expect that's what will have delayed his return then.'

They resumed their stroll, passing Vivien as she stood waiting for the hapless Bobby to return.

'You are a very wicked man,' Kitty murmured as soon as she was sure they were out of earshot. 'Do you think it was wise to tip her off that we knew that Bobby had met with Walter?'

'I don't think it will do any harm. It may make them more cautious if they are unsure of who might be observing them.'

Kitty glanced up to the window of her grandmother's suite as they reached the hotel entrance. She clutched his arm. 'Matt, look.'

He followed her gaze. Instead of the vase of red roses that had been visible from the street, a vase of yellow flowers stood in their place.

'Quickly, what does it mean?' Kitty hurried into the lobby and headed for the desk. 'Ellen, have I had any letters or deliveries whilst I've been out?'

The young receptionist's eyes widened at the urgency in her employer's tone. 'Only the flowers, Miss Underhay.'

'Yellow roses?' Matt asked.

'Yes, sir. I did as instructed, sir, and moved the other vase from the window. Have I misunderstood?' The girl looked worried.

'No, Ellen, that's fine. Did the flowers come with a message?'

'There was the instructions, miss, and I think there is a small card with them but of course I didn't open that.'

'No, of course not. Thank you, Ellen.'

'Who delivered them?' Matt asked.

Ellen frowned, clearly perplexed by the fuss. 'The florist's boy, sir, on his bike.'

Kitty hurried up the stairs with Matt close behind her, to see if there was anything on the card with the flowers.

Her fingers fumbled the key as she tried to put it in the lock and Matt had to take it from her to unlock the door. Sure enough, the red roses had been moved to the side table on the far wall and a fresh vase of yellow roses now stood in the window.

Kitty dropped her handbag and gloves down on the sofa and went to the flowers. A small florist's envelope stood propped up against the vase. She tore it open and eased out the small square of card.

Roses for my girl. Will see you soon, E

She sat down slowly on the sofa. 'More waiting, I suppose.' Her heart was still racing.

'At least you know he saw your message.' Matt examined the card. 'It's from the florist in town, so he's still close by.'

'Even if Inspector Greville can't find him.'

CHAPTER TWENTY-FOUR

The morning of the masked ball dawned dull and cloudy. Kitty rose early to supervise the decorators as they manoeuvred the huge pots of fronded palms and peacock-embellished screens she had ordered to decorate the ballroom.

The tables were grouped around the edge of the dance floor with greenery at either side of the stage and around the grand piano. Peacock feathers were also incorporated into the table decorations and the backdrop for Vivien's performance had been changed to one showing carnival masks decorated with gold glitter.

'What do you think?' she asked Matt.

He looked around the room. 'Very splendid, Vivien must be delighted that the Dolphin is going to so much trouble for her big finale performance.'

'The hotel has always been about providing entertainment for local people as well as our guests. It was one of the first things Grams taught me about managing the hotel. The holiday season can be quite short, and a bad summer could be a disaster if we didn't try to entice more paying customers through our doors. The tickets we sell for visitors attending our entertainment and suppers keep our accounts healthy.'

The staff left the room to go for their lunch break, leaving Kitty and Matt alone.

'Talking of Vivien and Bobby, have you seen them at all since yesterday?'

'No, I've been busy in here all morning.'

Matt produced a folded copy of the *Torbay Herald* from under his arm. 'Walter has certainly done his bit to publicise the ball.' He opened the paper out to show her. There was a picture of Vivien subtitled 'enchanting American chanteuse', and a glowing paragraph of praise for the promised delights of the masked ball at the Dolphin Hotel.

'Hmm, I do hope he's not trying to ingratiate himself with me again. Oh, perhaps this is what Bobby was handing to Walter.' Kitty rolled her eyes.

'But Walter is such a catch.' Matt grinned at her and stepped swiftly sideways when she lobbed a mock punch at his arm. 'And somehow I don't think it was simply publicity material in that envelope.'

Kitty's laughter was cut short by the arrival of Vivien to inspect her new set. 'Darling, peacocks, how quaint. I do hope they won't be unlucky though, the evil eye and all.'

'I'm sure you'll have a full house. You have a wonderful piece in the local paper.' Kitty reopened the newspaper to show her.

Vivien gave her an indulgent smile. 'Marvellous, darling, Bobby has done a great job. Did you say your grandmother would be here in time for the performance?'

Kitty shook her head. 'No, my aunt Livvy is very frail since her fall, so it's taking them longer than they thought to get here. You may get to meet her if they arrive before you leave to board your ship.'

Vivien pouted. 'I'd like to meet her. I heard so much about her from your mother. It must have been so hard for her when Elowed went missing, having all her things around her every day while she waited for her to come back.'

'Yes, I think she must have found it distressing.' Matt's tone was bland.

'I have very few things of my mother's, that's why it was so upsetting when my room was burgled, and my cuckoo clock was broken. It was one of the few things I had that had been hers.' Kitty wished now she'd kept the broken clock. Instead she'd asked the maid sorting out her room to get rid of it.

'Those ugly brown wooden things with the bears and such on the front are terribly old hat now, honey. I'm sure you'll be able to get something much nicer to replace it,' Vivien said lightly as she wandered over to the piano and idly pressed a couple of keys.

'Perhaps, but it won't have the memories.' Kitty wished Vivien would leave and let her get on with preparing the room. Her lack of sensitivity was as annoying as her soft, southern drawl.

Matt waited until Vivien had finished her tour of inspection and gone back to her room.

'How did she know what your mother's clock looked like?' he asked.

Kitty frowned. 'I don't know, I didn't notice that, I was too annoyed at how insensitively she was behaving over my mother's disappearance.'

'She was fishing to find out if your mother had any other belongings stashed anywhere. I suspect that's why she's keen to meet your grandmother.' Matt refolded the newspaper.

'Do you think she was the person who broke into my room?'

'She knew what the clock was like and Bobby could have been keeping lookout for her to make sure we didn't go upstairs. The way your room had been ransacked, it looked as if it had been searched in a hurry and there is no other way she could have described your clock.'

Kitty shuddered. 'That's horrid. Whoever broke my clock did it in temper; it looked as if it had been thrown against the wall. It could explain why Bobby always appears to be loitering around the lobby too.' The idea that it could have been Vivien who had searched her room and broken her clock angered her deeply.

'Good morning, Miss Underhay, Captain Bryant. I trust you've both recovered from your adventures the other night?' Inspector Greville strolled into the ballroom and glanced around at the decorations. His expression appeared to indicate he was impressed by the new décor.

'Yes, thank you,' Kitty replied. Her heart thumped a little faster. It was illogical, she knew, but she hoped he wasn't there to say he'd arrested her father, or that he'd somehow found out that she had the ruby in her possession.

'Any news on Cora or Hubert Farjeon's murders?' Matt asked.

'There's been a suspected sighting of Colin Wakes a few miles from here. Constable Jones is checking it out.' Greville paced up and down in front of them. 'I would like to have two of my men in attendance at the ball here tonight, Miss Underhay, if that would be acceptable?'

'I see. Not in uniform, I hope, Inspector Greville. My guests would be most alarmed at the sight of uniformed constables near the dance floor. The recent events in the town have already caused a great deal of concern.'

The inspector paused in his pacing. 'Your guests will be unaware of their presence, I assure you.'

Kitty swallowed the lump of fear in her throat. There was a sense of relief from knowing that the police would be on the premises, vying with a dread that there might be more events yet to come. 'Thank you, Inspector, that does reassure me. Do you anticipate any further problems during the ball?' She wasn't sure how to phrase the question.

He appeared to be considering what information he could share, his brow furrowing. 'I do have some concerns, Miss Underhay. Those are that whoever is searching for this gem is unlikely to cease until they either obtain it or are caught. I am also concerned that you personally may be in some danger.' His eyes appeared to bore into hers and Kitty's conscience gave her a sharp prick when she thought of the ruby, carefully locked away inside her grandmother's secret safe.

'I shall do my utmost to ensure Miss Underhay's safety,' Matt said.

The inspector raised his left eyebrow slightly in a thoughtful fashion. 'I don't doubt that, Captain Bryant, but I do not wish to see either of you hurt or worse. This person or persons have already murdered three people and violently assaulted another.'

'I understand, sir.' A look appeared to pass between Matt and the inspector.

'Please continue to be alert and report any suspicions to me. Good day, Miss Underhay, Captain Bryant.' He raised his hat and sauntered out of the ballroom.

'Do you think he really is expecting trouble at the ball this evening?' Kitty asked as soon as the door had closed behind him.

'I don't know. I can understand his concern. There will be a lot of people here tonight. Everyone will be wearing masks up until the midnight reveal. The potential is there for someone unscrupulous to try something.'

'At least the police will be in the ballroom. You and I will be there, and Mickey and the night porter will add to our security.'

'I'd still feel better if you weren't in possession of that damned ruby.' The ferocity of his muttered response did nothing to reassure her.

*

Matt too wondered exactly what Inspector Greville thought might happen, and what he had asked his men to look out for. It could be that he suspected Edgar Underhay or Colin Wakes might attend the ball, their identities safely concealed behind their masks. That same thought had come into his own mind, and he was pretty sure it had entered Kitty's too. He also wondered if the policeman suspected that Kitty had the ruby.

The staff returned from their lunch break to finish setting out the ballroom, and he escorted Kitty to the dining room for luncheon.

Vivien and Bobby were seated at their usual table and already finishing dessert as they entered the room. Matt noticed Vivien studiously ignore them as they were shown to a quiet table on the far side.

Kitty appeared preoccupied as she gave her lunch order to the waiter and he suspected that the inspector's warning was playing on her mind.

'Do you think your father will attempt to contact you this evening?' he asked, once the soup course had been set before them.

Kitty crumbled a small portion of her bread roll between her fingers. 'He would be mad or extremely reckless if he did, wouldn't he? There will be so many people around, and who knows who will be watching me, hoping to find him?'

On the edge of his vision, Matt could see Bobby. He thought the man appeared uncomfortable. He had his gaze fixed on whatever was outside the window and was fidgeting in his seat.

'What are you looking at?' Kitty asked, her voice soft.

'Bobby and Vivien. Especially Bobby, he's acting most oddly.'

'I can't see properly from here,' Kitty grumbled. 'What is happening?'

The waiter cleared their soup bowls and returned with the cheese omelettes and salad garnish they had ordered for their second course.

Matt continued to discreetly watch as another waiter approached Bobby and Vivien's table. He appeared to hand Bobby a note. As he opened the sheet of paper and read the contents, Bobby's normally florid complexion changed to ghostly white then to mottled purple fury. The waiter appeared to ask if there was a reply. As Bobby shook his head, the waiter took his leave.

Within seconds of the man withdrawing, Bobby's head was close to Vivien's and they seemed to be locked in a heated discussion.

'What's happening?' Kitty asked.

'Bobby has received some kind of note which appeared to upset him and now he and Vivien are having quite a conversation.'

'She had better not let me down tonight.' Kitty speared a piece of her omelette with her fork.

Matt wished he could follow Bobby and Vivien as they left the dining room. He would love to know what was going on. Instead, he called over the young waiter who had delivered the note to Bobby.

'You took a message to Miss Delaware's table a few minutes ago. May we know who the message was from?' Matt asked.

The lad glanced at Kitty in confusion as if unsure if it was permissible to answer Matt's query. On receiving her slight nod of consent, he started to talk. 'A boy brought it to the front desk, sir, said he'd been promised a shilling to make sure the gentleman dining with Miss Delaware got the message.'

'I see, I don't suppose you happened to catch sight of the message at all?' Matt asked.

The young waiter shook his head. 'No, sir, the gentleman seemed most put out by the note. Quite angry, he seemed, said there was no reply.'

'Did he say anything at all as he read the message?' Kitty asked. 'Please think, it could be very important.'

'He muttered something, miss, under his breath, like. I don't know if it's important or not, though. He said something about a pound of flesh.' The boy looked perplexed.

Kitty exchanged a glance with Matt.

'Thank you, you've been very helpful.' Kitty smiled at the waiter and he dashed back to his work with an air of relief.

'We had better stay alert. It appears that something is happening,' Matt said.

Kitty looked at Matt. 'I agree.'

CHAPTER TWENTY-FIVE

The masked ball was due to open at eight in the evening and to continue until one in the morning the next day. The house band was to play for the first two hours, followed by Vivien Delaware's performance for an hour. Piano music would play during the supper for the ticket holders, followed by the unmasking at midnight, with Miss Delaware singing once more for the grand finale of the evening's entertainment.

Matt had arranged to meet Kitty in her grandmother's suite so they would go down to the ball together. Since the burglary, she had been reluctant to return to her own room until all the new locks and security devices had been put in place, which had been delayed by the carpenter and his slow pace of work.

The muffled sound of voices from within the room reached him as he raised his hand to knock on the door. His pulse quickened. Surely her father had not managed to gain admission?

'Come in,' Kitty called.

To his relief, he discovered she was seated at the bureau, holding the telephone receiver in her hand, her mask beside her. 'Yes, Grams, it's Matt. We're about to go downstairs to the ballroom now. Did you wish to speak to him?'

Matt raised an eyebrow in enquiry.

'Yes, of course. Matt, Grams would like to speak to you.'

He accepted the receiver from her as she stood and walked away to stand in the window that overlooked the river.

'Mrs Treadwell, good evening.' He watched Kitty as she carefully tidied the roses her father had sent her. She looked so slender and delicate as she worked.

'Matthew, Livvy and I hope to be at the hotel by late afternoon the day after tomorrow. Kitty assures me that this Inspector Greville is providing protection for her within the hotel. Is this correct?' Her tone was anxious.

'Yes, two men will be stationed within the ballroom this evening. Don't worry, the guests won't know who they are.'

'She said that scoundrel, Edgar Underhay, has had the temerity to try to contact her.'

'Indeed, Mrs Treadwell.' He glanced at Kitty. She had her back to him as she stared out at the night, her delicate gold dress shimmering and sparkling in the light of the side table lamps.

'Captain Bryant, Matthew, I beg you to take care of her. She can sometimes be too much like her mother; soft-hearted, impulsive and headstrong. That man is a manipulator and a rogue. I lost her poor mother, please, don't let anything happen to Kitty.' Her voice quavered on the line.

'I will do my best, Mrs Treadwell.' Her plea made him uncomfortable. Hadn't he already pledged those same words to another parent? His own darling Edith's widowed father had made the same request of him on their wedding day. 'Promise me that you'll take good care of my girl.' His father-in-law's words still haunted him even though he knew there was nothing he could have done to prevent what had happened to Edith and Betty in those grim, dark days of the war.

'Kitty told me about the tunnels. I always wondered and worried for years that Elowed might have been taken into one of them.' The old woman's voice cracked. 'It's the not knowing that is the hardest. Thinking I see her on the street, passing by in an omnibus, walking in the park.'

'I understand.' Sometimes he thought he saw Edith. So many others had also lost loved ones, sons, brothers, nephews, during the war. *Missing; believed killed.* No body to bury, no grave to mourn at, and the faint, desperate hope that somehow, somewhere, they might have survived, perhaps concussed or injured, with no memory to guide them home.

'That Colin Wakes was always a bad lot. His father was the same; in and out of prison. Poor Cora was too weak with Colin, always giving him money, making excuses, poor soul.'

'You think he may be involved in the murders?' Matt asked.

'He would sell his own granny for a shilling, so I don't doubt he is up to no good, but murder? Well, murder is another matter, Captain Bryant.'

Mrs Treadwell's warnings rang in his ears as he walked down the broad oak staircase to the lobby with Kitty, her hand on his arm. They had carefully donned their masks before leaving the suite. His mask was plain black velvet, covering his eye area and the bridge of his nose. Kitty's mask was gold and glittery to match her dress.

The sound of the band greeted them as they descended the last few steps. Everywhere was a hive of activity, with guests arriving for the evening's entertainment. Ladies in fur stoles chattered and kissed cheeks as they greeted each other, while the men shook hands and looked pleased with themselves. The night porter stood by the front door, and along the corridor, next to the cloakroom, was Mickey, resplendent in an ancient evening suit.

Moving into the ballroom, they threaded their way past masked gentlemen in evening attire accompanying mysterious ladies in glamorous gowns as colourful as the peacock feathers in the room decorations. The ladies' masks were the more fanciful, adorned with sequins and feathers, like Kitty's.

Matt swiftly identified Inspector Greville's men despite their disguises. There was something about them that immediately said 'police' to his trained military gaze. Walter Cribbs was also present, accompanied by a photographer as he worked his way around the tables chatting to the great and worthy of Dartmouth. He looked more like a black beetle than ever, with his mask covering his eyes under his glasses.

He had to admit that Kitty's hard work had paid off, the additional greenery, painted backdrops and altered layout adding to the ambience of the room. The exotic peacock feather theme in green, gold and blue shimmered in the electric light of the glorious glass chandeliers. The dance floor was already full of people moving to the music provided by the house band.

The bright, young things of Torbay were out in force, their dresses daringly shorter than the more conservative length that Kitty favoured. The young men accompanying them had pomaded hair and wore evening suits in the latest wide-lapelled style. Cocktails and champagne appeared to be flowing.

Kitty had darted off to admonish a young waitress who appeared to be wearing her uniform in an improper manner, so Matt wandered between the tables listening in to snatches of conversation and looking for anyone who might be Colin Wakes or Edgar Underhay.

A faint fug of cigarette and cigar smoke hung in the air and the staff had opened the diamond leaded windows to allow the night air in to circulate around the room. Matt collected a glass of champagne from the bar and continued to monitor the room. He kept a careful watch on Kitty as she too worked her way around, greeting guests. He'd thought the gold colour of her gown and her distinctive short blonde hair would be easy to spot in the crowd but there were so many people it proved harder than he had thought, which worried him more than he cared to admit.

*

Kitty checked the tiny gold evening watch her grandmother had given her for her twenty-first birthday. It was almost time for

Vivien Delaware's first set of the evening. Everything appeared to be going well. The room was full, and her guests looked as if they were enjoying themselves. It seemed as if the night would be a success but she was aware she couldn't congratulate herself entirely until it was over.

She began to make her way towards the stage, ready to give the announcement. The side of the conversation Matt had held with her grandmother continued to play on her mind. Perhaps she was foolish for not handing the ruby to Inspector Greville and telling him of the communication with her father. All her life though, she had been curious about her father, where he was and why he hadn't ever come forward. Until she had seen and spoken to him, she knew she couldn't bring herself to hand over the ruby.

The letter he had sent had been full of tender concern for her well-being. It hadn't held the tone of someone who wished her harm. She pressed through the throng on the dance floor, narrowly avoiding having a glass of champagne spilled on her gown by some enthusiastic revellers.

Bobby was at the side of the stage, partly concealed by one of the giant pots of fronded palms. She barely had time to notice him mopping his brow with one of his coloured silk handkerchiefs whilst sipping from a silver-coloured hip flask, before the band stopped playing and she was on stage.

'Ladies and gentlemen, for the final night of her sell-out run here at the Dolphin Hotel, I give you the wonderful Miss Vivien Delaware.' She stepped away from the microphone and down from the stage as Vivien made her entrance.

Clad in a fitted emerald-green, glittering sheath-like gown, in a gold and purple mask with tall peacock feathers in a band encircling her head, she was a truly exotic creature. Not for the first time, Kitty marvelled at how someone like Vivien had married someone like Bobby.

The spot where he had been standing was now empty. She looked around the room for him, but the dance floor had refilled, and she wasn't tall enough to see across the crowded space to find either Bobby or Matt.

On stage, Vivien was singing, her tall, elegant figure swaying to the rhythms created by the house band and her own jazz musicians. Kitty's feet had started to ache from all the standing and walking she'd been doing all day and she searched around for a vacant chair. Spotting an empty seat at a table tucked inconspicuously beside a pillar, she sat down gratefully and eased off her shoes beneath the cover of the white linen tablecloth. She wriggled and stretched out her stocking-clad toes and sighed with relief.

'Champagne, Miss Underhay.' A glass appeared in front of her, placed on a paper napkin.

Startled, Kitty turned to see who had delivered it but there were no waiters in sight. She lifted the glass to take a sip and realised that there was a note folded into the napkin. She glanced around to see if anyone might be watching her. Satisfied that she could see no one, she palmed the folded paper into her hand, and, using the tablecloth for cover, swiftly slipped the message into her stocking-top under her garter. She would read it later, in private, where no prying eyes could see.

She had no sooner completed the transfer and smoothed her gown back into place when the masked leering visage of Walter Cribbs loomed in front of her.

'Miss Underhay, Kitty, my dear, I've come to claim my dance.' His breath smelled of stale onions and whisky and Kitty wrinkled her nose in distaste.

'I'm sorry, Mr Cribbs, my feet hurt and I'm taking a break so I'm not dancing this evening.' *Or ever with you*, she added silently.

Even behind the mask, she noticed his expression change. His eyes glittered and his mouth took on a petulant twist. 'Then you must allow me to keep you company while you rest.' He slid onto the seat opposite hers and she suddenly regretted choosing a chair with its back to the wall as she was now effectively trapped.

'Are you enjoying the ball?' She took a sip of champagne and hoped the note that had accompanied it wasn't a warning not to drink it. Although, if Walter didn't go away soon, she would require something stronger to drink.

'I'm enjoying it all the more now I've finished my work and I'm with you, my darling,' Walter leered and made a grab for her hand.

Fortunately, she moved more swiftly than Walter and managed to whisk her hand from the tabletop before his sweaty fingers could entrap her.

'Mr Cribbs, I thought I had made my feelings perfectly clear to you at Christmas.' Her tone was glacial as she tried to peer around him, hoping Matt would spot her. Not that she needed his aid with Walter, but she had no energy or desire for a prolonged conversation with him.

'Ah, but my circumstances have changed since then, my love. I can understand your previous reluctance to make a match which you may have considered beneath you in financial terms, but I can assure you that my fortunes have improved materially for the better. As my wife you would have no fears of being disadvantaged in society.'

Kitty stared at him, her mouth falling open at his extraordinary speech. 'Mr Cribbs, I can assure you that any material assets you might or might not have will never and have never entered my mind.' Surely the man was not proposing marriage to her?

'Then you can have no objection to my courtship, Kitty dearest.' Walter smirked.

Kitty's mouth closed with a snap. The man had lost his mind, or he had consumed far too much whisky. 'Mr Cribbs, I apologise for my bluntness, but I have no desire to be courted by you. Ever. Under any circumstances.' She felt for her shoes with her toes to try to slip them back on again to make her getaway. The man was a lunatic.

'My dearest Kitty, you can't be serious. And please, you can call me Walter. People will think it strange for an engaged couple to be on such formal terms.' He made another dive for her and captured her fingers in his moist hand.

'Please release me immediately, Mr Cribbs. I have no intention of becoming engaged to you. I can only ascribe your behaviour at present to an overindulgence in alcohol. I have never knowingly given you any cause to believe I had any romantic interest in you.' Her shoes now back on her feet, she attempted to stand and extricate her hand from his.

'Do sit down, my dear.' Walter's voice took on a new, more menacing tone and he tugged her back down onto her seat. 'I'm sure you would not wish to draw attention.'

A jolt of fear ran through Kitty. 'Please release me, Mr Cribbs, I have work to do and no more time to spend on this nonsense.'

In response, his fingers tightened on hers, causing her to flinch. 'You need have no fear that I will hold your questionable parentage against you when we are married. I would never reproach you on your father's lack of patriotism or criminal record.'

'Mr Cribbs, for the last time, release me and desist from this absurd conversation.'

'After all, my dear, you wouldn't wish your father to come to any harm, would you?' Walter leaned closer towards her and she instinctively shrank away.

'Why would my father come to any harm?' She continued to try to free herself from his grasp as the icicle of fear grew larger at the implied threat in Walter's demeanour.

He drummed the tabletop with the fingers of his free hand. 'My sources tell me that Inspector Greville's men are not the only people keen to speak to your father concerning a certain missing ruby and Hubert Farjeon and Cora Wakes's deaths.' He tightened his grip still further on her fingers, forcing a tiny squeak of pain from her lips.

'Mr Cribbs, you are hurting me.'

He relaxed his grasp just enough to stop the pain. 'I'm so very sorry, my love. But I just want you to understand. It would be terrible if those other people searching for your father should find him before Inspector Greville and his men.'

Kitty swallowed. 'Do you know where my father is?' she asked.

Walter smiled like a plump, unpleasant cat toying with a mouse. 'Oh yes, I think I know.'

'Then I suggest you inform Inspector Greville.' She made another attempt to extricate her hand.

'Not so fast, my love. There is the small matter of the ruby. After all, it is not just your father that shouldn't fall into the wrong hands.'

She gave another impatient tug, and to her satisfaction, managed to free herself. 'I know nothing of a ruby, Mr Cribbs, and if you do know where my father is then you must go to the police. Now, I must return to my guests. Please do not ever trouble me again with your unwanted affections.' She quickly stood and slipped past him before he could prevent her from leaving. Her legs trembled and she forced herself to keep moving, anxious to find Matt and update him.

CHAPTER TWENTY-SIX

She had not gone many steps when she walked directly into Matt.

'Kitty, I've been looking for you.' He took hold of the tops of her arms to halt her progress.

'Then where were you when that beastly Walter Cribbs was proposing marriage to me?' she demanded, her voice breaking as a tear escaped onto her cheek.

'What?' Matt stared at her; concern mixed with bewilderment in his eyes.

'Mr Cribbs renewed his very unwelcome romantic advances, then, when I rebuffed him, he tried to coerce me by threatening my father's safety. He said he knew where my father was and implied he would reveal his whereabouts to others who were searching for him, and the ruby.' Kitty dashed the tear from her cheek with the back of her hand.

'Cribbs knows where your father is hiding? Are you all right?' Matt was already looking around the room for the reporter.

'I'm fine, I think. He could have been bluffing. He didn't give me any kind of proof that he was telling the truth.' Her fear was subsiding now, replaced with increasing fury that Walter Cribbs had dared to lay his hands on her and threaten her in such a way.

'What else did he say?' Matt asked.

'He assumed my reason for declining his proposal was due to his lack of means, but he claimed he was soon to be wealthy.' Kitty scowled. 'The nerve of the man is incredible. I swear he was drunk.'

'He has expectations of money soon. I wonder where or who from.'

Kitty glanced at Vivien, still performing on the stage. 'Bobby?'

'Perhaps Hubert Farjeon is not the only person trying a spot of blackmail.'

Kitty sniffed and shuddered. 'Vivien is finishing her first set. I must make sure that the staff are ready to serve supper. Could you find Inspector Greville and let him know what Mr Cribbs has said, please?'

*

Matt went in search of Inspector Greville's men. He intended to make sure that Walter Cribbs was questioned as soon as possible about his claim to know where Edgar Underhay might be hiding. He found one of the constables near the entrance to the supper room and passed the message on. There was no sign of Walter in the ballroom and Matt guessed he must have left once Kitty had rebuffed his advances.

The pianist was now on stage for the supper break, so Matt decided to take a stroll out through the lobby to the embankment and check that there was nothing untoward outside the hotel.

Mickey nodded to him as he passed the cloakroom. 'Evening, Captain Bryant.'

'How's it going, Mickey? Any concerns?'

Mickey glanced around at the busy corridor and lowered his voice. 'I dunno if you would say a concern, like, but that man who's here with the singer came past in a hurry a bit ago. Looked proper mad, he did, and he hasn't come back.'

'Thanks, Mickey.' Matt clapped the older man on his shoulder and continued to walk towards the lobby.

The entrance was quieter now that most of the guests were taking supper before the unmasking and Vivien's finale. The night porter was still keeping watch near the desk and he nodded to Matt.

'Have you seen Bobby, Miss Delaware's agent, this evening?' Matt wondered if Bobby might have re-entered the hotel and headed upstairs to his and Vivien's suite.

'No, sir, he went out about an hour ago and hasn't returned.'

'Keep a look out for him, would you?' Matt couldn't say why but he had an uneasy feeling building in his stomach. Bobby always stayed near the stage during Vivien's performances. 'Any sign of Walter Cribbs, the reporter chap from the *Herald*?'

'Yes, sir, he left too, a minute or so ago, not much after the other one.'

Cool air met him as Matt stepped outside the hotel and onto the embankment. A few couples had also come outside, and he heard a girl giggling tipsily at something her companion had said. He decided to stroll towards the boat float.

The further away from the Dolphin he went, the quieter the streets grew. He could hear the river lapping against the banks and smell the faint salt tang of the sea in the estuary. When he reached the marina, he decided to turn back, he was worried about Kitty. There was no sign of Walter Cribbs or Bobby.

On his route back he could see the hotel and the silhouette of the castle on the hill beyond the customs house. Light spilled from the windows of the Dolphin, illuminating the people entering and leaving. As he drew nearer to the hotel, he passed a small, dark entryway.

A fragment of coloured cloth caught his attention and he pulled out his cigarette lighter to see further into the shadows. As he did so, he heard a low moan.

'Bobby!' He leaned into the entry and saw Bobby sprawled, half sitting, half lying in the gutter. His jacket was ripped, his mask missing, and an ugly swelling had begun to form around his right eye.

'Here, let me help you.' He dropped his lighter back into his pocket and with some pulling and shoving, managed to get Bobby into a position where he could help him to stagger back to the hotel.

Their arrival in the lobby caused something of a commotion. The night porter rushed to help him seat the unfortunate Bobby in the small back office behind the desk, away from the guests.

'Bobby, what happened?' In the brighter light of the office it was clear that Bobby had been assaulted. His head was cut and bleeding and the black eye Matt had noticed in the alley would certainly be sore in a few hours' time.

The night porter returned with a measure of brandy and one of the police constables from the ballroom. 'Out taking the air. Fella jumped me from behind,' Bobby muttered.

'Do you want me to get Vivien?' Matt asked.

Bobby's head shot up and alarm spread across his battered features. 'No, she has to finish her performance. No point upsetting her yet.' He took a sip of brandy, grimacing at the taste. 'Sure wish you had some bourbon.'

'Were you robbed, Mr Delaware?' The constable had his pocket notebook at the ready.

Bobby fumbled for the inside pocket of his jacket, wincing as he tried to move his hands. 'Wallet is gone.'

Matt noticed he still had his watch, which looked as if it was quite an expensive piece. 'Would you like us to call a doctor?' he asked as Bobby let out another groan.

'No, no quacks,' he snapped.

'Did you see your assailant?' the constable enquired.

Bobby carefully shook his head. 'Nope, told ya fella jumped me from behind. I did my best to fight him off, but he kicked me when I was on the floor. It was dark and it happened really quick.'

'Why were you on the embankment?' Matt asked. 'I know you usually stay and watch all of Vivien's performances.'

Bobby squinted at him irascibly through bloodshot eyes. 'I needed some air. It was kind of muggy in there.'

'At what time were you attacked, sir?' The constable licked the end of his pencil, ready to add to his notes.

'About half an hour, an hour ago? I don't know, think I passed out.'

In the distance Matt could hear cheering coming from the ballroom and guessed the partygoers were removing their masks. He slid his own mask off and tucked it in his jacket pocket. The constable followed suit.

'Was your wallet the only thing the assailant took?' Matt asked.

'My watch is still on and my silver hip flask is in my pocket. I had about fifty pounds in my wallet.'

Matt's eyebrows raised slightly at the sum Bobby had been carrying. 'I think Vivien has just started her final set. Would you like some help to get you to your room, to get you cleaned up before she comes offstage?'

Bobby drained the last of his brandy, pulling a face as he did so. 'No, I'll be just fine.' He struggled to his feet, swaying slightly. 'Any more questions, officer?' he asked the police constable.

'Not for now, sir. Will you be available tomorrow if the inspector wants to check anything with you?'

'Sure, I'll have to wire my bank for more money, so I won't be going anywhere till we're due to board our ship home.' He staggered to the door and a few minutes later they heard him clumping his way up the staircase.

'What do you think, constable? Any local villains likely to have set upon Mr Delaware?'

The policeman looked pleased to be asked for his opinion. 'That were a fair sum of money he had in his wallet, but that watch looked expensive and the flask would have been easy to pawn.'

'Perhaps the attacker was interrupted?' suggested Matt.

'Maybe, sir, or maybe they were satisfied with the cash once they saw how much there was.'

Vivien had changed into a crimson dress for her final hour, with a gold headband studded with red stones. Matt wondered how she would take the news of Bobby's assault and robbery. It could have been a random attack, but something about it didn't add up. Bobby had stormed out of the hotel in a bad mood, maybe to meet someone who had demanded money. Walter Cribbs had also left the building and Colin Wakes and Kitty's father were also still around. He didn't like it; he didn't like it at all.

CHAPTER TWENTY-SEVEN

Matt found Kitty sitting at a table near the bar sipping a cocktail. Her mask lay in front of her. She frowned at him. 'Where have you been?'

'It's a long story.'

She was shocked when he told her what had happened to Bobby. 'That is so strange. On the other side of town where the poorer houses are, I'm sad to say you expect more crime, but this part of town is very safe and there were so many people about tonight because of the ball.' She glanced at the stage. 'Vivien will be very upset.'

'Bobby didn't want to tell her until she'd finished the show.'

'Do you think this is to do with the ruby?' Kitty asked.

Matt helped himself to a sip of her drink, drawing an indignant glare from Kitty. 'Could be. Perhaps they wanted to search him and when it wasn't in his pockets, they took his wallet instead.'

Kitty glanced at her watch. 'Vivien is about to sing her final number.'

He took hold of her hand. 'Dance with me.' He had enjoyed their last dance together; it had been a bright moment in an otherwise scary time.

She frowned, uncertainty playing in her eyes at his unexpected request. 'All right.'

He led her to the dance floor, and he placed his arms around her as Vivien's soulful voice filled the room.

'You're a better dancer than Walter Cribbs,' Kitty teased.

'Why thank you, Miss Underhay, I'll take that as high praise.'

She laughed as he swept her around the floor. She moved well and he allowed the nightmare of the tunnels to be replaced with happier thoughts and the feel of her slender frame next to his.

The music finished and Vivien began her farewell speech. Kitty and Matt eased their way to the side of the stage, ready to intercept her afterwards. The band leader presented her with a huge bouquet on behalf of the Dolphin and the show ended.

'Vivien!' Kitty hurried up the couple of steps to the stage.

The chanteuse frowned when she saw Kitty and Matt. 'Thank you for the flowers, Miss Underhay.'

'They were my pleasure; you have a truly wonderful voice.' She paused before adding in a softer tone, 'Vivien, I have some bad news for you.'

The older woman paled and swayed on her high heels. 'What is it?'

'I'm so sorry but Bobby has been attacked tonight outside the hotel, on the embankment. He's all right but rather battered. The assailant took his wallet.'

'Where is he?' Vivien asked, alarm showing in her dark brown eyes.

'He insisted on returning to your suite, he refused a doctor,' Matt said.

Vivien clutched her flowers to her. 'I must go to him. That fool man will get himself killed one of these times.'

'This has happened before?' Matt asked.

Vivien's mouth twisted in a bitter line. 'He's a white man married to a black woman; we are no strangers to violence.' Her voice was harsh.

'Would you like us to come with you?' Kitty asked.

Vivien was already walking off the stage. 'No, thank you. I can take care of Bobby.'

*

It was after three a.m. when Kitty was seated with Matt in her grandmother's suite, her hands around a large cup of warm sweet milk laced with whisky.

'What a night.' Matt had taken off his tie and undone the collar of his shirt. Kitty was too tired to fight her eyes, which kept stubbornly straying to the dip at the base of his neck.

She kicked off her shoes for the last time and stretched out her toes. 'My feet have been killing me for at least the last six hours.' As she moved, the note she'd tucked into her stocking top hours earlier crackled against her skin. With all the other events of the night she'd forgotten about it.

Exhaustion tugged at every part of her and she couldn't face looking at the contents of the note right now and discussing it with Matt. If it was from her father, she wanted to read it by herself and see what he had to say before sharing it with anyone else.

Matt rose and walked towards the door. 'I'll say good night, you look all in. Thank you for the dance.' He smiled at her and her heart gave an unexpected flutter.

'Good night, see you tomorrow.'

Once he'd gone, she locked the door and pulled the table in front of it to ensure it was secure. She carried the remainder of her drink into the bedroom and undressed. Once she was settled in bed, propped up against a pile of pillows, she sipped the rest of her drink and opened the note.

> *My dearest Kitty,*
>
> *I had hoped to be able to spend some time with you this evening, but circumstances are against me. I fear that I have to leave this area soon for both my safety and yours. I would dearly love to see you for just a few minutes before I go. It would have been nice if you had found the ruby that Elowed had been guarding for me, but if it's not to*

be then that is fate. There are others looking for it who are quite dangerous, and I cannot risk any harm coming to you, my dear child. I have done much in my life to be ashamed of and little to be proud of; you are the one thing I am most proud of, dear girl. I will be at St Saviours church tomorrow night at 9.30 p.m. after the bell ringers finish their practice. I understand the church will be open for a short while. If you could find it in your heart to meet me there to say goodbye, you would make an old man very happy. If not, then I will understand. I wish you health, wealth and happiness, my dear, for all of your life.

Your father, Edgar Underhay. xx

Tears ran freely down Kitty's cheeks as she read her father's note and she was glad she hadn't shared it with Matt. It was deeply personal, and his sentiments had greatly affected her. She was not so naïve as to believe that he might not have an ulterior motive for wanting to see her and that he might still hope she'd bring the ruby.

She read the note once more before folding it carefully and slipping it inside the Bible she always kept in the drawer next to her bed. She turned out the light and snuggled down to sleep, unable to keep her eyes open any longer. She would decide what to do and whether to tell Matt in the morning.

Kitty rose late, her thoughts still no clearer on what she should do. She desperately wanted to see her father, if only to hear his side of events. She longed to know more about his marriage to her mother and if he could shed any light on what might have happened all those years ago.

If what he said in his note was true and he really was about to leave, then this would be her one and only chance to speak to him. She might never get to see or hear from him again. If she told Matt, she knew he would try and dissuade her from going, or worse still, tell Inspector Greville.

Kitty moved the table back into its rightful place and called reception to request that her breakfast be brought to her room. There was also the question of what to do with the ruby. To her mind, it would be much simpler if her father took it and it was gone from her possession. Surely with both the gem and her father gone, normality would return.

The maid knocked the door and entered with her tray. Kitty settled herself at the small table her grandmother used for dining and tucked into her scrambled eggs and bacon. She never had been good at thinking on an empty stomach.

By the time she had drained her second cup of tea she had started to feel much better. The more she thought about the murders, the less likely it seemed that her father could be responsible. He didn't know Hubert Farjeon and could hardly have been blackmailed by him. It appeared far more likely that Colin Wakes was the most obvious suspect in all cases, given his record and what they knew so far. It was entirely possible that he had been responsible for assaulting Bobby, especially if he was desperate for money. He wouldn't have taken the flask or Bobby's watch in case he was recognised if he tried to pawn it.

Meeting her father would be a big risk and she would have to find a way of leaving the hotel without Matt discovering she had gone out. Was it foolhardy? Yes, but some things in life were worth taking risks for and she wasn't stupid.

By mid-afternoon a dull grey drizzle had set in and Kitty's nerves were starting to fray. Vivien had dined alone in the dining room at lunch time, having ordered a tray for Bobby who seemed to be keeping a low profile.

'I need to attend the bank,' she said to Matt, who had joined her for lunch. She wanted to get out of the hotel to clear her head.

'Would you like me to accompany you?' Matt asked. She knew he would find a way to insist on going with her even if she said she'd rather go alone. In truth, she didn't mind, she would feel safer if he were there. It would also mean he would be less likely to think she would go out alone that evening.

It was still raining, a soft, light rain, when they left the hotel. Kitty held her sturdy black umbrella over both their heads. 'I really don't wish to ruin another hat. I fear this one has never properly recovered its shape after my last outing in the wet.'

Their route took them past the entry where Matt had found Bobby a few hours earlier. Kitty couldn't resist taking a peep as they walked past. What had he been up to? He must have gone outside to meet someone.

The town was quiet as they walked past the boat float towards the Butterwalk. The dreary day had obviously deterred the day trippers and holidaymakers. Instead, mostly town folk were busy about their daily affairs. Kitty smiled and said hello to a few people she knew in passing.

Her business at the bank did not take long and once concluded, she rejoined Matt outside the florist's, ready to walk back to the hotel. Matt discovered he had a small errand that he needed to run at the post office as he had been carrying a letter around with him for the past few days which he needed to send to his mother, so they varied their route for the return journey.

'We can cut through here,' Kitty said, pointing out a narrow entryway which connected the street they were on with one which ran almost parallel to it. 'It's a little quicker and might shelter us from this beastly rain.'

The alley did give some shelter from the drizzle and as they emerged onto the street the other side, Kitty gasped and clutched Matt's arm. 'Matt, over there, I'm sure, yes, it's Colin Wakes.'

She recognised Colin from when he used to call for Cora after she'd finished her shifts at the hotel. Now he looked in bad shape. His coat was dirty, and he was unshaven.

'Stay here,' Matt ordered, and set off towards Colin.

Colin locked his gaze with Kitty and realised he'd been sighted. He immediately began to run, back towards the more run-down area on the far side of town.

'Hi, you, stop!' Matt raced after him.

Kitty ignored Matt's instruction and followed them as quickly as her heels and skirt would allow. Her breath came in harsh gasps as she rounded the corner in time to see Matt grab hold of Colin's jacket.

Colin immediately tried to wriggle free and failing, aimed a punch at Matt. Matt dodged out of his way, but his balance shifted on the wet, slippery cobbles. Colin spied his chance and gave Matt a hard shove, knocking him into the side of the building against a wooden post.

Matt released his quarry as he fell, and Kitty hurried over. Colin seized his chance to run off, disappearing into the maze of alleys that made up that part of the town.

'Matt, are you all right?' Kitty stooped to see Matt wincing and clutching his shoulder.

'I had him, damn it. This wretched shoulder.' He managed to get to his feet.

'Are you hurt?' Anxiety gripped her as Matt continued to clutch his arm, pain etched into his face.

'I'll be okay, I've injured this arm before.'

'Come on, let's get back to the hotel. I'll call the doctor and we can tell Inspector Greville that Colin has been sighted.' Kitty bit her lip. Matt's face had paled, and she could see he was struggling with every step. She was relieved when the half-timbered façade of the Dolphin finally hove into sight and Matt was able to take a seat in the small office behind the front desk.

CHAPTER TWENTY-EIGHT

Kitty called the doctor and Inspector Greville. The inspector arrived first, the doctor being delayed at a house call to a woman having twins. Matt had recovered a little of his composure at least, with the aid of some brandy, when the inspector entered the office.

'I came as soon as I received your message. My men are out searching house-to-house in the town. Tell me what happened?'

Matt gave the policeman an outline of the events leading up to Colin making his escape. 'I swear he was the man in the tunnel.'

'And now you are injured?' The inspector looked concerned at Matt's obvious discomfort as he tried to support his injured arm and shoulder.

'Just rotten bally luck. I took a bullet on this side in the war and I think I hit the corner of the building right on the injured spot. My pride is smarting as much as anything else.' Matt attempted to play down his pain.

'You have to catch this man, Inspector,' Kitty said. 'He's obviously our murderer.'

The inspector stroked his moustache. 'We are doing our best, Miss Underhay. I agree he is clearly very dangerous.'

There was a knock on the door to the office and Doctor Carter was shown into the small space. 'Sorry I was delayed, two healthy baby boys safely delivered.' He beamed at the group from under the brim of his hat. Kitty thought he looked like an innocent middle-aged baby cherub, with his smooth round face and bright blue eyes twinkling behind his little round spectacles. 'Now then, let the dog see the rabbit.' He placed his bag down on the table and peered at Matt's arm.

'I need to get back to the station. If there are any developments, I'll let you know.' The inspector addressed the last part of his remark to Matt who was being assisted to remove his jacket, somewhat gingerly, by Doctor Carter.

Kitty was about to make her excuses to slip out so the doctor could remove Matt's shirt to examine him privately when Doctor Carter commandeered her into the role of nurse.

She felt somewhat awkward standing by, handing the doctor rolls of bandage, tape and scissors as he cut off Matt's vest and began to strap his chest and shoulder. She took a sneak peek and saw the white raised ridges of scar tissue all around Matt's shoulder blade. He had clearly been much more badly wounded during the war than she had realised.

Matt had his eyes closed tight while Doctor Carter did his work. A few times she heard his breath escape through his teeth in a hiss when the good doctor was a little firm with the strapping. Eventually he was done, and the doctor assisted him with his shirt over his good arm, before securing the heavily strapped injured arm in a sling.

'Here.' Doctor Carter produced a small brown bottle containing a few pills from his bag. 'Take a couple of these now and two more tonight and rest that arm. By tomorrow it should start to ease a little, but it will probably take a good week before you can remove the strapping.'

Matt didn't look very happy with the doctor's prognosis as Kitty thanked him and showed him out of the office into the lobby.

'You heard the doctor. You'd better go to your room and rest. Would you like me to have a tray sent up to you?' Kitty bustled around collecting his things.

'This is ridiculous. I can't believe Colin managed to get away.' Matt winced as he stood ready to leave.

'The cobbles were very slippery, and he got you off balance,' Kitty soothed as she helped him up the stairs. She escorted Matt to his room and insisted he rest. She organised a tray of tea and for the daily papers to be sent up so that he might amuse himself, listening to the radio and catching up with the news whilst he rested.

She knew Matt wasn't happy at being out of action. In a way it would make it easier for her to leave the hotel unseen later on that evening after work. She assuaged her feelings of guilt at not sharing her father's letter with Matt by justifying to herself that he needed to rest.

Alone in her grandmother's suite, she secured the door and made her preparations. Taking the ruby from the secret safe in the window seat, she wrapped it well inside an old handkerchief. Deciding against a handbag, she picked out an old, dark blue coat and made a small slit in the lining just large enough for the ruby to fit inside. It nestled between the rough woollen coat fabric and the satin lining in a small pocket. She would be able to retrieve it and hand it to her father, but if anyone were to hunt in her pockets, they would find nothing except a clean handkerchief and some small change.

Kitty hunted through her shoes and found an older pair with a slightly lower heel in case she needed to make a quick getaway. She selected the hat she'd been wearing earlier and her sturdy umbrella as both protection from the rain and any possible assailant. Much as she hated the thought, one had to be practical.

For her final precautions, she sat at her grandmother's bureau and wrote a couple of notes, sealing them into envelopes and writing times and names on the front. One was to Matt and one was to Inspector Greville.

When the time approached for her to meet her father, Kitty dressed carefully in her chosen outfit and went to the front desk to hand over her notes. 'Please ensure these notes are delivered at exactly the times written on the front of the envelopes. No earlier and no later.' Her voice was stern as she instructed Alice, who was looking after the lobby.

'Yes, Miss Underhay.' The young girl's eyes were round at the unexpected and unusual instruction.

Kitty glanced quickly around the lobby to ensure both the night porter and Mickey, the maintenance man, were temporarily absent, and slipped out of the front door. She was glad of the protection of her umbrella as she made her way back through the town, past the boat float and to the foot of the small hill leading to St Saviours. The sound of the bells had been pealing all around her as she walked where the ringers were practicing their rounds.

Now though, the sound of the bells had ceased, and she waited in the shadows of the stone wall of the church as the ringers came out, calling good night to each other as they left. She expected the verger would be along to lock up soon so she wouldn't have much time with her father.

When she was satisfied that the last of the bell ringers had gone, Kitty hurried up the slope and into the entrance of the church. St Saviours was one of the oldest buildings in Dartmouth. It dated back to the early middle-ages. The great oak-planked door was at least seven hundred years old; the ornate brass decorative work adorning it had been added a few centuries later, along with the carvings of animals. She had always thought it was beautiful, but now her emotions were too fraught to admire it as she usually did. The porch light was on but inside, the church was dark with only a few candles burning on a black wrought-iron sconce at one side. The air inside the church was damp and cool, smelling of flowers and lavender and beeswax polish.

The faint light from the candles cast shadows across the flagstone floor and the painted and carved wooden panels and pillars of the church. She held her breath when she noticed the figure of a man, his head bowed as if in prayer, sitting in the shadows at the far end of the back pew.

'Father?' Even as a whisper, her voice seemed to magnify and echo around the empty space.

The man raised his head and Kitty strained to see his face in the shadow cast by the brim of his hat. 'My darling girl, you came.' His voice was softer than she remembered from their last meeting.

Her knees trembled as she slid onto the wooden pew next to him. She recognised him immediately as the man who had called himself Mr Kelly when he'd met her in the town and at the launch of Miss Delaware's engagement at the Dolphin.

'We don't have long, my dear. The verger will be by soon.' Her father took her hand in his. 'My darling, I'm so sorry to have brought all this trouble upon you. I know that I owe you an explanation. I was shocked when you told me about your mother. I had no idea that something had happened.' He sighed. 'When the war came, I had to decide whether to stay and fight or return to America. Your grandmother has no doubt told you her opinion of my choice and I cannot defend it. I returned to America as I had prospects of money and business there and no desire to risk my life on the front line. I fully intended to send for you and Elowed as soon as I had sorted out some problems and obtained a house for us. The war was supposed to be over by Christmas, but time went on and it wasn't possible for me to return.'

'So, what happened? There was nothing in my mother's things. No letters, no photographs, no trace of you. All I had was a copy of my mother's marriage certificate and my birth certificate.' Kitty's voice shook. The whole of her body trembled as she was finally able to ask the questions she'd always wanted to ask.

'The war didn't end by Christmas. My business affairs became more complicated. In truth, Kitty, I was in a lot of trouble with some people who it wasn't wise to cross.'

'Was that when you took the ruby?' She saw the corners of his mouth lift in a small humourless twist.

'No, your mother already had the ruby with her when she came back to London before I returned to America. I had been holding it as collateral for a gentleman, in settlement of gaming debts. He unfortunately met with an accident with several bullets and I felt it prudent to lie low and to keep you and your mother out of danger.'

'You didn't know where she had hidden it?' Kitty asked.

He shook his head. 'She assured me it was safe. She wanted nothing to do with it but was afraid for my safety, and for you. We both thought it might give us some kind of financial security for the future. It was an uncertain time.'

Kitty thought about his answers. 'Why didn't you write?'

'I wrote a few times, then I didn't get any replies. I feared your mother had decided that being married to me was no longer what she wanted. I was moving around America and Canada. There was reports of bombings on London and other parts of England.'

'Vivien said you went to prison at one point,' Kitty said.

He sighed once more. 'Yes, I did for a short time. I was in the wrong place at the wrong time in the wrong company. That must have been when your mother disappeared. I used to get some news from England from my sister, your aunt Hortense, but she and I are not on good terms. She disapproves of me.'

'I have an aunt?' This was news to Kitty; she had always thought her grandmother and her aunt Livvy were her only family. Her mother and grandmother had never mentioned anyone else.

'Yes, my dear. Your aunt is Lady Medford, she has a daughter, Lucy, a year or two younger than you. They have an estate near Exeter. My sister has, sad to say, virtually disowned me. Her husband, Lord Medford, threatened to set the hounds on me the last time I called.' He gave a small chortle at her dumbfounded expression. 'It is a lot to take in, I know, my dear.'

'Do they know about me?' Kitty asked.

'They do now. I sent a telegram to my sister today. I knew she would probably burn a letter, but she would never ignore a telegram.'

'What do you plan to do now?' Kitty asked, her mind still reeling with the news that she had an aunt and a cousin only a few miles away in the same county.

'I have plans to leave the country for a time. I have some friends to assist me and I shall return to America. I would like to stay in touch with you, if you would allow me. And I would very much like to try and find out what happened to Elowed. You are very like her, you know.' He touched her cheek tenderly with a finger.

'I would like that,' Kitty breathed, tears starting to well up in her eyes unbidden.

Conscious that their time was almost up, they rose, ready to leave the church.

'Father, before we say goodbye. I have something for your journey.' Kitty paused, ready to feel for the ruby hidden in the lining of her coat.

The sound of footsteps on the floor of the porch sent them both darting into the shadows next to the ornately carved oak staircase that led to the upper balcony and bell tower.

'You may as well both come out. The game is up.' Walter Cribbs's reedy voice piped around the church as the outer door slammed shut and the electric lights came on overhead.

CHAPTER TWENTY-NINE

Kitty blinked in the sudden brightness of the electric light. Beside her, Edgar gave her hand a quick comforting squeeze.

'Walter?' She could see Walter standing just inside the porch entrance with another figure just behind him. To her horror, on the floor, inside the locked wooden door of the church lay the prone figure of the verger.

'Walter now, am I, Kitty my love?' he mocked her as he moved nearer. Kitty shrank back, closer to her father. 'If I'd realised a little scare might enhance your affections then I would have tried something earlier, rather than Colin's feeble attempt to scare you with a little traffic accident.'

'What do you want?' Edgar asked.

Walter tutted. 'Why, the ruby of course. You don't think I've gone through all of this for nothing, do you?'

'Gone through all what?' Kitty asked. She dreaded the answer to her question, even as all the pieces of the puzzle began to tumble into place.

'My dearest Kitty, didn't I tell you my prospects were on the up? Ever since Colin here told me about the ruby, I've been making plans.' As he spoke, Colin Wakes moved into the light. She felt her father stiffen. 'You! You double-crossing blackguard!'

'What have you done to the verger?' Kitty hoped and prayed the man was merely unconscious and that nothing worse had befallen him.

Colin stirred the man's body with his foot. 'He's just having a little nap.'

The verger emitted a low groan and Kitty's knees sagged a little with relief.

'You know we don't have the ruby, don't you?' She turned her attention back to Walter.

His eyes gleamed behind his glasses and Kitty realised she was looking into the gaze of a mad man. 'I think you know where that stone is, my darling fiancée.'

'I am not your fiancée. I never will be. If you were the last man in Dartmouth, I would not marry you.'

At her words, Walter lunged forward as if to grab her, but her father placed himself between Kitty and Walter. 'Keep your hands away from my daughter.'

'Get him, Colin!' Walter ordered and Kitty watched, horrified, as Colin darted forward and began to grapple with her father as Walter looked on. Colin, being younger and fitter than Edgar, despite his rough living over the last week, soon had the upper hand and her father dropped to his knees.

Incensed, Kitty grasped her umbrella firmly in her fist and almost without thinking, brought it down hard on the back of Colin's head. There was a loud crack as the umbrella broke in two with the force of her blow.

Colin paused mid-punch and Kitty's heart leapt into her mouth when she thought she had not hit him hard enough to make him desist. He turned a surprised face towards her before crashing to the floor. She let out a little scream as he fell across her feet.

Her father managed to stagger to his feet, a cut near his eye streaming blood as he went towards the door of the church, only to see that the large iron key was gone from the lock.

'Now that was very foolish.' Walter tutted.

Kitty swung her attention back towards him and with a cold wave of realisation, saw that not only did Walter have the key in one hand, in his other he held a gun. He waved the key at them before dropping it back into his coat pocket.

'I do hope you haven't hurt Colin too much; he has proved most useful so far.' He gave his unconscious colleague a kick.

'How useful? Did he murder his mother and kill Hubert Farjeon and Mr Blaas?' Kitty's voice wobbled.

Walter waved the gun at her father, indicating he should rejoin Kitty. 'Cora knew too much, she wanted Colin to stop. She had to go once her usefulness at providing information and creating diversions was at an end. I cannot allow Colin the credit of killing her however, he was foolishly attached to the old woman. It was far better that I dealt with the matter and convinced him that you, my dear Mr Underhay, had done the deed. Mr Blaas was surplus to requirements.' Walter smirked as if pleased with himself, and bile rose in Kitty's throat.

'And Mrs Craven? Who attacked her?'

Walter sighed. 'I had to search her house after Colin's mother informed us that there was a chance that the ruby might be there. I sent your dear grandmother notes urging her to hand over the stone. Her friend's injuries were her fault really; she should have done as I asked. It would have been better if Mrs Craven hadn't survived. Witnesses can be such a bore.' His eyes gleamed again, and Kitty suddenly realised that he was counting herself and her father as witnesses, and now that he was confessing, he had no intention of leaving them alive. She couldn't believe he'd been the hand behind the anonymous letters.

'And Hubert Farjeon?' Her father placed his arm around her waist, and she drew strength from his presence.

The maniacal smile on Walter's face grew larger. 'Very satisfying. So much blood from such a small, withered-up old man. He had the temerity to blackmail me. Me! As if I would allow that to happen. He had seen me from his booth, I let him believe I was going to pay up and cut him in on a share of the money from the ruby. He was so unsuspecting when he opened his booth. It was so easy.'

'Where do Vivien Delaware and Bobby fit into all this?' she asked. She just had to keep him talking for long enough to find a way to get the gun, or for Matt and Inspector Greville to get the notes she had left for them. She felt almost clear-headed now that she had a purpose to concentrate on.

A sneer twisted the corners of Walter's mouth. 'Bobby is an idiot. Mr Blaas gave us some very interesting information as we dispatched him – I really didn't want him encroaching on my territory, not when I had already hired Mr DeVries for that job. He informed us that Bobby was on his way, a representative of some American crook he is in the pay of, the same gang that had hired Mr Blaas. It seems Vivien saw you, Edgar, at that nightclub in London where you met with Colin and she and Bobby put two and two together. They are after the ruby too.'

Kitty's father seemed to sag next to her. 'It's all my fault,' he whispered.

But Kitty wouldn't allow herself to despair, she had to keep Walter talking. 'Why was Bobby giving you money, though? He was giving you money, wasn't he?' She wondered what the time was. The notes she'd left saying where she'd gone should be with Inspector Greville and Matt by now.

The barrel of the gun gleamed as Walter waved it around. 'Oh yes, he proved a very satisfactory source of income. It's always dangerous when you work for the wrong people, especially if those people think you might be double-crossing them. He wouldn't want any whispers getting back to his taskmasters. I reminded him of that.' Walter giggled.

'And was he double-crossing them?' She could see that Walter was revelling in what he saw as his cleverness and relishing the opportunity to boast about his crimes.

'Of course. Bobby and Vivien wanted the ruby for themselves. They caught up with him though, didn't they?'

'There is no honour amongst thieves,' Edgar said sadly.

The verger groaned and began to stir. Walter stepped over a pace and aimed a kick at the man's head. The toe of his shoe making a sickening crunch as it met the verger's skull. Kitty winced, closed her eyes and huddled into her father's arms.

'Now, enough of this. Where, my darling Kitty, is the ruby?'

Impelled into action as Walter turned his malicious attention to Kitty, Edgar moved forward slightly, partly shielding her with his body. 'My daughter has told you she doesn't have it.'

'Stay where you are!' Walter ordered and waved the gun once more. 'You must know then. Where is it, old man?'

Edgar sighed. 'My wife had the ruby in her possession for safekeeping when she came back to Dartmouth. I never knew where she'd hidden it. That's the truth.'

Walter's eyes glittered. 'I don't believe you. You came back to retrieve that stone so you must have had an idea of where it was.'

'Did my mother's disappearance have anything to do with the ruby?' Kitty asked. Walter would have been a child at the time of course, but she had clearly underestimated his skills for uncovering secrets.

Her question appeared to take Walter by surprise. 'How would I know anything about your mother vanishing when she did?'

'You work for the *Herald*, you must have looked back in the newspaper files for some clue?' Kitty persisted. She thought she had heard the faint sound of footsteps on the gravel outside the front door of the church.

The expression on his face altered and she could see he had been searching the records. 'Obviously I looked for clues. After all, the woman could have taken the ruby with her, sold it and made a new life for herself somewhere.'

'And?' She coughed as loudly as she dared, hoping that if someone was outside, they would stop and listen and not try the door to the church.

'Nothing. Nothing to indicate why she might have run off, and nothing about the stone.' He waved the gun once more at Edgar. 'Now, where is that ruby?'

Kitty swallowed, she was hoping against hope that there was someone outside the church, and they could hear something of what was happening.

'I don't have it. Elowed vanished before she could tell me where it was. My letters went unanswered and until I came back here, I didn't know what had happened to her. Your henchman there,' he nodded towards Colin, 'had kept that news from me. He led me to believe she was alive, well and still here at the Dolphin with Kitty and her grandmother. It wasn't until I arrived in Dartmouth that I realised I had been deceived.'

A smirk crept over Walter's face. 'Yes, Colin did his job well. How fortunate that you happened to run into him when you did and decided he would be useful to you.'

Kitty was certain now that she'd heard a small sound from within the church itself and her spirits lifted a little. She had to keep Walter engaged and feeling pleased with himself for just a little longer. 'You planned it all, didn't you? My father didn't meet Colin by accident. You had him meet him, prepared with some story to get him to tell you where the ruby was. But how did you know my father was in England, and make all the connections?'

'Ah, my dear sweet Kitty, you see now what a brain I have, and the great honour I did you by asking you to be my wife. Though truth to tell, that was luck as well as genius.' Walter cackled. 'I have many connections through my job as a reporter. I was asked to look at the passenger lists of a certain liner as a very famous film star was supposed to be aboard and coming unheralded into the country. A nice little scandal involving a secret baby and a married member of parliament. Well, I found my lady, and I also found your father. Your surname is not that common, and a few checks soon helped me put the pieces together and helped me to plan.'

'And how did you know about the ruby?' She had definitely heard a tiny sound, closer this time.

'I have sources in America and the obliging Colin of course.' Walter stopped talking and peered into the dark body of the church behind Kitty and her father. 'Who's there?'

No response came back. He moved to press the switch which would illuminate the main part of the church. Before he could flick the switch, her father had moved also, making a dive for Walter's arm. As they grappled together, the gun went off with a deafening roar and the light bulb above their heads shattered, sending shards of glass raining down on them as they were plunged into blackness.

CHAPTER THIRTY

Kitty froze, trying to work out their positions in the darkness. The only light showing now was the faint gleam of candles just inside the secondary door to the church, near the pew where she had sat earlier with her father.

'Papa!' She cried out. The two men were still scuffling and, in the gloom, she couldn't see who was who. She tried to edge around the protagonists but stumbled against what she realised must be Colin's prone body.

'Kitty, the door,' her father called and she heard something metallic hit the floor. Acting swiftly, she dropped to her knees and groped around for what she hoped was the key. If she could just find it and get the door open, hopefully Greville's men would be outside.

As her fingers closed over the large metal key, a heavy foot crunched down on her hand and the electric light in the main body of the church came on. She looked up, wincing from the pain in her fingers, to see Walter leering down at her.

'I don't think so, do you?' He waved the gun at her. 'Get up.' He released her hand and she scrambled to her feet. Her father was slumped against the stairwell to the upper level, the wound to his face pouring more blood, red and sticky, down the side of his face.

'Papa!' Where was the person they'd heard in the church? There had been someone in there with them. Or had she imagined it? 'What have you done to him?' She went to go to her father.

'Stay where you are. He's all right,' Walter commanded. She derived a degree of satisfaction from noticing that Walter himself had not escaped unscathed from the fight. There was a streak of blood below his nose and one eye had started to swell.

Her father groaned and moved. Relief raced through her. Walter jabbed Edgar hard in his ribs with the barrel of the revolver. 'Time to move.' He turned to Kitty. 'You too.' She picked her way past Colin and went to her father's side so he could lean on her for support. Her fingers hurt where Walter had stamped on her hand and she wondered if her little finger was broken.

'Move.' He waved the gun at them once more and forced them to walk in front of him towards a small side door.

Kitty had the bulk of her father's weight against her as they walked, and his breath sounded raspy in the cool air.

'Walter, this is madness. What do you plan to do?' She received a hard poke in her back from the nose of the gun for her question.

'My plans do not concern you any more, my dear Kitty. You refused my offer of marriage, remember? Now you must live with the consequences. Or rather, not.' He giggled as if he'd said something amusing. 'Open the door.'

That awful giggle, high and girlish, must have been what Mrs Craven had heard. Reluctantly, she stretched out her hand to unlatch the door in front of her, trying to delay the moment for as long as she dared. She knew that once they were inside whatever room or cupboard lay behind the door, their fates would probably be sealed.

Just then, she heard a great hammering and rattling at the door of the church behind them. 'Police, open up.'

Walter scowled. 'Open the door, hurry,' he barked.

The thuds at the medieval door grew louder. Her hand fumbled the key below the latch, and it dropped to the floor with a metallic ping. Walter's attention was distracted between the noise at the front door and trying to hurry Kitty along. Her father appeared barely conscious.

'Pick that up,' Walter snarled. She awkwardly leaned her father against the wall and bent to do Walter's bidding. As she did so she saw movement behind Walter in the shadows. Whoever had entered the church earlier had worked their way around to get closer to them. It had to be Matt. She scrabbled for the key, deliberately making her actions clumsy.

'Get a move on or your old man gets a bullet now,' Walter pointed the gun at her father.

'My fingers hurt from where you stamped on them,' Kitty said.

At that, a figure burst from the shadows and slammed into Walter, knocking him to the floor and sending the gun out of his hand and skidding towards the foot of the stairs.

'Kitty, the gun,' Matt commanded.

She ran forward, leaping over Colin, and grabbed the revolver. 'Stop!' She pointed the barrel at Walter and tried to keep her hands steady. Walter froze in the face of the merciless weapon, allowing Matt to kneel on top of him, pinning him to the floor.

'Good work, Kitty.' Matt grimaced and she could see the pain he was in from his injured shoulder. She kept the gun trained on Walter who wriggled futilely under Matt's weight as she collected the key to the main door from the floor. In a few seconds the door was open and Inspector Greville's men piled in from the porch.

As soon as Walter was in handcuffs and Kitty was relieved of the gun, she hurried to her father's side.

'Papa.' She assisted him to a pew as Matt limped across to join them. Walter was half led, half dragged between two burly constables to the waiting police car, swearing and screaming.

'Doctor Carter is on his way. I sent a message to him as soon as I received your note.' Matt closed his eyes and drew in a breath through his teeth. 'Thank God I found an open window. What the hell did you think you were doing?'

'Catching a murderer.' She watched as the police directed the ambulance men to move the verger, who had now come around, out to the waiting vehicle. They then returned with a stretcher for Colin. 'I didn't kill him, did I?' she asked.

'Unfortunately, no. Though no doubt he'll face the hangman along with Walter Cribbs for all his crimes.' Inspector Greville stood looking at the three of them. 'I'll need statements from all of you when the doctor has attended you.' He moved away to supervise his men.

Doctor Carter entered the church clutching his dark brown leather medical bag. The vicar accompanied him, wringing his hands as he inspected the doors and the church for any damage. Doctor Carter's round, cherubic face was flushed pink with excitement. 'What on earth has been happening?' he asked as he placed his bag down carefully on the pew next to Edgar.

'It's a long story, Doc.' Matt winced as he spoke.

The doctor pursed his lips, a frown creasing his forehead. 'I see you didn't follow my instructions.' He popped open his bag and began to attend Edgar first, cleaning the wound on his face and checking his reflexes. 'No lasting damage, and you have escaped sutures.' He applied a dressing to his head and secured it with a bandage.

'I have quite a headache,' Edgar complained meekly.

'Compared to what it could have been, a headache is nothing.' Kitty felt sick when she thought of what could have happened.

'I suspect Colin's head will feel far worse when he comes around. You broke your umbrella, my dear,' her father observed, wryly.

'So, it was you who bashed Colin over the head. I might have guessed,' Matt winced as the doctor looked at the strapping he'd applied earlier to Matt's chest and shoulder. He grunted as Doctor Carter tutted and clucked while adding more strapping to his torso.

'Now, Miss Underhay, your injuries, if you please.' The doctor tied the knot firmly on a fresh sling around Matt's neck and turned to Kitty.

'My hand. Walter stamped on my fingers. I can't move my little finger very well.' The doctor gently eased her fingers straight so he could examine them.

'I think they are just badly bruised. Pop along to the hospital tomorrow and we can take a look in case it needs splinting. I'll strap it for now and I suggest some cold compresses to keep the swelling down.'

Inspector Greville returned. 'It's very late. I suggest you return to the Dolphin to get some sleep and I'll be there at ten tomorrow to take your statements.'

Kitty glanced at her watch and was surprised to see it was almost one in the morning.

'Allow me to give you a lift back to the hotel. My motor car is in the street.' Doctor Carter fastened his bag and beamed at them as if it were they who were favouring him rather than it being the other way about.

The doctor assisted Matt to the front passenger seat while Kitty aided her father to the backseat. 'Off we go then.' Doctor Carter started the engine and they hurtled through the deserted streets the short distance back to the hotel.

'Thanks, Doc,' Matt said as he carefully negotiated his exit from the car. Kitty was thankful the journey had been so short. Doctor Carter appeared to have two speeds, fast or at a standstill. She suspected longer journeys might be quite terrifying.

The night porter admitted them to the lobby. His shocked expression at their bloodied and battered state almost made her smile.

'Father, you had better take my room on the floor next to Matt and I'll sleep in Grams' suite again tonight.' She led the way to the elevator. The night porter came to assist with the metal cage to permit them entry. She accompanied them to the top floor and said good night to Matt before taking her father to her room. There was a strange emotion in Matt's eyes as he bade them good night, but she didn't have the energy to consider it just now; she had used up her stocks of bravery for the night.

'Thank you, Kitty.' Her father took her hands in his. 'You were very brave this evening. I'm so glad you came to no harm.'

She stood on tiptoe and kissed his cheek. 'Me too.' She freed her hand from his and felt inside her coat. 'By the way, I have something for you.' She reached inside the secret pouch she had fashioned in the lining and took out the handkerchief containing the ruby. She pressed the bundle into his palm. 'Take it, do what you will with it, so long as it is gone where it can cause no more trouble.'

His eyes, damp with emotion, met her gaze. 'I promise it will cause you no more grief, child. You look so much like your mother, and you have her courage and spirit.'

To her surprise she saw tears cloud his vision. 'My darling girl.' He stooped and kissed her forehead. 'Good night.'

She left him in her room, promising to send a maid with a tray of tea and toast in the morning before the inspector came to take their statements. She made her way to her grandmother's suite in a state of exhaustion. Her fingers hurt and her body ached. At least now that Walter was in custody, the danger was over. Soon her grandmother would be back with her aunt Livvy, and she might be able to persuade her father to stay a little longer now he was no longer under the threat of arrest.

CHAPTER THIRTY-ONE

Kitty woke the next morning to the rattle of the door of the suite opening, followed by a soft knock at her bedroom door.

'Good morning, Miss Underhay, tea and toast.' Alice, the little red-haired maid, set the tray down on top of the bedside cabinet. 'Shall I open the curtains and let the day in, miss?'

'Please. What time is it?' She tried to peer blearily at her wristwatch which she'd removed and placed next to her bed.

'Eight thirty, miss. Can I do anything else for you?' The girl turned back from opening the curtains and smiled cheerfully at Kitty.

'No, thank you.' She pulled up her pillows, wincing when she forgot the strapping Doctor Carter had applied to her fingers, then helped herself to tea and toast.

An hour later, bathed and breakfasted, she hummed to herself as she hurried upstairs to tap at her father's door. Receiving no answer, she tried the handle and discovered the door unlocked.

'Papa.' She walked in to see the bed neatly made and everything in perfect order. Two envelopes were on her dresser, one addressed to her and the other to Inspector Greville. There was a tap at the door, and she turned her head to see Matt's tall frame.

'He's gone, hasn't he?' she asked.

'You sound like you expected it?'

She nodded. 'I hoped he might stick around for a little while.' She touched the corner of the envelope he'd left for her with the edge of her bandaged hand. Her father's departure was disappointing but not unexpected. She had a feeling that he was a man who never lingered anywhere for very long.

'Has he taken the ruby?' Matt asked as he edged into the room and sat down carefully on a chair, nursing his injured arm.

'I hope so.'

He smiled. 'I'm sure life will be simpler with it gone.'

Kitty sank down on the edge of her bed. 'He left letters, one for me and one for Inspector Greville.'

'Inspector Greville will be here soon.' Matt stood and groaned. 'I'm starting to think jumping on top of Walter Cribbs probably wasn't my most sensible move last night.'

Kitty collected the letters to take down to her grandmother's suite. 'I'm very grateful that you did.'

They made their way together slowly down the stairs. 'Last night was so surreal.' Kitty paused outside the door of the suite. 'This strapping is annoying.' She fumbled with the key to unlock the door.

'Don't talk to me about strapping, I'm hoping no one looks too closely at my shave this morning.' Matt followed her inside the room.

She placed the letter for Inspector Greville on the bureau and used the paperknife to open the letter with her name on it.

'I've ripped it.' She tugged the note free of the envelope.

> *My Dearest Kitty,*
> *I'm sure you'll understand that I can't stay. Your grandmother and aunt will be home soon, and I suspect that I'm not the houseguest your grandmother would wish to receive. I promise you that I will write with my address once I am back in America. I hope that you will hear from your aunt Hortense and cousin Lucy. I think you will like Lucy; she is a very modern young woman I believe. I expect that my leaving in this fashion will cause your grandmother to say*

that a leopard does not change its spots. Perhaps she is correct.
But always remember, my darling girl, that this old leopard
loves you dearly.

Till we next meet, take care, all my love, your affectionate
Papa xxx

Kitty blinked and fumbled for a handkerchief. 'I know he's a disreputable old rogue, but there's something about him.'

'Who are aunt Hortense and cousin Lucy?' Matt asked.

'Lady Medford is my father's sister. Rather unsurprisingly they are estranged, and he has only just told them about me and me about them. They have an estate near Exeter.'

Matt pursed his lips and let out a low whistle.

Kitty laughed. 'I know.'

There was a knock at the door and Inspector Greville was shown in by one of the portering staff. He raised his hat politely to Kitty, and, at her invitation, removed it and took a seat.

'Will Mr Underhay be joining us?' he asked as the maid returned with a tea tray and biscuits.

'My father left this for you.' Kitty handed him the note addressed to him.

The inspector opened the envelope and removed several sheets of paper. He read them in silence, only the occasional raising of his eyebrows indicating his thoughts on the contents. When he'd finished reading, he refolded the note, returned it to the envelope and tucked it in the back of his notebook.

'Your father appears to have left a complete and detailed statement of events, Miss Underhay. Naturally I shall need to take a statement from you and Captain Bryant about the events of yesterday evening.' He looked at Kitty as she proffered him the plate of biscuits.

'Of course.' She took a biscuit herself and nibbled at the corner.

'Mr Cribbs is in police custody, although he has been seen by a psychiatrist and there is a feeling that he may be sent to an asylum. The events of last night appear to have sent him completely over the edge.' The inspector brushed crumbs from his tie and looked hopefully towards the biscuit plate. Kitty took the cue and offered him more biscuits.

'Colin Wakes is under police guard at the hospital. He has now regained consciousness and is happily singing like a canary about Walter Cribbs.' The inspector bit down on his biscuit with a contented sigh.

'I'm glad Kitty is safe now, and Cribbs is locked up.' Matt set his cup back on its saucer.

'Will you be remaining at the Dolphin, Captain?' the inspector asked.

Matt exchanged glances with Kitty. She hadn't given much thought to what would happen now it was over, and the mystery was solved.

'Mrs Treadwell and her sister arrive today, so I will need to discuss things with her now that the immediate terms of my employment have been fulfilled.'

Kitty's spirits fell unaccountably at the thought of Matt leaving. It may have been dangerous and scary over the last couple of weeks, but she had felt more alive than she had for a long time. She also enjoyed Matt's company, even if he could sometimes prove annoyingly protective.

'Will you remain in the area?' The inspector looked somewhat mournfully at the empty biscuit plate. Perhaps he had skipped his breakfast.

'I have some plans,' Matt said, surprising Kitty.

'Good, good. Well, shall we set to business then?' The inspector put down his tea and began the lengthy process of taking their statements.

It took until lunchtime to complete the details. The inspector left and asked them to call at the police station in the next few days to check and sign the statements once typed. Kitty promised to let the inspector know if her father made contact so his statement too could be verified.

Once the inspector had left, they made their way to the dining room for lunch. 'You must go and rest after we've eaten.' Kitty was concerned that Matt had begun to look pale once more.

'For once, I shan't argue with that.'

Vivien and Bobby were at their usual table and Kitty noted that Vivien was dressed in her travelling costume. Bobby's face was a mass of purple and blue bruising that made Kitty wince. They were finishing their meal as Matt and Kitty were seated.

The waiter took their order and left. Bobby and Vivien came over to their table. Matt immediately rose and asked Vivien to take a seat.

'No, thank you, honey. Our car will be here soon, and I must supervise them loading the trunks. We heard that they caught the murderers last night?' She looked at Kitty's strapped up fingers and Matt's sling.

'Yes, Walter Cribbs and Colin Wakes are behind bars,' Kitty said.

'My maid told me that Edgar had been here too last night?' Vivien looked tired, Kitty realised; there were fine lines at the corners of her eyes.

'Yes, he was, but had to leave early this morning.'

Vivien looked at Bobby. 'Bobby felt I should come and apologise to you, Kitty. Our stay here wasn't entirely on the level and some things happened.' She paused and looked at her husband again. 'Well, let's just say I may have done things that I bitterly regret.'

Kitty realised that this was a big admission coming from Vivien. 'I understand.' Now that the ruby was gone and her father safe, she could even forgive Vivien for damaging her beloved clock.

Bobby gave a small cough. 'If you'll excuse me, I think the car may be here.'

Vivien watched him leave the dining room. 'Have you ever been in love, Miss Underhay?'

Kitty shook her head, colour stealing into her cheeks.

'Lots of folk don't get it, but I love Bobby. He rescued me at a time when I really thought I was going to die. The depression hit hard in America, especially amongst those of us who had little or nothing to begin with. Bobby saved me. Finding that ruby would have meant we would have been free. Free to stay in Europe – Paris, maybe – where we're more accepted. We would have been safe. Desperation makes folks do desperate things. Love makes you do desperate things.'

Kitty caught Vivien's hand in her undamaged one. 'I'm sorry. I do understand. Will you be all right?'

Vivien gave a small smile. 'I hope so. I wanted to explain, before we left. I'm glad you met Eddie. He's not a bad man, he just wanted a better life, I guess.'

Kitty released Vivien. 'I know. I hope you and Bobby have a safe journey and that things work out for you both.'

Vivien shook hands with Matt and stalked away, her head held high, to accept her furs from the staff as she left to supervise her luggage.

'I never asked you about your plans now this is over. Are you going to be staying in Devon?' Kitty asked, once their meal was before them.

'Actually, I've seen a house in Galmpton on the other side of the river, Churston, not far from the golf course. I've been at a bit of a loose end since I left the army and since, well, since I left London. My parents would like to see me settled and I have no desire to return to the capital.' His expression was bleak, and Kitty knew he was thinking about the past.

'Because of Edith?' She thought of what Vivien had just said about love.

'Yes.'

'What will you do?' She chased a piece of potato with her fork. It was proving difficult to eat with only one good hand. It made her unconscionably happy to know that he planned to stay in the area.

'I rather thought I might stay in the security and investigation business. A hotelier in Torquay I got talking to during the masked ball has already approached me to investigate a problem of some thefts from guests. Sometimes these things are too delicate a matter for the police.'

Kitty smiled. 'That sounds interesting. Of course, if you wanted any assistance anytime, where a woman's touch might be useful…?' She arched an eyebrow at him, her pulse speeding a little.

'Then I can call upon you?' He smiled at her.

'Absolutely.' She beamed back at him. 'I am terribly handy with an umbrella.'

'By the by.' He paused and wiped his mouth with his napkin and signalled to one of the waiting staff. 'I have a little something for you.'

'For me?' Kitty was puzzled.

The waiter returned, carrying a large cardboard box. She pushed her plate aside and the waiter set the box down in front of her.

'What is this?'

'Open it,' Matt said.

Curious, she carefully undid the flaps on the top of the box and parted the tissue paper. 'Oh, Matt, it's my mother's cuckoo clock. How on earth…? And it's been repaired! Oh, thank you!' She swallowed back the tears of joy that threatened to overwhelm her. The broken fret work had been replaced and it looked as good as new.

'I knew how special it was to you. There's no secret jewel hidden in it this time, though. The weights are both lead, and the timekeeping should be improved.'

'Thank you.' She stared at the clock. 'Do you think I'll ever find out what happened to her, Matt?' She couldn't begin to express how happy she felt having one of the last links to her mother returned to her.

'I'll keep it as an open case,' he promised.

The waiter returned bearing an envelope. 'I'm sorry to disturb you, Miss Underhay, but this just came.' He handed her a telegram.

Panic swept through her. 'Oh, I hope everything is all right with Grams and Aunt Livvy.'

She tore it open with shaking fingers. Surely nothing had happened to her father.

Invitation to stay follows. Can't wait to meet you. Cousin Lucy

She read it out loud to Matt before turning to the waiter. Relief rushed through her. 'No reply, thank you.'

'Very good, Miss Kitty.' The waiter left.

She wondered what her grandmother would make of the news that she now had other relations not too far away from her. It was strange that only a few weeks ago she had been wishing for more excitement and an escape from the hotel. It went to show that one should be careful what one wished for. On the positive side, now she had new relations to meet and the possibility of assisting with Matt's proposed new venture.

Matt raised his glass, a twinkle in his dark blue eyes. 'Here's to new beginnings.'

Kitty smiled back. 'New beginnings.'

A LETTER FROM HELENA

I want to say a huge thank you for choosing to read *Murder at the Dolphin Hotel*. If you enjoyed it and want to keep up to date with all my latest releases, just sign up at the following link. Your email address will never be shared and you can unsubscribe at any time.

www.bookouture.com/helena-dixon

The UK in the 1930s was a time of great change and contrasts, which adds an extra dimension to *Murder at the Dolphin Hotel*. I love Dartmouth and the Torbay area and I hope you enjoyed Kitty and Matt's adventures there as much as I loved creating them. Kitty and Matt's partnership will continue with more thorny mysteries and I hope you'll enjoy reading more about them.

I hope you loved *Murder at the Dolphin Hotel* and if you did, I would be very grateful if you could write a review. I'd love to hear what you think, and it makes such a difference helping new readers to discover one of my books for the first time.

I love hearing from my readers – you can get in touch on my Facebook page, through Twitter, Goodreads or my website.

Thanks,
Helena Dixon

nelldixonauthor

@NellDixon

www.nelldixon.com

ACKNOWLEDGEMENTS

I would like to thank the people of Dartmouth for all their kind and generous assistance in providing information and allowing me to fictionalise parts of their beautiful town. Dartmouth Historical Society were very helpful, and their archives are a wonderful resource. *Murder at the Dolphin Hotel* is the first of a series of stories I've wanted to tell for many years, and it wouldn't have happened without the support of the Coffee Crew, aka my wonderful author friends, Elizabeth Hanbury and Phillipa Ashley. My excellent and trusty beta readers, Sandra Forder, Kimberley Menozzi and Lisa Chalmers, all of whom are also wonderful writers.

I would also like to thank English Heritage for their help with information about Dartmouth Castle and its history. A special thank you also to the vicar of St Saviours church in Dartmouth who took time one cold January morning from dismantling the Christmas tree to show me around the church and tell me the history. It is a truly beautiful and special church.

Of course, it goes without saying almost that I need to thank some other special people; my husband, David, who is also my research assistant, and my daughters, Robyn, Corinne and Alannah, who are my cheer squad. Last but not least, the whole team at Bookouture for loving Kitty as much as I do, my excellent editor, Emily Gowers, and my wonderful agent, Kate Nash. All of you are superstars.

Lightning Source UK Ltd.
Milton Keynes UK
UKHW041024240120
357550UK00001B/86